LOVE IS IN THE EYE OF THE BEHOLDER

by
R. Antonio Matta

Albany, New York

Paperback ISBN: 978-1-7356064-5-3
eBook ISBN: 978-1-7356064-1-5

Printed by Lulu Press, Inc. in the United States

Content Done Write, LLC
90 State Street STE 700 Office 40
Albany, NY 12207
www.contentdonewrite.org

The Poetry Within

CORINTHIANS 13:2-8

"...though I have all faith, so that I could remove mountains, but have not love, I am nothing. And though I bestow all my goods to feed the poor, and though I give my body to be burned, but have not love, it profits me nothing. Love suffers long and is kind; love does not envy; love does not parade itself, is not puffed up; does not behave rudely, does not seek its own, is not provoked, thinks no evil; does not rejoice in iniquity, but rejoices in the truth; bears all things, believes all things, hopes all things, endures all things. Love never fails...And now abide faith, hope, love, these three; but the greatest of these is love."

Dedicated to anyone who has ever felt lonely, abandoned, heartbroken, lost, abused, underappreciated, forsaken and jaded.

PROLOGUE

"Let's give a warm welcome to an Ether Lounge veteran, Miss Dalesa Moreno." A petite woman stands on a medium-sized stage under warm lighting. She holds a black cordless microphone and smiles with brilliance, leading the audience in applause.

The woman's rainbow-colored dashiki looks beautiful with the luminous gleam of a spotlight shining down on her. She stands at center stage. Her reddish-brown afro is picked out with perfection—glistening from its sheen in the light.

The Ether Lounge is a restaurant and bar in New York City's Spanish Harlem. Every Wednesday night, poets, singers, and musicians pile into the establishment. They sign their name on a clipboard to be one of the night's performers at the open-mic event. As they wait for the MC to call their name, like Dalesa's just now, each artist prays with hope when they demonstrate their craft on the stage that night, it will be well-received.

Dalesa makes her way to the stage from the bar stool she had been sitting on while watching the other performers. She walks between scattered round tables, draped with tablecloths and candles flickering on top. Many of the customers in attendance know her from past appearances and smile with excitement watching her walk by them. They sip their cocktails as they finish their meals.

The Ether Lounge's ambiance is one of creative security and freedom—a place where individuals can express themselves as they are and feel safe in their skin without judgment. The Ether Lounge is a mellow place always full on Wednesdays—occupied with free-spirited people who enjoy the tastes of pallet-pleasing dinner platters, sentimental lyrics, moving instrumentation, rhymes, spoken word and sultry sounds of soulful singers and their melisma's charged with emotion and melodies. The Ether Lounge's signature libations are always satisfying. With their discounted drink specials exclusive for the weekly event, no attendee comes to the restaurant without a designated driver.

The petite, dashiki-wearing hostess waits for Dalesa as she gets closer to the stage. Behind her is a small ensemble of musicians. The band comprises a drummer sitting at a standard drum set and a woman behind a pair of conga drums. To the left of the drummers is an electric bass player. On the opposite side is a keyboardist. The quartet plays soft music as Dalesa steps onto the stage. The bass player extends his arm and helps her onto the platform.

Patrons admire Dalesa at the Ether Lounge for both her talent and loveliness. She turns the heads of the men there and even some of the women. She is beautiful—inside and out—with light-colored gray eyes and smooth, brown hair that hangs to her shoulders.

"Let's give it up again for Ms. Dalesa Moreno, ladies and gentlemen," the hostess introduces again, and the two women embrace in a friendly hug.

The hostess hands Dalesa the microphone and steps off the stage—leaving Dalesa alone in the spotlight. The band stops playing.

"Hello friends," she says in a soft voice to the audience. "It's a pleasure to be with you again this week. I've prepared something special to share with you tonight. I hope you enjoy it." Dalesa places the microphone on its stand at the foot of the stage. She opens a black and white composition notebook and flips to a page she had dog-eared while sitting at the bar.

Dalesa turns her head to look behind and give the band an okay to play something. It's typical of the musicians to start out playing unorganized, yet harmonious sounds as they let the poet speak a few lines. They play this way for only a few moments to get the feel of the piece the performer recites. In this way, they can better accompany the artist and their work.

So, the bass player plucks a few notes, while the drummer hits his hi hat and cymbal with his brush-tipped drumsticks. The conga player strokes the drumheads a few times, and the keyboardist plays a nice chord or two. Dalesa closes her eyes and feels the music a few seconds before speaking. Then, she opens her eyes, clears her throat and reads her spoken word poetry to the crowd.

TICK TOCK

The touch of its hand is cold.

The saying, "Cold hands, warm heart" does not apply to it.

It has no warmth, for it has no sympathy or compassion.

It does its thing regardless of consequence.

It is impatient, ceaseless and demanding.

It asks for me to keep up and regulate life to its pace.

Yet, it will not slow down to let me catch up.

It may not show kindness, but it heals.

It is the succor to my not-so-seldom languishing and misery.

It is the medium of my oscillations between exasperation and

contentment.

It is the plug for the gaping hole in my soul.

It mends the aching cavity in my heart from adversity.

It rejuvenates and heals by its Universal grace—yet it is impersonal.

Not even the Most High can alter its ways.

From the moment its measurement was created by humankind, it's

been going non-stop ever since—as my heartbeat has for decades,

unfailingly.

God has a distinguished way of dealing with it.

The rest of us have our way—no matter how inadequate.

It is the "Real Deal."

Its existence is of the essence.

Its persistence in existing and sustainability increase my resilience.

Even though, its generosity is limited.

Each person gets only an allotted share.

In it, maturity is an occurrence—a possibility for all that are subject

to it.

Even though, wisdom is not guaranteed.

Many get lost in the days.

Perfection can come from its tides and creation can evolve and grow

freely with its longevity.

It is wasted with idle minds.

People gamble with it in their attempts to challenge fate—even

though they fail to realize their authorship.

It is perseverant and independent.

It continues even when we stop.

It never looks back and never stalls.

It is a continuum of actuality.

Time keeps ticking away—tick tock.

The sands of the hourglass pour endlessly.

It ages in spite of facelifts and anti-age creams.

It allows the opportunity for resolution, restitution, realization, and

rehabilitation.

Its continuity builds on the past but cannot promise a future.

Oh, Time!

The firstborn of Mother Nature and religion's, Father God

It gave way for us primates to evolve.

Time has nurtured civilizations, guided spiritual journeys and ripened

the fruits of patience and love.

Yet, we still try to speed it up, slow it down, put it on pause.

All in order to cling to the memory of how we used to be or grasp the

tail of an often-distant dream of how we want to be.

Time and Love complement each other.

Love is kind and compassionate.

Time heals all wounds.

Love is patient.

Time waits for no man.

Love never fails.

Time never ceases.

Can those seeking love find it?

In time

Tick tock

CHAPTER ONE

Susan Cox, a middle-aged woman, sighs as she looks out the window of the Broadway Café—a little dive in upper Manhattan. She wears a blue blouse that is open like a flower's petals sprouting from a stem at her bosom. Light from the afternoon sun makes the diamond stud earrings in her ear sparkle. Her hair is in a bun, and a bang flows down the left side of her face, which ends with a slight curl. Finally, she turns her face away from the pedestrians she was watching on the street and gives her attention to the woman sitting across from her—a woman who has been waiting in anticipation for Mrs. Cox to respond to the question she has just asked her.

Mrs. Cox breaks her gaze at the woman and lowers her head. She seems to be distracted by the faint rise of steam from her cup of coffee on the diner's table. "I'm sorry for my hesitation, Ms. Moreno, but in all honesty, all I can say is that without it," she pauses. She looks up. She feels herself becoming warm inside with emotion and continues, "Without it, I have no idea how I could have made it through. I believe it conquers and heals all things."

Dalesa Moreno, a journalist for a popular variety magazine, *American Memoirs*, looks at Mrs. Cox with intent and listens with interest and empathy as she tells the reporter her story. This intimate meeting makes it the fourth interview conducted by Dalesa for her latest article on families affected by the U.S. "War on Terror."

"So, Mrs. Cox, are you saying that love has helped you deal with your son's passing?" Dalesa asks.

"Passing? No, Ms. Moreno, it was murder," Mrs. Cox says in a firm tone. Her hand begins to tremble as she picks up her cup of coffee. Noticing her body's reaction to the devastating thought of her son's death that has entered her mind, she places the cup back on the table. "You can say it. It's okay. Murder. My son was murdered by an Iraqi soldier. And yes, it is love that helps me get through each day without him. It was love that led him overseas. He loved his family and loved his country. That is why he was willing to fight for you…me." She points a finger towards a couple at a table across from them. "For her and him too. I believe there is no greater act of love than to sacrifice your life for the salvation of another."

Mrs. Cox picks up a napkin to wipe a tear that has drizzled down her cheek. Dalesa still has a few more questions for the solemn mother, but she decides to end their interview. She has most of what she needs to complete her article, and she doesn't want to push Mrs. Cox any further than her emotions will allow.

Dalesa places her hand on top of the woman's and says, "Thank you so much. It's so interesting to hear your beliefs on love. It's very refreshing." She removes her hand and presses "stop" on her digital recorder that has been on the table. As she is about to put it in her bag, Mrs. Cox grabs her hand.

"Refreshing, Ms. Moreno? I must ask. Why do you say my beliefs are refreshing? Pardon me, but have your own gone stale?"

Caught off guard by her question, Dalesa hesitates to answer. She smiles and responds, "It's just that I always hear stories about the power of love and how great it is. I guess I've never experienced a love grand enough to compare."

Mrs. Cox says, "Sweetie, love is already in you." Both women stand. "Just as your heart has been beating non-stop since the day you were born; love has been there waiting for you. You must open not just your heart but your mind, body, and spirit to receive it—even though it is already inside of you."

Dalesa's heard thousands of Billboard Hot 100 Pop songs over her lifetime describe some manifestation of love. She's sat and heard different ministers behind pulpits or at altars preach what Mrs. Cox has said. Dalesa feels touched by her sweet words, but that is all they are to her—mere words. She doesn't let her skepticism show and graciously thanks the woman for her time. Mrs. Cox leaves the restaurant.

Dalesa sits back down at the table and takes a few more sips from her tea. Then, she digs in her purse to get money to pay the bill. She reaches for her wallet and her cell phone rings. Before she looks at the Caller ID, she silently prays it isn't the office. She's been trying to avoid a call from her editor all day. The article was due this morning. Dalesa is in a race against time, but she isn't too concerned because she has until the evening to get her piece ready for print. When she looks at her phone, the Caller ID reads "Richard." Relieved and with immediate delight, she answers the call. It is her boyfriend. "Hey, baby. Perfect timing. I just finished my interview with Mrs. Cox."

"How was it?" Richard asks.

"It got a little intense when she started describing what the officials told her about her son's death. It was very touching, to say the least."

"That's the emotion you were looking for, right?"

"Yes! Absolutely! Richie, you don't know how glad I am the magazine finally allowed me to write something so sentimental. I'm gonna call the exposition 'American Pride and Matrimony: 'Til Death Parts.'"

"That sounds amazing, babe. Keep up the good work," Richard says.

"Thanks," Dalesa replies and picks up the receipt her favorite waitress has just placed on the table. "I'm leaving B.C. now. Linda just handed me the check."

"Linda's there? It's early. I thought the Broadway Café's best waitress only worked in the evening," Richard comments.

"Guess she's doing overtime. It's Twenty-ten. We're recovering from a recession, you know. People have to make money any chance they can get."

"You're right about that."

"Anyway, I'm heading straight home to continue writing. The article was due this morning, but I've managed to avoid my editor, Mr. Glasgow, all day long. He knows that I'll submit my work. Even still, I'm sure he is fuming that he hasn't heard from me, yet. I'll get the story to him soon."

"I can't wait to read it," Richard says.

"Well, I'll let you be the first person to read it tonight when we hook up—even before Coreen. How does that sound?" she asks.

He answers, "Even before your roommate? That sounds fantastic. I can't wait. I know you've put in a heck of a lot of time for this story. Don't laugh but for a couple of days I was jealous of your pen and your laptop."

"That's so sweet," Dalesa says. "How about this? For every day I sacrificed our quality time, I'll let you pick an activity for us to do. You can pick anything you want—except skydiving." She and Richard laugh. Dalesa places a ten-dollar bill on the table and waves goodbye to Linda.

She leaves behind the calm of the Broadway Café and walks out into the chaos, clamor, and commotion of the city streets. "I can't wait to see you, honey. I have something important to talk to you about."

Dalesa all too late realizes she shouldn't have said anything about having something important to tell Richard. She didn't consider the curiosity and concern it would spark in him. She shakes her head and sighs—wishing she could take back those last words. She lifts her arm to hail a cab. Two taxis, with no passengers, drive past her.

"I hope it is nothing bad," Richard says. He had been arranging books on a bookshelf during their conversation, but he's stopped now—concerned about whatever it is his girlfriend must tell him.

"There's just something I want to tell you. That's all, Richie," she says. She hopes by reiterating that, it appeases his concern, but at present, she is becoming aggravated by the millisecond as the traffic light signal changes and two more cabs pass her. She almost forgets that Richard is on the phone and huffs out of frustration as she walks to the other end of the block. She waves her arm in a way that looks as if she were a bird trying to fly with one wing. It's an amusing sight to any onlooker.

"What's wrong? Why do you sound annoyed? Is it because I'm a little apprehensive about what you have to talk to me about?"

"No, baby. I'm not annoyed with you. I'm annoyed with New York City taxi service right now. I'm trying to get home."

"Okay. I guess I will just have to wait 'til tonight," Richard says.

"Sweetie, I need to get off the phone. I have got to get home, and it seems like taxis are not stopping for women talking on their cell phones or ones wearing slacks and pumps. Either that or they have gone on another strike." She tries to laugh off her irritation.

Richard chuckles, "I sure hope they aren't pulling another stunt like that again. Well, I hate to have to get off the phone with you but okay. I'll just finish with these books in my office. You know something? Maybe you should take the train instead. Go green and save some green. Love you."

"You're right. Uptown Bronx-bound number 6 train, here I come! Love you, too, baby. Bye." The two of them hang up.

No sooner does she put her phone in her bag, does a car speed pass. It rolls over a pothole filled with filthy water from the April shower yesterday. The water splashes onto the sidewalk like a small ocean wave on an expanse of sand and much to Dalesa's disgust, all over her slacks from the knee down. She takes in a few deep breaths. Refusing to let something not life-threatening, albeit, unfortunate, demolish her day, she walks back down the block and returns to the diner to clean herself off.

"Wow! Stop the presses! Dalesa Moreno makes an appearance twice in one day. What an honor," Linda kids once Dalesa enters the restaurant. Noticing the journalist's wet clothes, she asks, "Honey, what happened to you?"

"Some idiot driver and misappropriated tax dollars by Mayor Bloomberg and the city to fix the streets. That's what happened," Dalesa says in a sarcastic but bantering way and hurries toward the ladies' room.

"Ain't that the truth," Linda says with a smirk on her face. She sneezes after refilling the pepper shaker on a table.

"Bless you. Going to use the restroom quickly, Linda," Dalesa informs.

"Okay, love. Ah-choo!"

Once inside the restroom, Dalesa tears off a hand full of paper towels from the dispenser and wipes herself off to dry her clothes as best she can. When she finishes, she looks herself over in the mirror. As she is about to leave the restroom, she checks the time on her cellphone. She is sure that she can have the article typed up in time but decides to call Mr. Glasgow, anyway.

Reluctantly, she dials the office number on her phone and waits for him to answer. He picks up after only a couple of rings. "Mr. Glasgow, it's Dalesa… I know it's late… Don't worry. I'll email you my story before you leave for the day."

Of course, Mr. Glasgow doesn't let her off that easy. Before hanging up, Dalesa gets an earful from him as to how he had better receive the article in his inbox by sunset. He also reminds her of the importance of deadlines and how risky it is to wait until the last minute to turn in work. Knowing full well that Mrs. Cox's story will add a unique element to the edition, she doesn't allow herself to be bothered by him and his reprimand. Besides, deadlines and pressure are a part of a journalist's job. Even in Mr. Glasgow's frustrated tone, saturated in his words, she could hear that he trusted Dalesa's ability to produce quality work and that it will be worth the wait. As they hung up, it is his confidence in her that she connected with—not the yelling. She inspects herself again and exits the restroom.

"Thank you," Dalesa says to Linda as she leaves the restaurant for the second time. She waves goodbye.

"See you tomorrow, honey," Linda says. She waves back.

Although a cab ride would save some time, Dalesa makes no further attempts to get car service. She walks to the train station and hops on a train in less than eight minutes.

As she sits in the subway car, on her way home, she tries to focus on "American Pride" by writing edits on her memo pad. However, all she can think about is the talk she's going to have with Richard and what she is going to say to him later tonight.

Richard had a right to be concerned, but Dalesa didn't want him to worry while they were on the phone. She has had "The Talk" with a few men before him, but she had never been in love the way she is now with any of them. The others did not take the news well, and she hopes that with Richard, it will not be a replay of those conversations. In the past, she had failing relationships spawned from unrequited commitments to the partnership. They broke up with her because of what she shared and without any hint from them of eventual acquiescence to what was or could have been; there was no love.

Dalesa wonders if Richard will be the same. Is the love they have strong enough to withstand the test that awaits them? Should she risk disclosure? Their relationship feels right to her the way it is now. She thinks to herself how respectful he is and considerate. She thinks of how understanding he is with the demands of her profession.

Is she wrong to want to wait just a little while longer to have this talk? Internally, she battles with herself because she wants to justify holding on to the way things are in their relationship at this very moment. The way Richard says her name makes her melt. He has no foreign accent or southern drawl to give her name any special intonation, but he is so dreamy that if he were to read the Yellow Pages to her, she would get moist. His touch brings about a sensation throughout her body that feels like a warm vaccine for loneliness has been injected into her bloodstream and the fluidity of his love coming from his warm body courses through her veins. So, what if they could talk for hours? So, what if she has opened to him about some aspects of her life that before knowing and meeting him, no one else knew occurred or could even imagine Dalesa experienced? 'No! No!' She screams in her head. She couldn't risk losing the dream—the manifest destiny personified in him every time he walks up to her, and they kiss.

WARMTH OF YOUR LOVE

Look at me.

Do you see?

I hope you see what it is you've done to me.

I'm snuggled in the warmth of your love.

You have opened up a part of me that I thought was closed.

That valve of my heart was on lockdown—obscured from light and the world around me.

Before you entered my life, I thought that love would never find me.

For many years, my body was not a temple but a brothel.

I sacrificed commitment and true intimacy for artificial supplements that fed my starving esteem.

I lived out my romantic and erotic thoughts and desires through sitcoms, movies, and cyber-land.

If only you knew how intensely I desired companionship and for how long.

Nonetheless, here you are, now.

Your arms have held me tight.

You have lifted me from loneliness and given me hope.

Hope in something I'd seen only in my dreams.

The consensual delay on our physical communion makes a fire burn deep within me.

How I wait patiently for the day, we make love.

I ache for you to embrace me passionately and allow our bodies to

melt into one.

Who would have thought today would have come when it did?

Today, I stand with you.

I want nothing else to quench my thirst for living but you.

The secrets shared between us give me assurance there is trust.

The closeness between us is intense and beyond just our flesh.

Take a good look at me and see what it is you've done.

You have taken a neurotic, often troubled, lost and lonely soul,

hungry for change and given me hope and direction.

You have shared with me a sip from your cup of friendship and given

me a bite of bread baked in the warmth of your love.

Outside of her thoughts, she hears the announcement for the passengers to stand clear of the closing doors. Dalesa wonders if by having this talk, she would be closing the door to a chance at true happiness. The subway car doors close shut, and the train starts moving again. It is then that reality swooshes in and kills the little unicorns, rainbows, and carriages made from pumpkins that were in her fairytale. The darkness upswings from the shadows of fear and doubt that had never been absent from her dreams of a happily-ever-after. She is reminding herself of her selfishness if she were not to have "The Talk." She wants to cling on to the perfection she's found in a romantic relationship—an ideal held so with a secret that is dense in its necessity to be shared still concealed from Richard. It will only do the "ideal" more damage if she prolongs a disclosure.

She thinks back to the first day Richard told her he loved her. It was on her 30th birthday about a month ago, in March. Dalesa was dealing with something dark during that time. Her foster parents she just found out died in a car crash only four weeks before her birthday. She was battling some inner demons as it related to their death. Issues began showing in her work and surfaced in personal relationships. She had doubts about her career—not the choice but mostly regarding a measurement of success. It could have been the birthday blues, hormones or something spewing from a boiling tank that held all her suppressed feelings about herself and the life that at that time she felt was devoid of any true meaning and purpose.

It wasn't the first time that Dalesa had gone through severe depression, but it had been years since it escalated that much. Who was there during that period for her through every breakdown, bouts of sadness and saline tears? Richard Delgado.

Richard listened to her talk about her most obscure, obtuse, irrational and intense thoughts. She felt comfortable sharing her feelings. On her birthday, after dinner, she got a little lost in emotion, and he comforted her. He provided a sincere shoulder for her to cry on. Dalesa remembers how Richard took her hand and said that from that moment on, he would be committed to loving her every day until she was able to believe it and on her own, feel that she deserved to be loved. He said that it would be his personal goal in life to make her happy. No one had ever said those words to her. A huge part of her felt she didn't deserve any of it, especially happiness and love. When Mrs. Cox was talking about love earlier today, Richard did cross her mind. Maybe she had found something legit.

UNEXPECTED POSSIBILITY

Often, we come across paths that have been tread before.

Familiar footprints in the sand not washed away by the tide

So many lives

So many destinies

Some with common ground and others contrasting

All interwoven to create a meshed layer of existence

Similar or not, my experience in life is not like your experience.

Tears from heaven have poured down, and I'm drenched.

However, two people can feel the same thing.

What's shared is unique and special.

Like being caught in the wind from the flap of an angel's wing

As priceless as this is, I cannot forget before.

The world I knew before was one of loneliness.

I feared tomorrow and today a little more.

I would sit alone in the darkness.

Feeling like excreted mass

Taking up space

Sealed to a life of uncertainty by Destiny's kiss

Insignificant and unwanted

I would call out to something greater than myself.

Tried to move on but the past still haunted.

It felt like the Supreme Creator had muted my prayers.

Then one day someone came to pull me up.

Brought me up through all the oppressive layers

This person took me by the hand and now abides with me.

Now, the pressures of life seem to lessen.

It's no longer just my footprints in the sand by the sea.

My will to live is rejuvenated.

I can continue to walk the path I started.

Life is no longer solitary and understated.

I have a partner now.

An extra set of eyes to see the world for what it is.

Another pair of ears to hear love's sound.

Another heart that beats and can feel what I'm going through.

Another soul to be set free by what is true.

A different path is trodden.

An avenue of life that doesn't have to be dark and painful.

Together, my love and I can have a life filled with possibility.

Richard's intentions have seemed clear and as far as Dalesa is concerned, have been trustworthy. Dalesa would rather cling to Richard's words of devotion and love than wrestle with worry. She smiles with her optimistic choice to accept that his words are true and that he will love her—no matter what. As the train approaches her stop, she allows a calm to come over her. Trust now solidifies faith bred hope in the love she has seen, sensed and stroked.

Once at home, Dalesa breezes pass Coreen, her roommate, who is sound asleep on the couch. She rushes into her room to begin typing.

As she types, reviewing notes, and sound recordings, the words flow like fluid from her frontal lobes. Images of the Pentagon and the Twin Towers in ablaze come to her mind. Candlelight vigils and evening news television broadcasts of fatality reports, flash in her thoughts. She thinks about the emotional impact the war has had on the citizens of the United States and the rest of the world. She thinks of all the conspiracy theories implicating political involvement in the attacks of 9-11. She recalls images of Middle-Eastern children holding firearms. She thinks of Mrs. Cox. She thinks about love—the love of money, power, materialism, God, family, lovers. Her fingers fly over the lettered keys of her laptop, about 60 words-per-minute as she pours more and more of her objectivity and patriotism into her writing.

Dalesa works fast. It only takes about two hours, after reading, re-reading, editing, re-reading, editing and re-reading again before she feels comfortable sending the final copy to Mr. Glasgow. She waits for the editor to confirm he has received the email. He replies quickly. She takes in a deep breath, holds it a few seconds and then enjoys the exhale, as she has completed something so beautiful. With a grateful heart, she sees the beauty in everything around her. She finds beauty in having a job at the magazine. She sees the beauty in having a residence in one of the grandest cities in the world. She enjoys the beauty of being in love.

Dalesa looks at the time. She is supposed to be meeting up with Richard soon. So, she freshens up and finally changes out of her damp clothes. She's ready to leave in mere minutes—completely defying the stereotype of how women take an unreasonably long time getting ready to go someplace. Before leaving the apartment, she kisses Coreen on the forehead and exits in exuberant bliss with the highest expectations for a great evening.

CHAPTER 2

"If our time on this planet has taught humanity anything, it is that life should be appreciated. Too many of us allow material gain and the pursuit thereof to dominate our thoughts and passions. Greed impairs our judgment and charity comes with hidden intentions. We wage war to protect our pride, predatory patterns of possessiveness and prejudices but put on a label that says it is patriotism," Richard recites, reading aloud Dalesa's article. He finishes the last sentence to himself. Then, he places his right elbow on the table edge and holds up his chin with his knuckles. He smiles with an amorous grin as he looks with astonishment at his lovely date for the evening.

After a few seconds of his fixated gaze and admiration, Dalesa who has been blushing the entire time looks away finally. "Why are you staring at me like that?" she says.

"Baby, that was exceptional. I'm really impressed," Richard praises. "Actually, I shouldn't say impressed because that implies, I expected something other than amazing." Dalesa's cheeks have yet to return to a normal color.

"Thanks, Richie," she says, smiling back at him. "I'm really proud of it, myself."

"As you should be. What I just read…wow! It's some of your best writing other than your spoken word poetry—from the little you let me read. It's all good. I know you are selective with what you share on those rare occasions," Richard says, teasing her a little. "You're probably too modest to consider this, I'm sure, but I wouldn't be a bit surprised if there isn't Pulitzer buzz when this hits newsstands," he says with an apparent conviction. Dalesa shakes her head, but the seed is now planted in her mental soil of possibilities. Richard places his napkin on top of his remaining rigatoni and motions for the server to come to the table. "Are you ready to go?"

Dalesa grabs her purse. "Yeah, sure. Let me go to the ladies' room first." She excuses herself from the table.

In the restroom, Dalesa washes her hands. As she checks herself in the mirror, she begins to feel apprehensive about the remainder of the evening. She knows it is only a matter of time before Richard asks her about "The Talk." She pats down the sides of her hair with her hands and lifts her chin. She puts her shoulders back and lifts her chest. Then, she walks out of the restroom to return to the table.

When she returns, Richard is signing the credit card receipt. Dalesa puts on her coat. Richard stands to help her. Then, he puts on his jacket and kisses her. He places his arm around her waist and escorts her out of the restaurant.

The two of them take the first cab they can get. The ride is quiet except for the static and poor reception of the driver's dispatch radio. Dalesa feels exhausted after having such an exciting day. She rests her head on Richard's shoulder and closes her eyes. He strokes her hair and wonders to himself what it is that she must tell him. His mind has been running around in circles all afternoon and evening trying to figure out what her important news could be. The anticipation has him on edge, and he hopes she will be ready to talk once they arrive at his place.

The ride isn't long to Richard's apartment in Co-Op City. They ride the elevator of his building to the 18th floor. After entering his home—being the gentleman he is—he takes Dalesa's coat and hangs it on the coat rack. Dalesa slips out of her shoes. She enjoys how the plush carpet feels between her toes. She walks over to the sofa and stretches out long ways, letting the back of her head rest on the arm of the couch. Richard puts on some music and lights a few scented candles in various places in the living room.

"Do you want anything to drink, baby?" Richard asks.

"Do you have any more of that tea I like?" She answers back.

"You mean the one with the rose petals?"

"Yeah. I love that stuff—especially since it has the chamomile too."

It takes Richard only a few minutes to brew the tea. He returns to the living room with two cups. Dalesa sits up straight on the couch—once again enjoying the feel of the carpet brushing between her toes when her feet touch the floor. Richard hands her a cup. "Be careful, baby. It's hot," he cautions. She makes ripples on the surface of the brew while blowing on it to cool it some. After a minute, she takes a sip. "Mmmm…Oh, this tastes so good. Thank you."

"You're welcome, sweetie," Richard says. He places his cup on the coffee table to cool. "Sit back. Relax."

Dalesa takes one more sip before returning to her lounging position with outstretched legs on the sofa. Richard elevates her legs just enough for him to slide and sit beneath them. With her legs lying across his thighs, he begins to massage deep into the muscles of her calves and feet.

Dalesa moans with a soft breath, adoring the touch and heavenly release of tension in her body underneath his fingers. Richard allows Dalesa time to enjoy the ambiance he's created for her—the Zen-ful taste and aroma of the tea, dim lighting, the fragrance floating in the air from the candles, the soft music playing on his stereo and the mollifying massage. However, after some time—him getting lost in the moment as well—he drifts away to another place and finds himself in a meditative trance.

'What does she want to talk to me about?' Richard says to himself. Then, comes in a subtle sudden rush of combustible-like anxiety and curiosity which have become passive-aggressive assailants to his peace of mind since their phone conversation earlier in the day. He says, "So, babe. What's up? You had something important to tell me, right?"

As if being shaken awake from a lovely nap, Dalesa snaps back from the serene place Richard's magical massaging hands had transported her. She swings her legs off his lap and sits up. She takes a large sip of her tea. Heat seems to be rising from beneath her blouse as if a radiator was attached to her belly. She straightens her back. Attempting to conceal her sudden ill at ease, she looks at him with her light-colored eyes—windows into her hidden apprehension and fear. However, with a smile of sweetness and calm, she asks, "Do you love me?"

"Of course, Dalesa," Richard replies.

"I love you, too. That's why this is both challenging and necessary to talk about," Dalesa says.

If there were a cardiograph in the room, the reading would show a sudden spike in Richard's heart rhythm. 'I haven't been preparing all afternoon for *bad*. I prepared for a *not-so-good* maybe, but this sounds like the beginning of bad news,' he thinks to himself. He says, "Whatever it is, sweetie, you can tell me. I will either a, understand, b, forgive you, c, won't judge you or d—all of the above." He gives a cheesy grin.

Dalesa chuckles at his endearing wit. "You're so cute." Hoping that his understanding is unconditional, she makes her first attempt to start "The Talk." "Richie, I want to thank you for being patient when it comes to intimacy," Dalesa begins.

Richard smiles. "Is that what this is about? Sex?" Richard interrupts. He sighs in relief. "Baby, I know you have a 'Getting to Know You' period, and I respect that. No pressure. If you need more time, I…"

"No, it's not about that. Don't get me wrong. I'm glad to know you're open to that, but that's not it," Dalesa says. Then, she suddenly thinks to herself, 'C'mon girl. This is 2010. People are much more open-minded these days. Relax, Dalesa. Here goes.' She then says to Richard, "I'm HIV positive." Richard is unresponsive at first. Then, he stands to his feet.

"You're what?" he asks. There is a moment of uncomfortable silence as he stares at Dalesa with a look of intense disturbance. "I can't believe this! I respected your stupid waiting period, and now you tell me that you are infected. You mean to tell me that you won't have sex with me, but you can with someone else? Then, as if the betrayal wasn't enough, he gives you HIV! What kind of crap is this? Is this some joke? This has got to be a joke, right? You're kidding me!"

Dalesa doesn't know what to do or what to say. Richard's excitement is borderline outrage. Of course, she must explain, but first, she feels the need to defend herself. "I did not cheat on you, Richard. I know that this is a shock, but I've been infected for eight years."

Richard's jaw drops. He shakes his head in disbelief and starts to pace the room. "This just keeps getting better. I can't believe this. You had this when we met? And you are just now telling me?" Richard walks in a small circle, rubbing the sides of his head with his palms. His voice seems to get louder with each step. "What's the matter with you, Dalesa? How could you do this?"

As she watches her hysterical boyfriend, Dalesa is petrified. She doesn't know how to appease the situation. She doesn't know if he is upset that she's sick, that she finally disclosed or that she didn't tell him right away.

"Why are you just now telling me?" Richard yells.

"I can't talk to you if you keep yelling at me," Dalesa says.

"I'm sorry. I'm sorry. I'm sorry," Richard says, lowering his volume with each apology. "Dalesa, what do you expect?" Richard stops pacing and stands a few feet away from her with his arms crossed.

"That's the reason for the 'Getting to Know You' period. I was afraid that if I told you sooner, I would lose you," Dalesa begins to explain. She moves to sit on the couch closer to the end where Richard stands. Richard steps back away from her. "Maybe I was wrong for not being forthcoming from the start, but things were going so well between us. I wanted to hold on to it for as long as I could, I guess."

"You guess? Dalesa, you were selfish and manipulative," he says. "I'm so disappointed in you."

"Disappointed? I know this isn't pleasant to hear but most guys when I tell them, they show a little sympathy."

"Oh, so what? You expect me to feel sorry for you?"

"No. Not *sorry* per se. Maybe sympathy was the wrong word."

"The wrong words started with *HIV* and ended with *positive*."

"Richard, you aren't making this easy. If you care about me then…"

"Then what?"

Dalesa doesn't respond and looks at Richard. She can see the hurt in his eyes. She also understands the anger. She hasn't seen this side of him before. This man standing in the room isn't the same man she'd fallen in love with over the last several months.

"Baby, I know this is no little thing, but we can make this work. Many couples have survived with this disease in their lives," Dalesa says. She stands.

"That's the thing, for over half a year, you stripped me of the right to decide if I wanted it in my life," Richard says. He walks to the hall closet to grab Dalesa's coat.

"Richard, I'm sorry I didn't tell you sooner," she says.

"Sorry isn't working for me, 'Lesa."

"Richard, can we talk about this? I thought you loved me."

Richard has calmed down but still filled to the brim with intense emotions. "I can't be in love with you." He returns to the living room and throws her coat at her. "You don't respect me, and you are deceptive. How can I love that? I won't watch you die. That's what HIV does isn't it?"

"It weakens a person's immune system but…" Dalesa attempts to answers.

"I don't need a lecture," Richard says. "What kind of future could we possibly have? What about the risks? And kids. You know I want kids one day."

"Richie, couples can have a negative child if one parent is positive" Dalesa explains. "You want me to leave?" Richard doesn't say anything. Dalesa starts to cry. She picks up her shoes. "Maybe we can talk about this some more tomorrow. Things don't have to end because of..."

"Will your illness go away tomorrow?" Richard starts walking to the front door. Dalesa follows.

"You know very well that it won't but..."

With his back to her, he says, "Then I will have nothing to talk to you about tomorrow." He puts his hand on the doorknob. He looks as if he is going to open the door, but he stalls. Dalesa is only a foot or two behind him. He turns around. "My parents were married for 15 years before my mom had an affair. She didn't tell my dad about the infidelity until she had to explain why her blood came up HIV positive when she got pregnant with my little brother. He came out positive."

"Oh, Richard, I'm sorry," Dalesa says.

"My parents divorced three months after my brother died."

"I'm sorry," Dalesa says and touches him on his shoulder. Richard removes Dalesa's hand and releases it quickly. He opens the door and says, "No. I'm sorry. That disease has destroyed my family and my life but not this time."

Dalesa crosses the threshold. She turns back around to face Richard. She wants to say something, but she feels so hurt. No words come out. Richard closes the door shut. Tears erupt from her eyes and drip like rain onto Dalesa's pant leg as she bends to put on her shoes. Her vision is impaired, and her crying is profuse, as she walks down the hall toward the elevators.

She knows that Richard is hurting, too. She wishes she could travel back in time to fix this. Would having told him sooner have made any difference to the finale of it all? Maybe betrayal, disappointment, and anger would be absent, but the severance of their relationship would more than likely still have occurred. She had no idea how this illness had already affected his life.

While Dalesa waits for the elevator to come, she prays no one comes down the hall to see her in the state she is in or that no one is in the elevator when the doors open. After a half minute of agonizing wait, the elevator comes. The cab is empty when the doors open. She walks in but does not press a button for any floor—just the "door close" button. She stands inside weeping.

She has been rejected because of her status before—on more than one occasion—but she didn't expect Richard to react the way he had. Where was the love and understanding that she had known to come from him for all those months? He was a different person, now. The gentle, caring, compassionate man that had swept her off her feet has now turned his back on her.

Eventually, she presses the elevator button for the lobby. When the elevator opens on the main floor, she walks outside and goes to the bus stop nearby. Then, as if the wet from her tears weren't enough, or the splash from the puddle downtown earlier today wasn't enough, it starts to rain. She doesn't remember there being rain in the forecast. Then, again the weather can be just as unpredictable as people. The bus stop has a shelter, but she stands outside of it and lets her clothes get drenched. Her hair gets soaked as the raindrops infuse with her tears.

A bus arrives moments later. The driver opens the door. He says, "Left your umbrella at home, I see. Awe." Dalesa steps onto the bus, finally becoming protected from the rain but not from the broken heart. Cordiality is a treat and rare when it comes to New York City bus drivers, but she doesn't respond to his comment. She pays her fare and walks to the back of the bus, dripping.

Once at home, Dalesa heads straight for her bedroom and throws herself onto the bed—face down with wet clothes and all. Finding it difficult to breathe after a few moments with her face buried in her comforter, she turns on her side and curls herself into a fetal position.

Dalesa feels no one will ever love her because of those three scarlet letters of infected status tattooed on her life. Even with her sanguine hopes, deep inside, she expected her disclosure to Richard to be welcomed with an adverse reaction. Something, however, inside her still wanted to believe that he would be the exception. She didn't want to let go of the hope. She wanted him to be the one that truly meant the words of everlasting love he had often spoken. She wanted to have found someone that could look beyond his fears and embrace all of her—who she was with adoration and affection. Now, she has given up on such a silly and senseless fantasy in its entirety. She convinces herself that her life was predestined to be devoid of intimacy and acceptance.

Dalesa's eyes begin to burn from her tears. Pain is in her stomach—like a knife piercing her gut. She can't take this. How many times will she be let down by her hopes and dreams? How many times will she trust in imagined happy endings? How many times can she give in to the temptations of trust that cause her to believe the words that people say? This was it! No more! She is done.

She sits up and wipes her face, using her hands as a towel. She gets out of bed and goes to the bathroom. A bottle of Norvir is sitting out. She forgot to put her HIV medication back in the medicine cabinet after she ate breakfast. Seeing the white bottle enrages her. She opens it and empties its contents into the toilet. She opens the medicine cabinet and grabs her other two HIV medications, Reyataz and Truvada, which make up her cocktail —chemical life support. As she flushes the toilet, she dumps the other pills down the porcelain vacuum.

Next, Dalesa opens a bottle of NyQuil and drinks well over half of it as if it was water. She turns on the faucet. Dalesa grabs the package of Unisom sleep gels in the cabinet. She opens it and puts all of them in her hand. She bends down to drink from the faucet as if the water running from it was a water fountain. Dalesa swallows each pill—as many as she can with each gulp. She finishes all of them but does not stop there. She grabs from the medicine cabinet the Advil and Bayer aspirins. She drinks dozens of the pills—popping them in her mouth as if they were Tic-Tacs. Dalesa gags a few times from drinking them so fast and so many all at once. Coreen had surgery not too long ago and still has a bottle of OxyContin. She helps herself to a handful of capsules. She has no remorse for robbing her best friend of pain relievers, but the opiates are the cherry on top.

When she feels satisfied with the number of pills, she has provided her liver to detoxify and hopefully self-destruct, she turns off the water. Dalesa rests her hands on the sides of the sink and leans in a little. Then, she stares at her reflection in the mirror. She spits on the glass. What a pathetic human being she sees staring back at her. Dalesa frowns her face and shakes her head with shame. "You disgust me," she growls. After a moment, she turns away. She cannot bear to look at herself any longer. She does not bother to put away any of the bottles and packaging before returning to her room. Her stomach aches and she finds it difficult to walk without a slight uneasiness or dizziness. Dalesa stumbles on her way back to her room—using the walls as support.

In her bedroom, surrounded by darkness—with only a glowing hint of the moon seeping into the room from the window—the silence is disturbing but loud with her thoughts. She lays with her back flat on the bed and stares upward. She hopes to end it all—her final thought, her last heartbeat, her last breath, the final second of her life. Even still, in her lamentation, she feels the need to leave something behind before her desperate departure—a word or two to the friends and family she will be leaving. She turns on the lamp by her bed and picks up a pen and notebook that is conveniently on her nightstand.

With all that is left swelling within her soul and amidst the storm of emotions pouring down on her heart, she begins to write. The chemicals from all the medication she just took cause her eyelids to feel heavy. Her stomach's aching causes sensations throughout her body that are weakening and nauseating. She tries to find the right words—if there are any. With a contrite heart, she says goodbye to the disappointing and abusive world.

FAREWELL TO MISERY'S COMPANY

I don't know how I'm going to do this.

Please forgive me, but I must say goodbye.

It's been a bumpy trail all the way from unfavorable infancy to a

meager maturity.

To my dismay, I've come to see what's real and true.

This is when I say I'm through.

I've given the best I can.

Sadly, it seems my best hasn't been good enough to remove from my

life, the touch of Destitution's hand.

What I've done tonight could very well be the most selfish act ever

done.

I hope that in time you can forgive me and see that my race had been

run.

I gave all of me—unconditionally and sometimes naively.

Disappointingly, reciprocity seemed always to be lacking.

Now, I am free.

You don't understand the pain.

No drug or prayer could ever seem to alleviate the rain.

The turbulent storms continued ceaselessly.

Couldn't you see how I was drowning in discontent and despondency?

Everything about me—genetically, mentally, financially—reminds me

that life isn't good for everyone.

I'm Adversity's perpetual victim.

In the cosmic book of life, it is written.

It is done.

A part of me doesn't want to go, but it's my only choice.

I'm surrounded by sorrow.

Peace no longer recognizes my voice.

I call for it, but it never comes.

No light waits at the tunnel's end because the pain has darkened the

sun.

Misery doesn't always love company.

So, let me go.

Hold no memory.

Let me die.

Goodbye.

With the last stroke of her pen, sedation trounces Dalesa, and her eyes close. As she drifts away, she feels her heartbeat slow down. Her breathing becomes almost imperceptible. It is not too much time before she is at complete rest—her body as well as her consciousness.

CHAPTER 3

Around seven in the morning, Coreen returns home from work. Her discovery of the mess in the bathroom happens in a manner of minutes. Curiosity sets in at the sight of leftovers from Dalesa's toxic dinner of pills.

Fearing the unknown but thinking the worst, Coreen rushes to Dalesa's room. She knocks hard on the door, but there is no answer. She turns the doorknob and enters. Dalesa appears to be sleeping. She walks toward the bed. She picks up the notebook off the floor that had fallen out of Dalesa's hand. She doesn't read it entirely, but her eyes seem to be guided by words like "die," "goodbye," "free," "done." Coreen tries to wake her by saying Dalesa's name and pushing on her shoulder. Her best friend doesn't flinch. Coreen then shakes her by both shoulders, which makes Dalesa's head wobble back and forth with the rigorous force, but still, her roommate is unresponsive. Coreen gets nervous and scared. Realizing that Dalesa is unconscious, she picks up the phone by the bed and calls '9-1-1.'

She tries her best to inform the operator of the situation, but she is panicking. Reciting every Bible verse, she can remember, Coreen places two fingers on Dalesa's wrist to check her pulse, as instructed. She can feel the blood pumping through the cephalic vein of Dalesa's wrist, but she tells the emergency operator that it is faint and slow.

Paramedics arrive at the apartment soon after Coreen hangs up the phone. They transport Dalesa to the hospital. Once in the care of the Hippocratic Oath, the doctor and nurses begin procedures to bring Dalesa back from the purgatory her consciousness wades in. The attendants slide a tube down her throat and into her stomach. Through the gastric lavage, they rid her stomach of its objectionable contents. However, it does not awaken or rouse Dalesa from her profound state of unconsciousness.

Dalesa remains in a coma for two days. It is midday when she finally awakens. The sun shines brightly into her room. As her eyes adjust to the light, she can make out a figure sitting beside her bed. Thinking that she has died and gone to Heaven, she believes the person to be an angel about to welcome her to the glorified heaven where she has longed to be domiciled for so long. Dalesa finds comfort at the thought of finally being at the pearly gates that would be the entrance to eternal serenity. As she sits up, she sees no wings. She sees no ethereal glow. The reality is, there is no messenger of the Most High sitting in her presence. It was just an ordinary man—a psychotherapist by the name of Dr. Romeo Sylvian.

"Ms. Moreno, can you hear me?" Romeo asks.

Dalesa looks around the room and feels disoriented. She doesn't answer him at first. She slowly begins to realize something went wrong. She was supposed to be in Heaven not in a hospital.

"Ms. Moreno?"

She clears her throat and murmurs, "Yes?"

A nurse enters the room. She seems happy to see Dalesa awake. The nurse walks to the bed and adjusts the pillows behind Dalesa's head.

"Where am I?" Dalesa asks.

The nurse asks if she is feeling okay. Dalesa nods—beginning to become aware of her surroundings. The nurse leaves the room. Romeo pushes his chair closer to the bed.

"Who are you?" Dalesa asks. She leans back a little.

"Ms. Moreno, it is so nice to see you awake. You are at Montefiore Hospital. My name is Romeo Sylvian. Do you know how you got here?"

Dalesa lowers her head and with a dejected acceptance of her new reality answers, "Yes."

The nurse returns to the room rolling a blood pressure unit alongside her. Pulling the machine close to Dalesa's bed, she wraps inflatable cuffs around Dalesa's arm and puts a digital thermometer under her tongue. The nurse takes Dalesa's vitals. Once done, she leaves the room so Dalesa can talk with Dr. Sylvian in private. Dalesa, I'm a therapist, and I've been asked to speak to you. I've been hoping you would recover. Welcome back," he says most compassionately and charmingly.

Dalesa is caught off guard by his words, "welcome back." She, of course, is unaware of what day it is—let alone that she has been in comatose slumber for two days.

Romeo continues, "Earlier, when I asked if you knew how you got here, you said 'yes.' Can you tell me in your own words what happened two days ago?"

"Two days ago?" Dalesa asks—puzzled again by his word choice.

"You've been in a coma since the incident."

Dalesa wants to cry. Rolling on her side, she turns her back to Romeo.

"If you don't want to talk, now, I understand. Maybe tomorrow." Romeo stands and begins to gather his things to leave.

With her back still to him, Dalesa says, "I tried to kill myself. That's why I'm here. I failed. I'm not supposed to be here."

Romeo puts down his briefcase. "What you're not meant to be is dead. I'm interested in knowing what has happened to you to lead to this." He sits back down in his chair. "Don't think of it as a failure. Your death would have been premature. Dalesa?" He pauses in hopes that she will turn to face him.

She doesn't move. She only responds, "Yes?"

Romeo says, "I want to help you. I know you feel like giving up, but if you can find a way to trust in good things and good people again, I assure you we can deal with this together."

Dalesa turns to face her self-proclaimed advocate and says, "Trust? I can't trust anyone. Not anymore. People are not what they seem."

"I will always be open and honest with you. I say what I mean. I won't lead you on," Romeo assures her. He wishes to lessen her skepticism, but Dalesa remains quiet.

She turns flat on her back and looks at the fluorescent lights on the ceiling. Romeo waits patiently for a verbal response. Finally, Dalesa faces him and says, "My life has been cursed since day one. There is no hope for me."

"Yes, there is."

"No, there isn't Mr....Mr.?" Dalesa tries to think of his name.

"Sylvian," Romeo says.

"Mr. Sylvian, there is zero hope. I lost it."

"Well, Ms. Moreno, I'm committed to helping you find it. You are a beautiful woman and a brilliant writer from what I've heard."

Dalesa still stays silent. She returns her gaze to the ceiling. Romeo stands up. He reaches into his pants' pocket and pulls out his wallet. He removes from it a business card and places it on a stand by her bed.

"I will return here tomorrow so we can talk a little more. I'm glad you are still with us, Dalesa. Rest easy," Romeo says.

Dalesa closes her eyes and Romeo leaves. Later in the afternoon, the hospital moves her to a room out of ICU and into the psychiatric wing. They give her street clothes to wear but minus her belt and shoelaces. They are confiscated for her protection while on suicide watch.

STOP

Make it stop.

The heartache

Make it stop.

The pain

Make it stop.

The suffering

Make it stop.

The rain

Make it stop.

Misfortune

Make it stop.

The endless tests

Make it stop.

The failure

Make it stop.

Always being given less

Make it stop.

Uncertainty

Make it stop.

Temptation

Make it stop.

Empty promises

Make it stop.

Interest in life is done

Make it stop.

My heartbeat

Make it stop.

My breath

Make it stop.

God's contempt for me

Make it stop.

Life, I want death.

The night is long for Dalesa. Her thoughts are tormenting, but she makes it thru to another day—despite her missing desire to do so. As promised, Romeo returns. When he enters Dalesa's room, he finds her out of bed. She is peeping out the single caged window. A tray of food remains untouched on a table by the door.

"No appetite yet?" Romeo asks, looking at the cold food.

Dalesa turns around and gives him a little smile. "No, my stomach feels a tad uneasy." She walks to the bed and sits.

"Hopefully, it will feel better soon," he says. "I'm glad to see you smiling today."

"I'm sorry if I was rude to you yesterday, Romero," she says.

"It's okay. My name is Romeo by the way," he says like he's used to people mispronouncing his name all the time.

Embarrassed, Dalesa apologizes.

"Don't worry about it. I get that all the time. Now, let's talk about getting you out of here." He smiles.

Dalesa sits up straight and places her hands in her lap. She likes the idea of leaving. "I want to go home. Last night I had a chance to think about what you said. You know? About it not being my time? You were right."

"Are you gonna be safe at home?" Romeo asks.

"Yeah. What I did was stupid and purely emotional—out of pain and anger. I thought it was the only way to fix how I was feeling," Dalesa answers.

"Do you still feel that way?"

"Romeo, as I'm sure you know, I have HIV. Honestly, I believe that death is my only true redemption, but I can die some other day. Not now. Death is in my future just like anybody else's, but I feel it's a slap in the face to the Most High for me to try and escape the way I did."

Romeo seems pleased. "Nice answer."

For the first time, Dalesa notices that Romeo is very handsome. His skin has a masculine glow. His hair is dark and curly. His eyes are warm, and his smile is inviting. She begins to feel self-conscious as she sits in the presence of someone so attractive with her hair unkempt and her overall appearance so homely.

"How do you feel, Dalesa?" Romeo asks.

"To be honest, I feel a little embarrassed," she confesses.

"Why is that?"

"I've always thought of suicide as a selfish act. Yet, I get my heart broken, and it was my first reaction," Dalesa replies. She lowers her head.

"Dalesa, look at me," Romeo requests. He waits for her to lift her head. She is hesitant. "Please."

Dalesa looks up and into the kind sincerity in his eyes. Romeo says, "What you did is done. You can't un-do it, but I want to help keep you from doing it again. Do you understand?" She nods in agreement. "Good," Romeo says. "I want to see you once a week for as long as you need. Something more than heartbreak led you to do what you did, and I want us to explore what that is together."

Despite her despondency, Dalesa feels comfort in his words.

"Now, tell me again. Are you going to be safe to go home?" Romeo asks.

She smiles and says, "Yes, I'll be safe."

Romeo believes her. In the light color of her eyes, he sees hope. People who want to end their lives feel hopeless. He can see that Dalesa wants to go home. However, way more than that and entirely different from what he saw yesterday, he can tell she wants to move on—past the despair. He leaves the room and gives his assessment to the staff with approval for Dalesa's discharge. Dalesa is released the following day.

LET IT IN

When the road you are traveling is thwarted with snakes, snares, and

setbacks

Keep your head up, look to the sun and let the light in.

When the spin of the world seems increasingly fast, and you get lost

and knocked off track

Hold tight to that little strand of hope and let redemption in.

When you look in the mirror, and your reflection causes shame and

disappointment to surface

Peel off the mask of tragedy, cleanse yourself in the waters of

acceptance and let forgiveness in.

When the storms of life create turbulent winds and the downpour of

sadness and sorrow drowns you

Find shelter, dry yourself off and let peace in.

When uncertainty about choices in the past and worries about the

future rob you of stability

Release yourself from the chains of fear and let security in.

When you've tried all that you can to change the unfavorable and

misfortune into something good

Hang in there.

Try to keep yourself motivated and let perseverance in.

When everything around you just screams defeat and discouragement

Hold high a banner of positivity.

Deafen your ears to anything contradictory to your hopefulness and

let victory in.

When you feel alone, and it seems there is nowhere left to turn

Find refuge in Love's care and let comfort in.

Dalesa returns home. Corceii leaps from the couch when she hears the locks to the front door turning. She stands behind the door with her arms opened wide. When Dalesa enters, she walks right in between Coreen's arms. Coreen embraces Dalesa, squeezing her with all her might. She envelops her roommate with a tight clasp to her bosom, and they stay welded together for a couple of minutes— swaying their bodies from side to side. Coreen lets her go and then from nowhere, slaps Dalesa on the arm. Dalesa says, "Ouch! What the...?" She rubs her arm that burns a little from the unexpected impact. Her mind, on the other hand, is boggled from the abrupt flip in Coreen's warm and affectionate welcome to assault.

"Don't you ever scare me like that again," Coreen demands. "If you ever need to talk, you come to me. You got that?" Dalesa nods her head. Touched by her roommate's concern, her eyes begin to water. She gives Coreen another hug. "I love you," Coreen says.

"I love you, too," Dalesa replies.

Coreen kisses Dalesa on the forehead. Then, Dalesa goes to her room. She is overcome with a sense of something warm by Coreen's welcome. It makes her feel good. She suddenly has an overwhelming feeling of appreciativeness. She's glad to be home. It wasn't paradise, but a girlfriend whom she loves lives here. Dalesa sees new scratches from the cat on the frame of her bedroom door. She knows the damage will come out of the security deposit, but the thought of it doesn't bother her, now. She appreciates the scratches and the cat that made them. She picks up Iris, the tan and brown tabby who has followed her to the room. Dalesa kisses her and puts her back on the floor. She appreciates the smell of her room. She appreciates the oil painting of an ankh hanging over her bed's headboard. Dalesa enjoys the pile of dirty clothes in the corner of the room. She appreciates the overstuffed tiger she won at a carnival that is laying on the beanbag chair by her desk at the window. She sits on her bed. Dalesa appreciates the bed covers that are disheveled from when she was last at home. She realizes that she has a few things but grateful for many. She takes it all in.

Life appears different, now. 'Is this what it feels like to live?' she asks herself. Appreciating life and the things that are in it is such an amazing feeling. Is living seeing that there is more to life than just being troubled with the worries of the day? Is being alive being immune to the bites of the vampires of fear and doubt that are always trying to suck the life from her? Whatever she feels as she stands there in her room is something that she doesn't often feel and not recently.

With the quickness as if a blink of the eye, without her permission, she begins to imagine Coreen finding her unconscious body on top of her flowered sheets. She imagines the EMT and paramedics lifting her over-dosed body onto a stretcher. Her mind begins to paint unpleasant pictures of her failed attempt to end her life. Feeling overwhelmed, she decides to take a shower. Her imagination is taking too much control of her mind. She hopes to cleanse her body from the smell of Montefiore and clear her thoughts as well.

Standing under the hot and heavy spray of water coming from the showerhead, she tries to envision all her troubles, fears, and psychological ailments rinsing away. Although arising from her cerebrum, thoughts invade her well-being without her conscious cognitive clearance. Her mind wanders with recklessness and causes an unsolicited disturbance. She thinks of José, Louis, Khalid, and Richard. These four men have each taken a piece of Dalesa's esteem and pride—bit by bit. At one time or another, she found herself in romance and at various moments, emotional hostage with each of them. Without prejudice or proper discernment, she gave of her devotion and love. Each time she hoped her Prince Charming had arrived to sweep her off her feet and carry her away to a life of fidelity and love. Unfortunately, Dalesa found it impossible to make her dream a practical and tangible existence with either one of them.

Regardless of all the advancements in medicine to help those living with HIV, even though many of the infected can live long lives and even possibly bear children who are HIV negative, Dalesa mostly cares about finding love. She feels her last and only chance of finding true love was before she got infected. The men she's met have been turned off by the disease. Did they not like condoms? Were they ignorant? Did they not care about her enough to deal in a mature way with what she had put before them? Did it have to be dismissal?

Dalesa feels that it is all unfair. The disease has taken so much from her already, and it continues to take every day. She thinks about her experiences with swollen lymph nodes, cold sweats in the middle of the night, and excruciating muscle and back pain. She thinks about the persistent weakness and fatigue. Dalesa thinks about drinking pills to keep her CD4 T cell count away from a critical level and prays that her immune system will not come across any opportunistic infection that it's too weak to fight. She thinks of these things, and it is depressing and maddening. However, what eats at her and breaks her down is not even the fear of dying but the fear of dying alone without knowing true love.

Before telling Richard her status, what she had seen in him was in so many ways different from what she had seen in the men before him. José, Louis, and Khalid did not care about her career. They did not care about her past and the emotional wounds from which she still ached. They were interested in one thing, and it did not require Dalesa's intelligence, spirituality, personality or heart. They just wanted sex. However, once they found out her status, she became unattractive and undesirable to them.

Since Richard was not shallow or superficial, she thought that the news about her illness would be something he could handle. Richard and Dalesa had invested so much time in being open with each other and caring for one another that she feared losing it. She feels if she had kept the secret, maybe she could have enjoyed his *conditional* love for a little while longer. To her, it had felt limitless.

Isn't real love supposed to be fair, fearless and unrestricted? Perhaps, the love Dalesa longs for can only be given by a deity and not a human being. Some people tend to hide behind flowery, sweet-sounding declarations, pledges, and promises. They are guided by imagination and live in fantasy. When this is the case, love is fleeting and has no substance. These individuals create expectations and demand their partner meets them. Love is often confused with lust and submission. The vulnerability that accompanies that love affair is not offered willingly but instead prodded by coercive manipulation of emotions and seduction into psychological games. Dalesa, however, hoped she would find somebody who knew what it meant to love another person. With her hopes, she had given the possibility of receiving that love a platform to stand on and fertilize a dream of anticipation that someday the love would actualize.

Unfortunately, with Richard's recent rejection, she has torn down that altar at which she once worshiped these hopes. Now, she is convinced that love does not know her name. Dalesa believes that her heart, her prepared residence for sentiment, affection, and fidelity, will be vacant forever—lacking intimacy and be undiscovered for the rest of the years of her life that are left. They will be years in which she'll live with an intense yearning to give love, make love and be loved. Knowing, now, that she cannot give her love indiscriminately, she feels that she will never find anyone to share in a love-drenched, intimate relationship with her.

Dalesa scrubs and rinses her skin over and over. Her thoughts hypnotize her. She is mentally absent from the act of showering—adrift in myriad cognitions. She snaps out of it only when she hears Coreen knocking on the door and asking if she is alright. Dalesa has no idea how long she has been in the shower, but if Coreen got concerned, she realizes it must've been too long. Dalesa assures Coreen she is fine and turns off the water right away. She dries off and swaddles herself with the towel. She then goes to her room.

Dalesa is glad to be back home but despondent with her subsequent return to melancholia. She decides to take a nap and find relief for her troubled conscious mind.

CHAPTER 4

"Cursed since day one," Romeo says to Dalesa. "Do you remember saying those words?"

"I don't remember," Dalesa answers, as she adjusts herself in Romeo's client chair and looks around his small South Bronx office. It is her first session with him, and she is trying to get acclimated to it all—especially, being in therapy for the first time.

Romeo's desk is gray and made entirely of metal, which he has pushed flat against a wall. He sits in a swivel chair, and Dalesa is sitting beside his desk. On the wall, to the left of Dalesa, is a window and bookcase. On the wall to the right, is a circular analog clock and file cabinet. Across from Romeo and Dalesa by the desk is the door. The door has a window with closed blinds.

"It's okay that you don't remember. Let's see if I can re-create our dialogue that day. I was asking you for a little trust so that we could deal with your issues together and…"

Suddenly remembering, Dalesa says, "And I said there's no hope for me because I've been cursed since day one."

"Great! You remember," Romeo says.

"Yes, I do."

"So, can you tell me what you meant when you said that?"

Dalesa knows why she said it. She knows what those words meant, but she does not want to say. She only says, "That's just the way it is."

"No reason? It just is?" Romeo probes.

"Yeah." Dalesa drops her eyes and taps her fingers on her knee.

"Dalesa, this is only going to work if you are open with me. It may be hard at first but try. A little can go a long way in the sessions."

After a minute or two of silence, Dalesa finally blurts out, "I killed my mom." She turns her head to look out the window.

It was almost 31 years ago. June was approaching the Summer Solstice. Dalesa's mother, Dora, was 25 years old and working as a waitress at a moderately successful restaurant and bar called Sylvia's. It wasn't the famous Harlem soul food restaurant but a restaurant and bar on the Lower Eastside in Manhattan. Dora was a beautiful woman with shiny brown hair and light gray eyes.

She was a delight to all her customers. One patron took an interest in the Bachelorette and sat in her section practically every day. His name was Stanley Jenkins. He was in his late 40s. He worked as a realtor by day and a drunk by night. "You have beautiful eyes," he would always say to Dora. "How can anyone say 'no' to eyes as lovely as yours? Your eyes tell a story." Anyway, he could say it; he would find a way on each visit to let her know how fond he was of her and her "sexy eyes."

EYE SEE YOU

There's something I see when I look into your eyes.

There's something about them.

They tell a story.

They are so beautiful, but I'm sure you hear that all the time.

I can see into your soul.

From the iris to the cornea, to the pupil, straight through like a ray of

light to your retina

I see more of you than you do yourself.

I know you are vulnerable, but this spying in on your soul is no crime.

You give me permission when you look at me.

You've been hurt.

They didn't know any better.

So, don't blame them.

You can heal.

They are damaged and lost.

You will be triumphant over the push and shove of your back against

the wall; peace, you will find.

You have already glimpsed glory.

I bet the illumination of your eminence blinded you when you saw it.

When you recovered, you were frightened by the greatness you

witnessed.

Special beauty and light of love gleam in your eyes.

Their metallic flecks of hue are like no other kind.

You blush when I compliment you—a trait that you've had since the

chromosomes crossed at conception just three seasons before your

birth.

I find safety and trust when you speak and look me in the eye.

This trust in another human for me is rare and not given

indiscriminately, but this is what you've unearthed in me—the ability

to trust again.

Did you know you purify with tears?

Rain that washes your soul with the condensation of your emotions

Even still in your pain, there is a benevolence that will bring you the

love you need to find your way home—even if home is just occupied

by you alone.

No domestic partner

No offspring or displaced younger or older sibling

There's something that I see when I look into your eyes.

Windows to your soul that open their shutters to mine

I see what you don't see.

Let me continue to look you into your eyes so I can learn more.

Look into the mirror.

You won't come across vain.

You will have your day.

Your eyes tell it all.

Close your eyes, and you can see the light in the lidded darkness.

You will know that your eyes are beautiful.

I can't deny my covetousness that wishes they were mine.

I respect that those eyes are yours only with which to see.

To have seen

Your story told with each quarter of a second blink

It is, will be and has been.

Dora didn't mind his compliments. She thought he was innocent and harmless. She did, however, monitor his servings of alcohol. He would become a little aggressive with his flirtation when there was too much liquor in his blood. He would do little things like grab her behind or grab her hand and massage it when she came to the table. Dora still did not take offense, but if she noticed him becoming too fresh, she would have the bartender weaken the drinks she served him for the rest of the night.

On one summer evening, Stanley somehow figured out what she was doing to his drinks. So, he got his drinks directly from the bar. By the end of the night, he had gotten inebriated to a cautious level. His thoughts were under the influence of Seagram's and Bacardi. On this night, he left the bar late and loitered outside patiently for the neon "Open" sign to go dark and his light-eyed princess to exit the building.

After getting a few odd looks from customers as they were leaving, Stanley realized he should not wait in front of the restaurant. He was drawing unwanted attention and suspicion. So, Stanley waited across the street at the subway station and would come back to Sylvia's in a few minutes. He had a clear view of the building. Stanley leaned on a street sign while he waited. He wouldn't have been able to stand any other way.

As Dora was leaving the lounge for the night, she spotted Stanley waving to her from across the street. She waved back and went about her way. Stanley could not let her get away. He made a mad dash to cross the street and almost got himself hit by an approaching car, trying to get to Dora before she left the block. Stanley paid the driver's honk no mind and caught up with his favorite waitress. "Stanley, you ought to be more careful. My goodness, you nearly got yourself killed. Don't scare me like that," Dora said.

As if marbles were in his mouth, he muttered, "It would take more than a sedan to keep me from getting to wherever you are Dora."

"What are you still doing around here?"

"I'vvve been waiting forrrr you," he garbled.

"Oh. Is everything alright?"

"No, ma'am. No! Everrything is not alright. You know why? Because I ssspend every night mourning over unrequited love," Stanley wobbled closer to her and placed his hand on her shoulder. It was mostly to help with his balance but also a subtle excuse to touch her. "You know I love you, but yet every night you ignore that love."

"Stanley, you are a sweet…"

"You look at me with those intoxicating eyes of yours, take my usual order for the dinner special and tell Malcolm to put more ice cubes in my glass of vodka. Everything is not alright."

"Stanley, I'm sorry you feel that way but…" Dora said.

"I've given you more money in tips than I spent on my late wife the whole first year we were dating. I probably paid for those shoes you have on and maybe that hairdo you just got. It's not fair!" Stanley has the semblance of balance now and stands on his own. The word "fair" seemed to ricochet off the side of a bus that passed and shot her as if a pellet from a BB gun.

"With all due respect, I am a waitress, Stanley. Serving people…serving you is my job. Your gratuity pays for my day-to-day no more and no less than anyone else that eats at Sylvia's every day," Dalesa said. "I can see that I didn't have Malcolm put enough ice in your drinks tonight to weaken the booze that has apparently gotten you this way. Do you want me to call you a cab?"

"You can call me a cab. Call me a drunk. Call me a Democrat or rock star. I don't care. I'm done destroying my liver just to have a reason to come see you every night, and you just see me as a credit card holder and…and…auuuuugh!" Stanley interrupted himself with a retching sound as he vomited on the sidewalk.

"Stanley," Dalesa reached out to grab his arm as he bent over to regurgitate once more. "Are you okay?" Dora always takes a handful of napkins from the server's station at the restaurant before she leaves each night. So, she reached into her purse to get a couple to hand to him. He took the paper handkerchiefs from her hands and wiped his mouth and chin.

Dora waited for a moment and then asked, again, "Are you alright? Let's sit down. Do you think you can make it to the bus stop at the corner?"

Stanley cleared his throat. "Yes. Yes," he replied.

The walk was less than 100 feet to the bus stop. They didn't speak for several moments after they sat on the bench. "Do you live far from here? I can hail a taxi for you, now, or if you want to wait a few minutes. I can sit with you a little while longer," Dora said. In a very nurturing way, she rubbed him on his back.

"Dora, Dora, Dora. You are so kind," Stanley said in a sing-song tone. "Look at you. You must be an angel. Even after the way I behaved towards you, only a few minutes ago, you are still willing to sit here with me and wipe spit up off my Oxford."

"It's nothing," Dora said, humbly.

Stanley tilted to his side but sat up to say, "No. No. It is something. You are a real gift. That's what Dora means you know. A gift. I looked it up one day. Stanley's gift." He smiled in her direction but with his eyelids partially closed.

Dora smiled back at him with softheartedness "So, love, how are you feeling? A little better?"

"Around you Dora, things are always getting better," Stanley said. He hadn't stopped rocking back and forth for five seconds since the two of them sat down at the bus stop to convince Dora that he was up to a ride. So, she told him to stay put, so, she could go to the corner store and get him a small cup of black coffee.

He assured her he would stay put. Then he started singing a Spinner's song from the early 70s. As she walked up to the sidewalk, she could hear Stanley singing in the key of tone-deaf, "This is our fork in the road. Love's last episode. There's nowhere else to go."

Dora hurried back as quickly as she could with the coffee— hoping that the Java will help to sober Stanley up a little. As she crossed the street at the corner, she could hear Stanley's off-key vocals and a new song. Dora wasn't sure, but it sounded like Elton John. Whatever it was, she could tell from the way he bopped his head he was feeling a little better. Stanley seemed to sing louder once he caught sight of Dora walking from the corner.

"Mama don't want you. Daddy don't need you. Give it up baby. Mama can't buy you, love," Stanley sang.

"So, you're Elton John, now, Stanley?" she said, playfully. "Here you go." Dora handed him the coffee.

"Thank you," he said. Being muted by the acting of sipping, his singing became a hum, immediately, once the cup was in his hands.

As she sat with Stanley, she reminisced of her youth. Her mother would abuse alcohol regularly and get inebriated to a level past any state's legal limit to operate a soft serve ice cream machine—let alone a motor vehicle. So, on those days or nights of her drunken stupor, Dora, and her father would sit with her to keep her safe in the house. They would smile and sing, even when dolor seemed appropriate. It didn't matter what their plans were for the day, or how frustrated, angry or saddened they were with the alcohol abuse. They would sacrifice their happiness and convenience or secrete their emotions all in hopes to ensure that the world closest to Dora's mother was as safe for her as they could make it.

"So, do you have any children, Stanley?" Dora asked.

Stanley finally had stopped humming. His stomach was feeling better, and he realized that using his diaphragm to continue humming was a tad premature. "No, we never had kids," he answered. "My wife had ovarian cancer, and doctors said that it would be difficult, if not fatal for her."

"Oh, I'm sorry to hear that. I have one child—a boy. I want to have at least one more someday. I've learned so much about love raising my son over the years and from my family. It wouldn't be fair to not continue passing on what I've learned," Dora said. She smiled and hummed Elton John, as she thought about the possibilities.

"You should have my baby, Dora," Stanley said.

"See there you go talking that nonsense, again," she smiled. "I just got you to calm down," Dora nudged him on the arm. "It's getting late, Stanley. What do you say, we call it a night? I think you can manage from here."

"Don't leave me. At least ride with me to my place. This was our first date. You should see me to the door," Stanley said. He tried to stand up slowly.

"You got it? Can you stand?" Dora asked as she gave him support by holding his arm. He stood up and seemed to be okay. As if trying to fend off his inebriation, Stanley shook his head from side to side like a dog after a bath. Then he vocalized a loud, long exhalation of breath. Dora gave in to his plea for an escort home and said, "I suppose I will take the ride with you."

"Thank you. Such a jewel. What would I do without you?"

They walked to the corner. "You said earlier that you only come to Sylvia's to see me. So, without me, you'd probably be sober." They both laughed. In unison, they hollered for a taxi and, ironically, with synchronized arm movements, motioned for a cab.

Stanley only lived ten minutes from the restaurant. Dora wanted to have the cab driver take her back to the train station, but Stanley insisted that she come in for just a few minutes. "I don't know, Stanley," Dora said with the sincerest of contriteness in her tone for wanting to just head home.

"Please?" Stanley begged. He reached into his pocket to pull out his keys.

"Come on lady. Are you getting out or going somewhere else?" the cab driver asked. "The meter's running."

"Okay, Stanley. Just for a moment. They want me to come in early tomorrow at the restaurant. So, I should be getting home soon," Dora said. "How much is it, sir?"

"Don't worry about it. I got it," Stanley said, and he handed the driver money. They stepped out of the car and walked up to Stanley's building. He lived in a high rise. When they entered the building, Dora found the lobby impressive. She had no idea he stayed in a luxury condominium. 'I guess you can't judge a book by its blood alcohol level,' she said to herself. They took the elevator to the 8th floor. As they entered the apartment, Stanley took Dora's hand and led her to his living room.

A person's home is usually a reflection of their essence because his or her domicile is a place of solace and refuge from the outside world. Stanley's apartment was obviously a reflection of his sober self because it was sophisticated, stylish and stunning. It was large with hardwood floors that appeared to have gotten recent waxing. Large oil paintings hung on just about every wall. He had African and Chinese statues of all sizes just about everywhere. The place was an immaculate private museum that captivated Dora. Homes like Stanley's had only existed in her dreams.

"Your home is beautiful," Dora said.

"Thank you. But not as beautiful as you, Dora," Stanley said.

Dora blushed, and the two of them sat down on a suede sofa. After two minutes of silence, Dora felt a little uncomfortable with Stanley's quiet stare. Breaking the not-so-golden silence, Dora said, "I really should be going. I'm glad you are feeling better."

"You have beautiful eyes. The most beautiful eyes I have ever seen," he replied. "More pretty than that of my wife's. Rest her soul."

"I'm sure you miss her."

"Yeah. I do so very much miss her, but her eyes were nothing like yours."

Dora stood and said, "Thanks, sweetie. Well, look, Stanley, I'm glad you're home. Try to get some sleep. You may wanna take two aspirin before you go to bed to help with the hangover you may have in the morning. I'll see myself out."

Stanley took her by the arm and pulled her back to the couch. He leaned in and kissed her. Dora pushed him off her and stood up, quickly, to continue her walk to the front door. "What are you doing?" Dora asked.

"No goodnight kiss? Tonight, was our first date." Stanley stood up. "Let's stop playing games, Dora."

Defensively, Dora asked, "Games? What are you talking about?"

"Come on, Dora. I sit in your section almost every night and tip you handsomely," Stanley said as he walked towards her. Dora was practically at the door.

"Yes, thank you. You are very generous, but that doesn't mean I owe you anything in return."

Stanley reached out his arms as if he wanted a hug and said, "Dora, please don't go. You're right. You don't owe me anything." He walked toward her, while she slowly moved away from him. "Just one more kiss, please?"

"Stanley, no! I'm leaving," Dora said. She was nervous but tried to unlock the door.

"Don't do that," Stanley said with a little bass in his voice. He quickly grabbed hold of her waist and yanked her away from the door and pulled her close to him. Dora tried to fight him off, but his grip was too firm.

"You're hurting me!" she exclaimed.

"Shhhh…" Stanley said as he flipped her around to face towards him, and he went to kiss her, again.

Dora slapped his face and tried to knee him in the groin, but he moved out of the way. Her resistance angered him. He shoved her body back into the living room and pushed her onto the sofa. Before he could get any closer, she got up and headed for the door again. Stanley grabbed her legs and pulled her body to the floor. He climbed on top of her and pinned her down. The more she fought, the more forceful he became.

Dora kicked and tried to get from under his legs that had her body wedged in between them. Her fist landed on him with every blow Dora made but eventually, Stanley could handicap her movements and hold down her arms by her wrists. With the other hand, he reached underneath her skirt and ripped off her panties. Dora continued to fight the best she could for him to stop. Tears erupted from her eyes, and she pleaded with her assailant to let her go.

"Shhhh…It's alright, baby. I know this is what you want," Stanley cooed to the hysterical woman. He released his stiffening penis from his pants and just as quickly as Dora could plead for him to stop one last time, he made his blunt entrance.

He thrust his meaty member into Dora. She tensed up and moved her head from side to side saying, "Stanley! No! No! Please stop! Don't do this." Her appeal was in vain; the invasion had been executed, and she felt helpless. Her resistance only made Stanley's thrusts feel more painful. She relaxed her body—a state of physical limpness that was the antithesis to her uncooperative soul slipping into shock.

"That's right, baby. Take this loving. Take all of me," Stanley said.

She didn't ask for it, and she didn't want it, but she was taking what she was being given. Did this make her weak? Should she have stopped fighting? Should she have surrendered and accepted the sacrifice into her altar? This was not right but was she wrong for not harnessing some superhuman strength to cast off this pirate that was raiding her precious womb.

"My gift. My gray-eyed gift. Yes, baby!" Stanley crooned.

He pushed himself deeper inside her—pounding harder with each penetrating hump. Then, Stanley did something unexpected. He stimulated Dora's clitoris, but Dora couldn't accept that. Although willing to take Stanley inside her, she did not want to find pleasure in any aspect of this beastial violation. Dora just wanted it to be over. Since Stanley had released her hands, she could push his hands away.

"This is love, Dora. This is about us. Don't push me away," Stanley said. He continued his attempts to rub her.

Now, she had to fight another physical provocation that was titillating her senses and her sanity. She didn't want to speak. She just wanted him to climax and be done with her. No matter how much she wanted to be quiet, Stanley's attention to her sensitive tissue caused her to moan from the stimulation quietly. Dora wanted to scream from all the mixed signals surging through her body and mind. Eventually, Stanley's need to satisfy his own sexual hunger overcame him, which caused him to forsake further efforts to please Dora and penetrate her faster.

Dora just closed her eyes as Stanley ravished her for what seemed like an eternity. He finally ejaculated violently inside her. Dora's prayer for it to be over had come at last. Stanley got up and stood over her. He extended his arm to help Dora to her feet.

"Get away from me," Dora said. She stood on her own.

"What's wrong beautiful? We just made love. That's what you wanted. I could see it in your eyes," Stanley said. He seemed to feel that he'd done nothing wrong. "I didn't mean to hurt you."

"Stay away from me," Dora said as she ran to the door and left the apartment. Little did either of them know that it was at that moment of Stanley's climax, with all its impassioned fury, that Dalesa was conceived.

Dora had to quit her job at Sylvia's and kept quiet for days about her assault. The violation hung down on her like a veil. She didn't want to leave her home for anything—not even her room. Images of Stanley flashed in her mind throughout the days that passed. An atrocious monster replaced the middle-aged man with the gentle face she had served for all those months. Stanley was selfish and a thief.

Inordinately and in a deleteriously damaging way, he took what he wanted with no regard to the rules of sexual intercourse that state it should be consensual. Dora's kindness that once touched the hearts of many would no longer be given carefree. She found it hard to trust anyone. Dora found it hard to even ride the crowded train because she presumed the men sitting beside her to be a threat to her safety.

She spoke of the night in Stanley's apartment to no one. Despite being the victim, she couldn't help but feel culpable for the assault. The incident only came to light when Dora discovered that she was pregnant. It was then she confessed to her parents, who persuaded her to talk to the authorities. Stanley got arrested for sexual assault, and despite his fondness for Dora and his mistaken belief they made love, he pled guilty to the charges. The judge sentenced him soon after that in a prompt special hearing. The expedited trial pleased Dora because it meant she would not have to endure the evasiveness of a trial. Pressing charges was already emotionally debilitating having to relive the events of the night in writing for the police reports, and in testimony to the officers and assistant DA.

Dora and her family did not believe in abortion. She prayed day and night she would find a loophole in her religious conviction but the more she looked for ways to lose her faith, the more she got reminded of what conviction truly entailed. It was an unwavering of faith regardless of any contradictions or doubt. For nine long months—through morning sickness, weight gain, and maternity clothes—she carried around a constant reminder of that horrific night with Stanley.

Dora and her parents decided to give the baby up for adoption once it was born. Although she may not have wanted to abort the life growing inside her, she did not want to care for it either. Dora wanted nothing to do with the child. She knew that she couldn't give it the love any child should deserve, and she already resented it as a fetus.

During labor, Dora went into hypovolemic shock. She began hemorrhaging from a uterine rupture. The doctors performed a cesarean and blood transfusion to rescue Dalesa, but they were unsuccessful in preventing Dora's fatality.

A MOTHER'S LOVE

You went away to a place far from this earth.

All I have now is a void that cannot be filled by anyone else.

I imagine a love so special.

Did you love me the way the mothers do on the TV?

Would you have made me cookies for straight A's on my report card?

Would you have put money under my pillow when I lost a tooth?

What greater love is there than that between a mother and her child?

Surely, if not love, no greater bond

None can compare to what I'll never have again.

I wrestle with an insecure and feeble heart.

All I need now is your love.

Lead the way to a brighter day

I imagine a love so special.

None can compare to what I'll never have again.

I wonder how different my life would be if the Most High never took

you away from me.

I want to make it through the heavy rain, but it's hard without you.

I want to burst through heaven's pearly gates.

See your smile, feel your embrace but I can't

Are you looking after me?

Are you watching over me?

Am I someone you would be proud of?

Or has my life been a disappointment?

I think about you all the time, but right now I'm alone in the darkness.

Shine your precious light on me.

I dream of a love so special.

None can compare to what I'll never have again.

I wish that you were here today to hold my hand.

Be with me

Through the pain and through the tears

My heart goes on.

My love grows strong.

Through the years, I'll miss you.

Until we are together again someday

"If I were never born, my mother would still be alive. Why her? Why was my life spared?" Dalesa asks Romeo.

"So, if you had it your way, you would rather not exist?" Romeo probes.

"The musical group, Foreigner, said it best when they sang 'I Want to Know What Love Is.' I really do. I imagine what a mother's love would be like. I create a fantasy relationship with her, but the truth of the matter is my mom didn't even want me," Dalesa says.

"How could you possibly have known what your mother wanted or didn't want?" Romeo asks.

"My grandparents told me," Dalesa answers. "It's interesting. She loved God enough not to abort me but didn't have enough of God's love for her to want me."

"You can't blame yourself for your mother's death, Dalesa."

"Well, I'm sure she wouldn't have had labor complications had she not been in labor. She would have not been in labor had she not been pregnant," Dalesa says. She places her hand on her chest. "I take full responsibility for her death. I own that. I've lived with that for all these years. It's not a pleasant truth, but it's my truth."

"If you want to place blame, you could blame any number of circumstances. What about Stanley?" Romeo asks. "If it weren't for your father, your mother wouldn't have gotten pregnant in the first place. What about your mother's decision to work at that restaurant? Had she not worked there, the two of them wouldn't have even met, more than likely. There are infinite possibilities for the things that happen in our lives. The capacity of our minds is not that great to be able to come up with all the algebraic variables that make up such an infinite number of equations that equal our present circumstances."

"But Romeo, if what you say is true then I can only deal with the variables within my own mind's ability to comprehend," Dalesa responds. "In that space, I see myself, an unwanted child—the product of rape—ready to come into the world but by taking away the only person whose womb had been my only world until I was born."

"So, you aren't looking at all the possibilities—just at what you can see?"

"Yes."

"So, can you see that you are special?"

"If by special, you mean murderer, then yes," Dalesa says.

"I don't make any mission statements here today sitting with you that I will rid or attempt to rid you of all thoughts you may have that say you killed your mother. What I hope you come to see, with time, is that you are special. Special to have been born a survivor. From the day you were born, you have been able to survive and overcome calamity," Romeo smiles. "You couldn't even speak as a newborn, but your existence spoke 'victory.' That's special."

Dalesa didn't want to smile or allow herself to feel comforted in Romeo's words, but they touched her. She wondered to herself if he was a therapist or minister. Dalesa stays quiet.

"How old were you when you found out the truth about your parents?" Romeo asks.

"Seven," Dalesa answers. She looks at the floor. "I know they say that ignorance is bliss." She looks up and smirks. "I wish I had a blissful childhood."

After the death of Dalesa's mother and her father's incarceration, Dalesa immediately became a ward of the state—a motherless and fatherless child. Dora's parents were willing to care for their grandson—left behind by their daughter's death—but they did not have an interest in raising their daughter's illegitimate newborn. Not only were they not welcoming to a child conceived in the brutal way that Dalesa was, but they also blamed the innocent baby for the death of their only child.

The waters were a little less troubled, however, on the other side of Dalesa's gene pool. Stanley's parents were saddened and shamed by their son's sins. The Jenkins' seed had grown up to be a sexual villain and a disgrace to their family. However, they were willing to care for Dalesa and embrace her as the new member of their family. They were granted full guardianship.

Stanley's sentencing did not sit well with Dora's parents. He only got 11 years. The Moreno's tried to get him charged with murder, considering Dora died giving birth to a child resultant of his attack. The Moreno's attorney, however, could not see how he could get a conviction for murder considering the rupture that Dora died from came from a cesarean scar received from her previous pregnancy.

Prison terrified Stanley. He became severely depressed and made minimal attempts to adapt to his new home. When Stanley found out about Dora's death, he was devastated. The truth of the matter was that he adored Dora and only wanted to love her—not harm her. Stanley had gotten so intoxicated that night; he became an entirely different person. Maybe the beast he was then that ravished the person he held so dear was his true self. Stanley battled with himself about it ceaselessly in his cell. It got to where he was unsure of the person he was. He wondered whether he deserved to live when such an innocent life ended.

He wondered if he would see his daughter. He dreamt of what she looked like. Out of all the visits, his parents made to the prison during the first year and a half, not one time did they bring a picture of Dalesa. He wondered if he even deserved to see her at all.

Life became unbearable for Stanley. His guilt and remorse tormented him day and night. Finally, he broke down. As his cellmate slept one night, Stanley stripped his bed of its sheets. He stepped up onto the cell's steel toilet. Balancing himself on the rim, Stanley tied one end of his bed sheet around his neck and the other around a ceiling pipe. He slid the knot down the pipe as far away from him as his arm could reach. Then he stepped off the toilet. The next morning the guards removed his asphyxiated corpse from the cell.

"I thought my grandparents were my parents. I called my grandmother, 'mom,' and my grandfather, 'dad.' I didn't know any other reality because no one told me anything different. What started as a simple conversation with one of my cousins and an innocent inquiry into my last name turned into a dramatic change in the relationship I had with my guardians," Dalesa says to Romeo. "I asked my parents why our last names were different. I questioned why none of my cousins—not even my parents—had the same last name as I did. That's when they told me my parents were dead and that they weren't married at the time I was born. That's how I got my mother's last name. I guess they thought at age seven I could handle the truth."

"That must have been difficult to hear being so young," Romeo says.

"Yeah, but something changed from that point on for me. I wanted to know my real parents—not substitutes. At that age, I couldn't process the whole thing except that they lied to me about who my parents were and that both my real parents were dead. I was a fatherless and motherless child. It wasn't until I was much older that I found out the details about the rape, the labor complications, the suicide, and the Moreno's dis-ownership."

Dalesa often wonders if her life would have been different if she did not know the truth. Would it have been so wrong if she thought her grandparents were her birth parents? She thinks about the withered and wilted branches of her family tree. How could her mother's family completely discard her? She cannot help but feel bad knowing that the Moreno family despised her life. If she could, she would go back in time and stop Stanley from picking up the first glass of Bacardi on the night of the attack. If not then, she would find a way to get flushed from Dora's uterus before the second trimester.

Dalesa has battled with clinical depression since she was a teenager. She is only getting help now because she has never attempted suicide before—not even after finding out she had HIV. She has done good to keep many of the thoughts now surfacing in her session with Romeo suppressed all these years but talking and thinking about them now seems to only be worsening her depression.

This hour with Romeo is dredging thoughts and emotions that Dalesa has not entertained in any objective way ever. She knew she felt a certain way about her early beginnings, but she never articulated the feelings or thoughts to another living soul. This is the first time she's heard the words come out of her mouth. They are facts, admissible statements, now, no longer in the background.

Dalesa thinks of how it's been told that the truth will make you free. Free from what exactly and what truth? There is only one truth, but we seem to only know various sides of it—never the whole. Perception can reveal much of the truth and bring awareness, but with limited knowledge, it is often only in part. Love rejoices with the truth, but many people can hide for many years in the crevices of altered reality or untruth.

The unadulterated truth frightens many souls. Has Dalesa been lying to herself all these years to avoid the intimate reality of her suppressed feelings? Has she owned that which she claims? For some, it can disturb and disillusion to come face to face with how things really are when compared to the cropped and edited picture of what they had been held as truth in their mind. The world is full of customized realities, and only a few can take absolute truth as it is.

As Romeo guides Dalesa on their brand-new voyage, Dalesa will hopefully come to see that to love absolutely, especially to love one's self, there must be a yearning present to know the truth. To desire the truth means to accept what comes with it and that sometimes more than not, does not match with our previous versions. To accept that what may be real may also be unpleasant and then to embrace it is a courageous act. If truth is liberating and love rejoices with it, then this means the freedom given by reality is the freedom from one's own self and one's self-defending delusions.

Hiding from her pain is not healing from it. Maybe now, in talking with Romeo honestly and unequivocally about her innermost thoughts and feelings, Dalesa can eventually find a passage towards peace and happiness. Traveling this path of vulnerability about her emotions regarding the past would be unbearable if she walked alone, but she is safe with Romeo if she trusts in him. Romeo and Dalesa talk a few minutes more before bringing their insightful icebreaker session to an end.

"You touched on some heavy topics today, Dalesa," Romeo says. "I think you did well for our first time together in therapy. I want you to know that as we talk about the past, we are not doing so to change or relive it. It's to help us deal with the present only. You understand?"

"Yes. I got it," Dalesa responds.

"Well, I look forward to seeing you next week. Enjoy your evening, Romeo says. He stands to open his office door for her.

"Thank you. You too."

Dalesa and Romeo decide to have their therapy sessions every Wednesday, which also happens to be the open-mic night at the Ether Lounge. Richard first introduced her to the spot when he first heard Dalesa read to him some of her poetry. She had mostly always been private about her poems. However, Richard encouraged her to share her work and gave her confidence. Plus, the response she received from the audience the first time she read was overwhelming. So, now she looks forward to sharing spoken word at the Ether Lounge each week to a packed crowd and her fan base is growing.

After her first therapy session with Romeo, Dalesa becomes inspired to write on the train, as she rides downtown to the Ether Lounge. She decides to share the new piece with the audience.

THE FORGOTTEN EMBRACE

Ever feel you didn't belong?

Ever feel out of place and unnecessary?

Life is full of so many surprises and gives way to so many discoveries.

The most shocking finds are the ones under the veil that has kept

hidden what's inside you.

The lies we tell ourselves in order to live with ourselves are many.

The life we build on these lies can become blinding with all the

glittering gold.

A life so corrupt if the truth isn't told

So, we forget the truth.

Why not forget the sorrowfulness?

Forget the fear.

Forget the pain.

Yet, rarely does one forget that it all remains.

Every bit of it is collected, and it all comes together—no matter how

obscure.

There it remains.

The years compile as our body gets old and the things about

ourselves that we have chosen to run from cling to our soul.

We cannot let go when it still clutches hold.

Tight!

It forces us to flee or take flight.

War is waged between who we are and who we want to be.

Running away does not help.

The path tread is 360 degrees, and in 365 days you realize that

you've run nowhere far because the circle leaves you where you

began.

As the seasons change and the world turns, you must not forget to

embrace the truth.

Yet, we never forget to embrace the sorrowfulness.

Embrace the fear.

Embrace the pain.

CHAPTER 5

The following week, Dalesa and Romeo meet again for therapy. Romeo starts their hour by saying, "So, is there anything you wish to talk about today? Anything interesting happen this past week?"

"Nothing in particular," Dalesa says.

"Okay. Well, I have a question for you. Let me know if you don't want to answer. Okay?" Romeo says.

"Sure."

"I understand that you are HIV positive. When did you discover you were infected?" Romeo asks.

"It was about eight years ago. So, 2002, when I was in college," Dalesa answers. "I didn't think I would make it this long, but yet it still feels like I got the news yesterday."

"I'm glad to see you are taking care of yourself," Romeo compliments.

"I guess. But I shouldn't even have this illness. I've always practiced safe sex."

It was a Friday night eight years ago. It was Dalesa's senior year at Columbia University. She was leaving the library when one of her classmates, Carson Melon, ran up behind her. Stunned, she dropped the books in her hands. She turned to see who it was behind her.

"Don't do that, Carson," Dalesa said. She bent down to pick up her books. Carson made an animalistic grunt as he enjoyed the view of Dalesa's rear end snug in her jeans.

"Sorry I scared you, but this view was worth it. Dang, girl! Looking good, Moreno," Carson said.

"Don't be fresh," Dalesa responded, but she blushed—mildly fond of his brute flattery.

"I'm as fresh as they come. You know this," Carson said, as he laughed cockily. "Didn't mean to scare you, beautiful."

"It's okay. Next time, I'm going to hit you with one of these books, though."

"Did you watch those movies for Professor Dorian's class yet?"

"No. The copies had been checked out of the library already. That's what I get for waiting until the last minute. What can I say? I'm the queen of procrastination," Dalesa said with a laugh.

"Well, lucky for you, your highness, I so happen to have copies I rented back at my place," Carson said. "I was going to watch them tonight, but I think that maybe you should come to my crib and we watch them together."

Dalesa smiled and said, "Sure. That would help me out so much."

"You know what would make this spectacular? Is if you were to have dinner with me, too."

"So, what? Like a study date?"

"Yeah. I'll make my world-famous tacos. My roommate is staying at his girl's place tonight. So, we'll have the place to ourselves."

"Sounds cool."

"You got a pen? Take down my address and number," Carson said.

"Sure. Will you hold these?" Dalesa handed him her books, and she reached into her purse for a pen and piece of paper. "Here you go." Dalesa gave him the stationary.

Carson used the book surface to write on. "Come by around seven. My roommate should be gone by then," he said. He handed her back her things. "I got to go. See you later."

"Ok."

Carson and Dalesa didn't hang out much outside of class but were friends on each other's Myspace page. They had been emailing each other for a few months and had developed a relatively amicable relationship.

Dalesa didn't have any romantic interest in Carson but knew he had interests in her; either that, or he was just flirtatious by nature. She would entertain his sexual innuendos and unsolicited compliments, but she made it clear to him that her only interests were for a platonic relationship between the two of them. Carson seemed to respect the conditions of their friendship, but that didn't stop him from trying to psychologically seduce her with his wit, charisma, and playfulness.

The two of them met up that evening as they had discussed. Like Carson told her earlier, they had the apartment to themselves. "Welcome to my home. It's not much but make yourself comfortable," Carson greeted.

"Oh, no, Carson. It's a cute place," Dalesa said.

"The food is almost ready. Do you drink?"

"Socially, I guess," Dalesa answered.

The apartment was small. When you walk through the front door, you enter immediately into the living room. There was a partition with a countertop that separated that space from the kitchen and there were two bar stools up against the partial wall. Dalesa thought the couch looked comfortable but decided to sit on one of the bar stools instead.

Carson said, "Well, I have some beer or if you rather some Hennessey." He walked to the kitchen on the opposite side of the partition, and Dalesa sat looking at him as he opened the refrigerator and pulled out a bottle of Heineken. "You want?"

"Sure."

"I know I'm magnetic, but you don't have to sit there. You can sit in the living room." He laughed and looked in a drawer for a bottle opener.

"What's wrong with me sitting here? You don't want me watching you cook?"

"Yeah, pretty much. You don't go to the restaurant and ask for a seat in the kitchen," Carson said. He leaned forward with an arrogant smirk on his face. "But I can't blame you. It's been four hours since you saw me last and I'm sure you've been thinking about seeing me again ever since."

"You need to stop, boy," Dalesa said, as she rolled her eyes. Laughing at his cocky remark, she got up and walked over to the couch to sit. "Fine. These tacos had better be phenomenal." She sat and crossed her legs as she waited for her beer.

Carson found the bottle opener and brought her the libation. He went back to the kitchen and returned minutes later with dinner. He put on the first film they had to watch for their "American Cinema" class—which was *Casablanca*.

A few scenes, bites, and sips into the movie, Dalesa's stomach started to feel a little uneasy. "The food is delicious, but I think I've had enough," Dalesa said.

"Thank you. Okay. No problem. You only left crumbs, anyways. I wasn't offering seconds," Carson kids. He takes her plate and goes into the kitchen to put it in the sink.

Dalesa felt herself fading out. There was an uncontrollable succumbing for her to welcome darkness that was now entering the room and wiping out Humphrey Bogart on the television. Her eyes closed shut and when they re-opened the television was off, and she didn't see Carson.

Dalesa didn't remember finishing the movie but felt that something wasn't right. First, why was she laid out horizontally on the sofa? The last activity she could recall was sitting *straight up* watching Ingrid Bergman's first scene on the television. Then Dalesa quickly noticed that the button and zipper of her jeans were undone. She also noticed that her blouse was unbuttoned down to the gore between the cups of her bra.

Not sure what to make of her dishevelment, she fixed her clothing and called for Carson. "Carson? Where are you?"

He entered the room with a cheesy grin, shirtless, barefoot and with a towel wrapped around his waist. "Hey, Sleeping Beauty. You finally woke up."

"What time is it?" Dalesa asked.

"It's like two in the morning. You must have been exhausted. I tried waking you up, but you just laid there. So, I did my thing." Carson said with a smile.

"What do you mean by did your thing?" Dalesa asked, starting to feel paranoid.

"I finished Casablanca." He began singing, "You must remember this. A kiss is still a kiss. As time goes by." He laughs at his poor reinvention of the movie's classic song. "Then, I treated myself to dessert. Had me a nice piece. Yummy! Still, some left if you want. Watched the second video after that. Washed dishes. Then I went in for some more sweet stuff and just finished a shower."

"Why was my shirt unbuttoned?" Dalesa asked. She was feeling a little uncomfortable with the possible double entendre in his recapitulation of the last several hours.

"I don't know."

"And my pants?"

"Why are you asking me? Maybe you undid them after you ate. I know I'm slim, but when I'm full, I have to give my waist some breathing room sometimes." Carson chuckled.

"I'm going to go. Can I borrow the DVD's?"

"Sure. You should stay the night," Carson suggested.

"I don't think that would be a good idea," Dalesa declined. She was finding it difficult to think clearly. Not being able to account for the last four or five hours, waking up with her clothes the way they were and then seeing Carson with nothing on, but a striped bath towel wasn't sitting well with her.

"Okay," Carson said. He maintained the same smug grin on his face since giving Dalesa his alleged alibi for his hands and private parts. "It was nice having you." He opened the door for her, and she left.

"I returned the videos for him on that Monday. Carson talked to me like usual when I saw him the two days later," Dalesa says to Romeo. "That day and the days that followed, he would—in addition to his typical display of machismo—wear a certain look on his face. There wasn't subtle desire like there had been in their encounters before their study date. Now, what Dalesa saw when Carson looked at her was a sense of accomplishment. I stopped communicating with him on Myspace and never had another study date with him after that night.

"It's my word against his, but I know he slipped me something that night in his apartment. He was a clean rapist but sloppy re-dressing me. A month went by, and at a routine physical, my doctor asked if I wanted an HIV test. This year was the first year the rapid finger prick test was being used. I knew that I wasn't sexually active, but because I didn't know if Carson used protection or not, I agreed." Dalesa tears up.

Romeo sees that Dalesa is getting emotional and moves a box of facial tissues on his desk closer to the edge where Dalesa was sitting.

"When my PCP told me I was positive, I wanted to kill Carson. It confirmed my suspicions about that night because I knew I had not been with anyone other than my ex-boyfriend. Carson was my Stanley. I saw HIV as a penance for ever being born. In my inevitable deterioration, my death will serve as the retribution for my mother's demise."

MAYBE I DESERVE IT

Maybe I deserve it.

Misfortune

Waiting for the other shoe to drop

Why should I expect anything else?

Doomed since the genesis

Cursed to live out my days in misery

The silver-lined clouds above me are tarnished.

Hardship loiters around the corner.

It waits patiently for me.

I'm all alone and vulnerable.

Then, thuggishly disrupting the calm, it attacks viciously.

Ravishing me like a hunter's game

Pride ripped apart

Ego bruised

Spirit stabbed

What it doesn't know is that I'm already broken.

Damaged goods

It tears down; even more, someone tore apart.

Then it leaves but leaves a mess.

I'm left to bleed out hope.

Left in agony

Feeling not, in the least, worthy of a touch from Grace.

"Unprotected, forced, fornication in exchange for a shortened lifespan now filled with toxic medications that are keeping me alive," Dalesa says. Tears start to cascade down her face. She snatches up a couple of tissues from the box on the desk and wipes her face. "I don't know why I'm still crying like this after so much time has passed living with the disease. What are the stages of grief again? Shouldn't I be at acceptance by now?"

"What would you be accepting?" Romeo asks.

"Did you really just ask me that?"

"Yes. I want to know what you feel you need to accept. Do you think that you need to accept that similar to your mom, you got sexually assaulted? Do you need to accept that you contracted HIV? Do you accept that your birth created complications that killed your mother? Do you accept that separation from you and the loss of your mother led to your father's suicide? Do you accept that you are here with me because of your own suicide attempt? Do you accept that you have to take medication every day for the rest of your life?"

"Yes! Yes, to all of that!" Dalesa says. Her sinus cavities are filling with mucus from the crying.

"What about accepting that you are still alive? After eight years and counting, with this illness, you are still alive and healthy. What about accepting that you deserve to live a life in which you can be happy? You deserve to be happy. You've had a hard life, but you have a good life."

As a human being with emotions and compassion, Romeo wants just to hold Dalesa in his arms—hug her so tight that she feels in his arms is the safest place in the world to be. His heart goes out to her. He wants to comfort her completely. No matter how warm and powerful his words may be, he knows that it will take more than saying "Everything will be okay" or "It is okay to let it out." These words seemed so cliché and scripted to him.

There's a clinical explanation for what Dalesa is feeling. There's a textbook response to what she is saying. Romeo doesn't want to rely on any of that. He's been out of school for several years, and he knows, as a therapist, there is going to be a lot of stories and a lot of clients that will tug at his emotions.

However, there is something about Dalesa that has gotten to him—ever since seeing her in a coma a few weeks ago. All his previous clients have been conscious when they first met but not Dalesa. It was like looking at Sleeping Beauty or Snow White after she had bitten the wicked queen's apple. Maybe Dalesa had indeed taken a bite from a poisonous fruit—a fruit of her labor of which has had a deficiency of love. Romeo wants to cradle Dalesa in his arms and rock her back and forth as if she was an infant that was just being introduced to love.

Dalesa is not a helpless child, but just as a baby being left alone in the crib for the first time, Romeo wants to be like a parent that comes back into the room and somehow communicates to her that love will never leave her nor forsake her—if even with only a hug. However, Romeo has a responsibility to his *client,* not his daughter, sister, or girlfriend. As her therapist, ethically and professionally, he must sit up straight in his chair close to her, listen actively, offer a tissue for leaky eyeballs and manage to lock-in her trust to continue opening—with just his non-judgmental gaze and benevolent eyes.

Dalesa finally pulls herself together. "I'm sorry."

"Don't apologize. Our sessions are the perfect opportunity for you to do that," Romeo says.

"Thank you."

"After you got the results, did you ever confront Carson?" Romeo asks.

"I wanted to, but that wouldn't have done anything. I heard he died two years ago."

"So, Dalesa, what are your relationships like with people, now? Are they different after being taken advantage of in such a covert way?" Romeo asks.

"What do you mean?"

Romeo clarifies. "Do you have trouble with intimacy? Do you have trust issues?

"Well, I usually have a three-month waiting period before I have sex and tell a guy I'm infected," Dalesa says. "I call it my 'Getting to Know You' period. If after three months, I think the person is worth it, I'll disclose my status and then take it from there. With Richard, sex wasn't important to me at the time, and my condition was being managed well. So, it took me longer to take the risk in telling— inevitably, to lose him."

"This is a rather personal question but considering your waiting period, have you been sexually active since you found out your status?"

"Yes. I was pretty active with one guy I met a few months after I graduated from Columbia," Dalesa recalls. "It was a fling. His name was Khalid. It took me a while to even want to have sex again after I got infected. But I eventually met this guy, and we hit it off; there was a strong attraction. I told him my status early on, we used protection, and everything was fun. He ended up being a jerk, though. Not about the disease or anything but it was something else—not worth mentioning. It wasn't until after Khalid that I started the whole waiting period thing."

"So, that was eight years ago," Romeo says. "I know there was one guy recently, but have you dated many men since then?"

"Not many, no. I've tried to date a few times. The three months would come and well…let's just say, who I was as a person ended up not being worth more than what I could transmit to them—only transmitting to them if not being careful and precautious, mind you. I'm not a reckless individual, but who wants damaged goods? I've had very little sex."

As Romeo listens to Dalesa, he wonders to himself why this one woman is having such an empathetic pull on his heart. He wonders why his humanity has risen beyond its normal range for his patients when it comes to Dalesa. Listening to her describe herself as "damaged goods" bothers him and hurts him deeply to hear someone, another human being, refer to herself as damaged goods. That's something people say when describing merchandise. Her life—her individuality—was not up for commerce. He sees a beautiful woman with an autobiography that tells a story of events that many people could not have endured. Here she is. She is still pushing through, and she does not know her strength. She has been broken down by abandonment, manipulation, disappointment, and fear but still, she is able to sit before him to tell about it and is not beyond repair.

"Do you think you can ever have a healthy relationship in the future?" Romeo asks.

"If it wasn't for Richard," Dalesa answers.

"Richard?"

"That's the guy who was partly the reason I hurt myself. Well, if it weren't for him, I would say 'yes' my romantic forecast would have a stable, healthy relationship in my future. But Richard clearly showed me that love is nothing. It is a phantom sentiment—an overly glorified concept to keep sinners donating money to churches, families to have a reason to forgive one another, couples more federal tax credits and deductions and to have a 'four-letter word' that sounds better than the f- word." Dalesa crosses her arms. "I have given up hope on that. What is love anyway? Love is for romance novels and fairy tales. Oh, and it makes for great music and movies," Dalesa answers.

The other day, Dalesa got a visit from Richard. He wanted to return a few things that belonged to her. He still had them at his place.

They talked for a little while. Richard explained, calmly, why he felt things could not work between them. Dalesa wanted to tell him it could work. She wanted to tell him how he made history. She has had her heart broken before, but Richard was the first man to obliterate it. She wanted to tell him about her suicide attempt prompted by his careless way of giving a falsely advertised love. However, all she could say to his cowardly excuses for breaking all his promises of love and devotion was, "Okay, Richard. I understand. I'm sorry." He wished her well. She wished him better, and the two of them said their goodbyes.

As Dalesa speaks to Romeo in his office, she hears herself and her words sound jaded and hopeless. She recalls the interview with Mrs. Cox and the blessings of love that seemed to be bestowed upon her family—even in a loss. Dalesa is re-evaluating everything she has ever thought about love. Does she have a point of reference to know when there is love?

Love has the power to tear down, transform, teach and take away. It can rebuild, heal, and change perception—among other things. If a person were to understand that love is not just a feeling but energy— probably the very building blocks of creation—then maybe he or she would be able to harness its power and protect him or herself from the constant blows of misfortune, the imbalance of unexpected events, cruel intentions, and ailments.

Perhaps, Dalesa will one day be able to find comfort in the most seemingly harsh reality of her given circumstances. In the ideal relationship with love, a person must also learn to protect love. If love is to be a person's daily bread, defense, medicine, and guidance, then it must be guarded. It is a most prized possession of anyone that owns it.

Love is said to protect always. Should this be interpreted to mean that love protects those that are loved or should those that are created from the substance of love always protect themselves with love? The two of the most lethal threats to love are fear and doubt. They are enemies of courage and faith. One should try to protect the love within these adversaries. For a person to have something so precious and invaluable as love, which all humankind has ownership of—no matter how active or inverted it may be in them—one must tenaciously guard the essence of love.

Romeo asks Dalesa, "We're about to end for the day, but I have a question for you. Do you love yourself?"

"No. I despise myself."

"That's something we will explore more. Your homework for this week, however, is to think about your answer to my question and if you've accepted it as your final answer. That'll be all for today." Their session ends.

Later in the evening, Dalesa takes center stage at the Ether Lounge and shares her latest spoken word poetry.

THE LAST TIME

I took a chance.

Courageously, I stepped out on the ledge.

Beneath me, I see your arms stretched out ready to catch me.

I took the leap of faith.

I jumped off the ledge of my doubt and inhibitions.

As I was falling towards you, you lowered your arms.

I see you walk away.

My refuge, my net, my security, and hope, got up and left.

I fell to the ground.

Shattered and broken into pieces is my self-esteem and pride.

Wrecked is my heart and wretched I lay injured by the risks I took.

Time will heal, but I won't take that chance again.

I learned from my misfortune.

I know better now.

This is the way.

Not trusting in the love someone confesses

Promises have proven themselves made to be broken.

I vow to keep my heart from being hurt again by knowing better than

to trust the fables, folklore and fairytales of love.

I will hold tight to something.

Something strong, secure and everlasting

This I know, won't be love.

It has let me down for the last time.

CHAPTER 6

"Dalesa, tell me a little more about your childhood," Romeo says.

"What do you want to know?" Dalesa asks.

"Did your grandparents treat you well?"

"I never really saw them as grandparents. Up until I was seven, they were mom and dad. Then after they told me about my parents, they became more of my foster parents—better yet, legal guardians—than they were *grandma* and *grandpa*."

"Didn't that still make them parents? Caregivers? Family?" Romeo asks.

"Oh, Romeo, I like your new Japanese Zen garden. I used to have one of these."

Sitting on Romeo's desk is a mini sandbox with stones and a small, bamboo rake. Dalesa takes the rake and outlines a line between the rocks.

"Thank you. I'm glad you like it. The way you diverted from my question tells me the subject of Mr. and Mrs. Jenkins is a difficult one to talk about now or maybe always. Am I wrong?"

"Being a foster parent isn't the same as being a real parent or even an adoptive parent. I was a responsibility—a legal obligation and subsequently a paycheck to the Jenkins."

"You told me that they took you in when your mother's family refused. They weren't obligated to do that," Romeo says.

"True. I guess I ruined a good thing," Dalesa responds.

Stanley's parents had their doubts at the beginning about whether at their age if they could handle raising a child. However, Dalesa was their blood, and there was no one else in the family with the financial means or accessibility to accommodate the newborn. They treated Dalesa with tender care and managed to care for her as if she was their birth child.

Dalesa got spoiled from the very first bottle of milk she drank and rattle she was given and clutched. As a little girl, whatever Dalesa wanted Mr. and Mrs. Jenkins made sure she had. Perhaps, the overindulgence to be like the god and goddess of provision for their grandchild was due to contrition for Stanley's actions regarding Dalesa's mother.

If curiosity killed the cat and a cat has nine lives, what exactly does this proverbial feline represent? Are there nine opportunities to be curious? Not that humans are subject to the same instincts as cats, but if this curious cat does somehow represent some anthropomorphic entity of human nature, surely, at age seven, you wouldn't want your life to be over by questioning the simple, dissimilar life compared to those of your peers. Asking about her last name, wondering why the parents of her friends seemed less geriatric than her own and inquiring about the roles of her family members, practically ended Dalesa's childhood.

Parents should protect their children from dangers—especially avoidable threats to their livelihood. Dalesa's grandparents did not. Was there not a loophole in their religious beliefs to allow them to lie to a child about something that could devastate and disintegrate the very essence of the little girl? She was in the second grade. She hadn't even learned to write in cursive, yet. How could she possibly deal with knowing that her parents were both dead? Couldn't the revealing of that truth be delayed or altered in some way as to avoid introducing death and the cognizance of death to a child so soon?

Dalesa was too young to process deception and death altogether. A new world—an abstract reality—in which she had no living biological parents and was made to believe the people who fed her, clothed her, sheltered her and prayed with her were only pretending to be mommy and daddy. Whereas many of her classmates had parents but no surviving grandparents, she had the opposite. Since she thought her grandparents were her parents, who she thought was her brother, Dalesa then discovered he was her uncle, and that she wasn't the aunt to her cousins who she thought were her niece and nephew.

Maybe Mr. and Mrs. Jenkins were offended that Dalesa would even dare question the makeup of the family. Maybe that's why they told her the morbid truth. Maybe they couldn't keep up the lie any longer. Maybe the rest of the family—their co-conspirators—started getting confused at family reunions. Whatever the reason for the revelation, it truly killed Dalesa's curious cat—the **C**onfusion **A**bout **T**ruth.

For the following years, Dalesa learned to understand what grandparents were. As she matured and approached pre-adolescence, she became more aware of the roles within the family. The media—movies and sitcoms—was instrumental in the view she had of her placement within the immediate ecological system in which she was living. She also grew to understand more what death, deficit, and deception meant.

When Dalesa was close to eleven, there was one day that seemed to be the turning point of the Jenkins and Dalesa's interpersonal dynamic. Dalesa grew out of calling her grandparents "mom" and "dad," but for the Jenkins, she was still their daughter. On this Sunday afternoon, after a spirit-filled, Pentecostal service at their church, a woman spotted Dalesa and said, "Dalesa, your mother is looking for you."

Mrs. Jenkins came out of the church building the exact moment Dalesa repudiated the relation, and with a stern, straight countenance said, "She is not my mother." Dalesa had no idea what a detrimental impact those five truthful words would have on her relationship with the Jenkins from then on. For Mrs. Jenkins, Dalesa had publicly disavowed her relationship the way Mrs. Jenkins had seen it from Dalesa's cradle and teething—up until the purchase of her first training heel shoes Dalesa was wearing that day along with her Sunday dress.

From that moment on, Mr. Nathanieal and Mrs. Josephine Jenkins treated Dalesa as the orphan she was—a child of the state entrusted to their well-compensated guardianship. She was still family, but her care diminished to the bare minimum. It was just enough to satisfy basic needs the majority of the time—no more than enough to make signs of neglect imperceptible. They abused her in one of the most damaging ways. Metaphorically, they attacked her esteem by spanking her with thick leather belts of their legal power. They programmed and conditioned a vulnerable developing mind with psychological corporal punishment—often using bullying branches from trees of circumstance to hit her with their unexplainable contempt for her existence. Perpetually, they gagged and bound her to her emotions as they whipped her with torturous taunting tools of verbal degradation. Her subjection to secret mental and emotional beatings from her perpetrating legal guardians was equivalent in degree to the acts of brutal physical child abuse inflicted by biological parental assailants.

Physical wounds heal, but they can often be seen by others to alert people who could be potential advocates or aid. However, psychological and emotional abuse does damage that is imperceptible to the world that exists outside of the home. The lacerations of the heart, the broken pieces of the self-esteem, the submerges in waters of condemnation are so painstaking, the injuries and wounds could last a lifetime, and no one would know.

It wasn't that Dalesa stopped loving the Jenkins. It was just that she saw their relationship different. Although morbid, Dalesa rather lived in the reality that said she had no parents and was being taken care of by her grandparents. She wasn't disowning them in the least— just placing them in their rightful familial place in her life.

The Jenkins didn't see it that way. They wanted Dalesa to give them the love that a biological child would give their parents. The reality they wanted to live in was one that would allow them the love they were missing since their son was no longer alive.

Dalesa became a burden. Although no one ever said those exact words to her, the Jenkins' behavior spoke louder and more indignant than any words ever could.

On one occasion, Mrs. Jenkins didn't feel like cooking and ordered Chinese food. Mr. Jenkins wanted chicken and broccoli and an egg roll. Mrs. Jenkins was in the mood for shrimp fried rice. She didn't ask Dalesa if she wanted anything. She intended to give her some of her food.

When the food arrived, Mr. Jenkins took his white, Styrofoam container to his den to finish watching the Knicks game. Dalesa was in her room doing some homework.

"Dalesa! Come eat!" Mrs. Jenkins called.

Dalesa was starving. She flew down the stairs and into the kitchen. She didn't know they had ordered out. She loved takeout. Mrs. Jenkins handed her a plate of her shrimp fried rice. As soon as Dalesa saw the long-tailed crustaceans in the rice, she said, "No, thank you."

"Take this food, child," Mrs. Jenkins demanded.

"You know I have a severe reaction to shrimp, grandma."

"Take them out. This is dinner. I'm not cooking anything, and I don't want you using the stove."

"I guess I'm not eating," Dalesa said. She was about to return to her room.

"Oh yes, you are. You're going to eat this food. I don't want you saying to anyone that I don't feed you," Mrs. Jenkins insisted with authority.

"No, I'm not. It will have me vomiting all night."

"Oh well. What do I care? Eat the food little girl." Mrs. Jenkins put the plate on a small dining table that was in the kitchen. She pulled out the chair for Dalesa to sit.

Dalesa stared at the woman and then stared at the food. She couldn't believe her grandmother was going to force this on her. Dalesa would've been happy with just a peanut butter and jelly sandwich, but obediently, she sauntered towards the chair. Mrs. Jenkins had no patience for her sloth-like processional to the table. She grabbed Dalesa's arm and pulled her to the seat.

"Eat, or you're grounded! Don't waste my food," Mrs. Jenkins said.

Dalesa started to cry. She couldn't believe her grandmother was doing this to her. She took her first bite, and despite the taste—which she found pleasing—she thought of the aftermath. She thought to herself that this was a waste of food because the upset stomach she would have soon, would lead only to her vomiting it all up—emptying her stomach and leaving her to go to bed hungry in the end.

The family never ate meals together, but tonight, Mrs. Jenkins sat with Dalesa to eat her food. Dalesa ate as much as she could before starting to feel sick. She tried to clear the plate because of the disdainful glare she was receiving from her dinner companion. When Dalesa couldn't shovel any more rice from the plate to feed herself and felt the heaving in her abdomen, she got up from the table and went to the bathroom.

"Uuuuuuugh! Uuuuuuugh!" Dalesa knelt at the toilet and regurgitated her meal.

Mrs. Jenkins got up from the table and stood at the bathroom door that Dalesa left open and watched her granddaughter with apathy. She wiped her mouth with a napkin. "Look at you. Hmph! You want to know something little girl? You are nothing. You are worthless. Pathetic. You are nothing but a sad, helpless orphan. That's why your mother didn't want you and your father killed himself to keep from having ever to see your pitiful face."

"Uuuuuuugh! Uuuuuuugh!" Dalesa continued to throw up and now with tears pouring into the toilet bowl.

"She stood there and watched me for what had to be around twenty minutes. Twenty minutes I was there at the toilet—unable to leave a foot away from it because I couldn't stop puking. She enjoyed it," Dalesa tells Romeo. "Why did she say those things about my parents? How could she say those things about me?"

"Did she tell you bad stuff like that often? Did she subject you to any other harmful situations? Was it just her or did your grandfather do and say things as well?" Romeo probes.

"Yes. That was only one of many times in which they subjected me to degradation," Dalesa says.

When Dalesa was in high school, one day, she had to stay after for a meeting with the Forensics club of which she was Vice President. The meeting let out, and she headed home. When she got there, nobody was there. She was locked out. Her grandparents knew that she would be home later than usual on this day and Dalesa did not have a key. The Jenkins wouldn't allow her to have one because they didn't want her to have access to the house without their knowledge and permission.

They told Dalesa that morning that they had something to do in the evening but that they would wait until she got home before leaving. Dalesa was on time. 'They left early intentionally.' She figured. Dalesa sat on the front steps and waited. Ten minutes. Twenty minutes. Thirty minutes. Forty-five.

Dalesa had nowhere else to go. All she could do was wait. Every car that rode past she thought it was them pulling up. "Dalesa, hey!" a friend of hers, Tiffany, said as she walked up. "What cha doin'?"

"Waiting for my grandparents," Dalesa said.

"You locked out or something?"

"Yeah."

"Come hang out with me. It's gonna rain soon. You can have dinner at my place," her friend said.

"Oh, that sounds great! Thank you," Dalesa replied. She got up from the stairs and walked towards her. "Thank you."

"No problem."

Dalesa stayed at her friend's house for a few hours before going back home. It was kind of late. Dalesa had lost track of time. When she got back to her house, the Jenkins had returned. Mr. Jenkins scolded her for not being in the front of the house when he and Mrs. Jenkins got there. "Where were you?"

"I was at a friend, Tiffany's, house. You guys weren't here when I came from school," Dalesa explained.

"You don't have any friends, little girl. No one will care about you. Tiffany just pitied you because it would make her feel better about herself or to make herself feel good by pretending to care. You're such an idiot, Dalesa. You think these little girls around here or in your class are your friends. You got all that *book* sense but no darn common sense. If somebody in this world likes you enough to call you their friend, it's because they like themselves. You're nothing more to anyone than a liability. You should have waited here until we got here."

"I didn't know what time you were coming back. You said that you would wait until I got home before you left. It was going to start raining, and I didn't have an umbrella."

"You're talking back to me?" Mr. Jenkins said as his tone got dark. "You illegitimate little ingrate. We not now or ever will revolve our life around you. You keep thinking that we do if you want. You keep believing that anyone in this world gives any care about you and see where you'll end up."

Dalesa would ordinarily exit with her head down low and spirit bruised after an altercation like that—let him have the last word. This time, however, she made her often imprisoned voice heard. "If you don't care about me then why do you keep me around? Put me on the street. Let someone else get those checks each month," she said.

"Why would we do that? The bills have to get paid somehow." He laughed, heartedly. "Social Security isn't enough if you must know and want to be all up in grown people's affairs. You keep forgetting that everybody wants but to use you or benefit from you."

"So, that's all I am to you. A way to pay for the lease and insurance on your Lincoln Town Car?"

"Listen, child. Don't talk back to me. Go to your room. I don't want to see your face anymore tonight."

"I went to my room and cried until my tears felt like acid was coming out of my tear ducts. It's funny, though. I believed him—every word. It wasn't so much that he was saying such hurtful things to me, as much as, what he was saying was true. I didn't have many friends growing up. I don't have many now. Who cares about me? Nobody," Dalesa says to Romeo.

"Coreen cares about you. I care about you," Romeo replies.

"Does she? I pay half the rent. Apartments are expensive in New York City. She could be just securing my portion of the rent with some semblance of amity," Dalesa argues.

"Dalesa, in your heart do you feel there is any truth to that? She came to visit you every day in the hospital," Romeo reasons.

"Yes, I do feel that way. And you. You have to show empathy because my insurance pays you off," Dalesa responds. She hears what she's saying and has to check herself. Deep inside, she knows these words coming out her mouth are baseless and emotional. "Maybe I was all wrong feeling that my grandparents were poisoning and programming me to hate myself and maybe they were right," Dalesa says. "Yet, instead of accepting the degrading, demeaning and damaging things they said as truth, I resisted. Internally I fought it. I didn't want to believe that I was nothing and not worthy of love because I got care and attention from teachers, members of the church, and a few classmates. How could these people who aren't my family—who barely know me—care more about me than my sanctioned caregivers?

"I was confused and conflicted about what compassion was but maybe what these compassionate people—these perfect strangers— showed to me was the inevitable pity my grandfather could have been prophesizing about in his contemptuous dialogue all those years. For the first time, I see, now, how love abandoned me and consequently took out a restraining order against me from the second I was born."

"Didn't you say that your peers and teachers showed you love?" Romeo asks.

"How can I be sure that that was genuine love?" Dalesa questions.

"What did it feel like?"

"What I received from them seemed kinder than what I felt when my grandparents spoke to me. My teachers, even members of the church, appeared to have a personal interest in me, and their words were encouraging."

"Surely, that was an encounter with love. Wouldn't you say?"

"Romeo, I can't be sure. As far as I was concerned, I had no viable point of reference. The way I saw the world back then, if my loved ones couldn't love me, then how could I trust the care or concern of anyone else?"

English was Dalesa's favorite subject all throughout school and writing was something in which she excelled. She started creative writing in sixth grade, but it wasn't until seventh grade that her English teacher, Ms. Mayon, noticed Dalesa's potential as a poet, with remarkable use of the language and structure, upon grading a class written assignment one semester.

Dalesa longed to have something in which she could find confidence. The praise she received with each following assignment nurtured a fondness for the literary arts. She started keeping a journal and began writing all the time. She was private with her writings but did occasionally share a piece or two with her teacher.

Ms. Mayon would instruct on grammar and punctuation, but Dalesa was coming into her style and technique. Ms. Mayo always encouraged Dalesa to push the boundaries of her abilities and creativity each time she wrote. One day, after reading one of her poems which moved the teacher in an emotionally significant way, Ms. Mayon told Dalesa that she found her to be a real architect of the English language. This plainly stated but laudatory compliment given by her teacher resonated warmly within the budding adolescent and was like a beacon of hope for Dalesa that siad the Jenkins were wrong in their evaluation of her existence and being.

Ms. Mayon didn't want to force Dalesa to share her poems publicly if she didn't want to do so. She was, however, successful in persuading her poet protégé to join the Forensics club where she could read the work of other poets to an audience.

Dalesa enjoyed competing in competitions where she could perform poetry written by some of the greatest writers of American literature. She was exceptional in oratory and won some awards citywide and regionally. Although, not a first-place winner on the state level, she did manage to rank admirably high among other contestants at state competitions during her participation in middle and high school.

Her ability to connect with a poet's emotions and convey them dramatically to audiences eventually gave Dalesa the confidence to start performing her original work at competitions. It was the first time she was sharing her work with not just another person but with groups of individuals. Her original work was received well. However, she wasn't judged in the competitions for the content as much as she was for her dramatic reciting of the work.

Occasionally, Ms. Mayon would ask why none of her family came out to support her at the meets. Dalesa would give some plausible excuse and quickly change the subject. Just like the wicked intentions of Snow White's queen, there was one night during Dalesa's last year of middle school that provided the Jenkins with the venomous apple needed to dissolve what little self-esteem that had managed to be fertilized by the charm and influence of outsiders inside Dalesa.

Each year, Dalesa's middle school held a talent show, and Ms. Mayon wanted Dalesa to perform something original her eighth grade year, which the teacher was sure to impress the rest of the faculty,

PTA, and Dalesa's peers. Dalesa was apprehensive. She knew that the worse critics for any artist are the ones closest to them. No one at the school had heard or read any of Dalesa's work. They knew of her victories for the school from the competitions, but the competitions were always off campus, and Ms. Mayon was the only one of the teaching staff that attended the Forensics meets. The school newspaper asked if they could print one of Dalesa's poems for an edition of the paper, but Dalesa declined to have anything published—feeling that they were too private to share with the entire school.

Ms. Mayon insisted for weeks approaching the event that Dalesa signup to participate in the show. Seeing how much it would mean to her favorite teacher for her to do so, she eventually agreed. Ms. Mayon was so happy that Dalesa was going to perform that she gave her prized pupil a fancy pen and notebook as a gift.

The day before the variety show, Ms. Mayon blind-sided Dalesa by asking, "Your grandparents are coming tomorrow, right? I know they haven't been able to attend any of your competitions. So, surely they wouldn't want to miss your performance."

Dalesa wanted to tell her teacher that the Jenkins probably didn't care if she was illiterate, let alone that she was an award-winning orator and phenomenal poet. She didn't want to give any false hope to add to the already created expectation that her caregivers would be in attendance, but she also didn't want to demean the image of their presumed, nurturing upbringing and guardianship either. She just replied, "They are always active doing something with the church. So, they might be busy."

"Oh, I see. Well, I hope they can make it. I only saw your grandparents that one time for the parent-teacher conference and they seemed like such nice people," Ms. Mayon said.

When Dalesa got home that day, she presented the Jenkins with a formal invitation to the talent program. The Oprah Winfrey Show that had been captivating the Jenkins' attention for about a half hour went to a commercial break. So, Dalesa took the break as her opportunity to tell them about the showcase.

"The school has its annual talent show tomorrow night. I'm performing some poetry," Dalesa said—thinking that with the talk show off the air for a few minutes, she wouldn't be disturbing what had been a Jenkins daily ritual for years. However, her grandparents seemed to find the new commercial for Roto-Rooter to be more interesting than anything Dalesa was saying. That is until she continued by saying, "My teacher Ms. Mayon is really looking forward to seeing you there."

"Who is Ms. Mayon?" Mr. Jenkins asked.

"She's my English teacher and Forensics club coach. You met her that one time at the parent-teacher conference," Dalesa answered.

"What does she want us there for?" Mrs. Jenkins asked.

"Well, like I said, I'm reading some of my poetry. So, since Ms. Mayon has never seen you at any of my competitions, she thought you would probably want to come tomorrow."

"Did you tell her that we were coming?" Mrs. Jenkins asked with a tone that indicated there *was* a right and wrong response to the question.

"No. No. Not at all. I told her you might be tied up with the church or something."

"Is this program at the school going to be at a time when it would be believable that we would be at a church function?" Mr. Jenkins asked.

"I guess. I don't know when the universal church function time is but…" Dalesa began to say with an unintentional sarcastic undertone, but her grandmother checked her before she could finish the sentence.

"Excuse me? Are you being fresh with me, girl?" Mrs. Jenkins asked with a sharp inflection in her voice.

"No ma'am," Dalesa said, respectfully.

"You better not. So, what time does the program start?" Mrs. Jenkins asked.

"7:30. You know this is one of the last things I'll be doing at the school before going to high school next year. Maybe you will consider coming."

"Oprah's back on." Mr. Jenkins said. Then, it was as if Dalesa was no longer in the room. The attention they were giving her had an abrupt ending. Dalesa left the room inspired to write something in her journal about their reckless care of her emotions and lack of attention to her interests. Dalesa had no doubt they wouldn't attend the program tomorrow. So, she intended to write something truly profound and emotionally charged for reciting at the show that she would secretly dedicate to them in their absence.

The next school day came. The scholastic periods of the day prevailed with a mundane mental drudgery which made for a drawn-out day for the students. Whereas, the evening seemed to have come far too quickly for Dalesa. She was nervous about reciting her work for her classmates. When talking to Ms. Mayon before the program got started, her teacher found it ironic that Dalesa could captivate a panel of judges and an audience of strangers performing Robert Frost, Maya Angelou or even original poetry. However, when it came down to her teachers who knew her best and kids she's known since elementary school, she was about to have a panic attack.

All the participants, for the evening's event, sat in the first couple of rows in the auditorium to watch the other performers as they took the stage. The place was packed, but Dalesa felt isolated in her world. She could barely enjoy the acts that went on before her because she kept thinking about her performance. At first, it was the thought of speaking in front of her peers that gave her anxiety. However, after writing the poem last night she was going to recite tonight, it was her emotional vulnerability she was going to put on display that had her nervously shaking her leg and tapping her foot more than the tap dancing twins that had just bowed and walked offstage.

Dalesa couldn't remember which student she was supposed to follow, but she knew that it wasn't until after intermission. When she was able to exhale and breathe in the reality of her environment, she noticed that the audience was very receptive and supportive to all the performers that had gone before her. She found solace in a belief that they would show her the same encouragement. Even the sixth graders were enjoying themselves with a bit of maturity that was refreshing to her.

Gradually, Dalesa loosened up. The pricey fruit punch she had along with the basketball team's homemade cookies, she bought during intermission from the concession stand, helped to relax her some. After 15 minutes, the scattered about audience members returned to their seats for the start of the second half. The first performer was Tonya Robinson, whose performance had more influence on Dalesa's deescalated anxiety than the chunky chocolate chip cookies during the break. Tonya was small, meek, and most times quiet, as if she needed to be surreptitious. It was like night and day to see her perform. When she finished her rendition of Mariah Carey's "Hero"—belting out notes in a range and decibel level no one would have thought possible for little "Timid Tonya"—she had the entire audience jumping to their feet in ovation.

For moments during Tonya's performance, she and Dalesa seemed to make eye contact several times. Had they not locked gazes on such lyrics of the song as, "You can find love if you look inside yourself and the emptiness you felt will disappear" or "When you feel like hope is gone, look inside you and be strong" then, Dalesa wouldn't have thought anything out of the ordinary. Dalesa knew it was more than just engaging stage presence—it was divine intervention through music. The song was inspiring, but Dalesa felt confused by her emotional response. She didn't know if she should feel encouraged by the message or saddened by the awareness, she needed a hero—not to mention, her need to be that hero herself.

As she stood there standing with the rest of the audience clapping, Arsenio Hall inspired air-fisting and shouting praises, Dalesa remembered when she was supposed to go on stage. There was to be another orator from Forensics club, a dance group and then her.

She needed to start heading to the backstage area. So, she got up from her chair—along with four other girls that were also sitting in her row. As she stood offstage in the wings, she read her poem in her notebook. She was ready. She was no longer nervous. She was excited to be performing something so personal with the teachers and classmates that had shown her friendship, affection, and support during the school year.

The time had finally come. The MC announced her name, and she walked from off stage to stand before the crowd. When the audience was scattered in and out of the auditorium, during intermission, Dalesa could tell a lot of people were there. However, while she was sitting on the second row, making intermittent glances at the stage and then down again to her tremoring hands, she was oblivious to the number of parents, teachers, and peers seated in the rows behind her. Now, she sees them all and all of them see her.

"Good evening. I'll be reading you something I've written called, 'Monsters.' Thank you." As she was about to start, she heard a distinctive clearing of the throat out in the audience. It sounded like a gargle with a dry cough at the end. The auditorium was quiet—except for a few six graders who had finally started to get restless and fidgety in their chairs. Dalesa knew that sound, but it couldn't have been her grandfather, she told herself, because she had looked around for the Jenkins when the show began and didn't see them.

Dalesa couldn't speak. Her brain was telling her voice box to produce a sound, but nothing came out because in the back of the auditorium —— sitting in the very last row right by the doors—were her grandparents. She figured they had to have come in after intermission was over because she certainly wouldn't have missed them right by the exit. She started to panic about reciting the poem she prepared. It was fine to share in her grandparents' absence but not with them there listening—hearing.

The MC motioned from off-stage to get Dalesa's attention. Dalesa turned her head to look—pellets of perspiration were forming a low-resting liquid tiara on her forehead. He whispered loudly, "Are you ok, Dalesa?"

Dalesa nodded and turned her head back to the audience. She swallowed the lump that was lodged in her pharynx and it dropped like a block of hardened clay in her stomach.

MONSTERS

Frankenstein once created a monster.

Each day we construct creations within the laboratories of our mind

with expectations.

It's a grotesque reality when they are not brought to life.

Beauty had her Beast but are monsters merely characters made up for

books, horror films, and Halloween costumes?

Do they exist in actual reality or conceptualized fantasy?

If so, are they sworn to a monster's fraternity?

Is their devotion to an alliance that horrifies members of a community

with their cruelty?

Do they misunderstand the way things should be within society or are

they simply misunderstood?

Are they monsters because they were created as such by Nature or do

we create the monstrosity of their nature?

Could you spot a monster in a room?

A monster is considered extremely ugly and frightening.

So, couldn't a monster with any number of high-quality cosmetics and

dose of a calming, injectable antipsychotic then be able to display a

less scary behavior and appear more attractive?

Monsters.

They are as real as tumors.

I see those hideous, malignant spirits every day.

These creatures aren't the playground bullies that used to knock my

imaginary friends from off the see-saws and merry-go-round.

They wear fedoras and baseball caps.

They wear stockings and nibble on generic brand, ginger snaps.

They keep a Bible on the coffee table and keep a book of psalms and

prayers by the bed.

They know the scriptures as if the word of God was the alphabet and

apply holy oil on the sick's head.

They are resourcefully able to feed a hungry child with no fear of

personal loss or inconvenience.

Yet, they'd rather see an orphan go to bed hungry because to them,

having humanity is tricky in a sense.

There's a monster under the bed that awaits to show up after a good

night kiss.

The lights go out when lies kept the innocent ignorant and tucked in

darkness.

There are monsters in the closet, but they are hidden underneath and

behind façade and appearances.

Optics and optical illusions

Cloaked and casual clothing

Promiscuity with promises and politics

Routine and religion

Tax credits and children

Arbitration and assets

It's called self-preservation for them so that in society they do not

appear as a threat.

Some monsters are just as cunning as they are vile and manipulative.

They hide behind ambiguity, maintain the status quo and corrupt

what good others can give.

Delving deeply into the very darkness that they dispense—daring to

defy a doomed destiny—they demean and depreciate.

Leaving enough life and residue of love within the victim to avoid any

criminal charges of hate

They wear colorful, masks and opaque, veils as they toggle, day-to-

day, between masquerades and wakes.

Hopelessness cannot be the only disposition available for those naïve

and unsure of what's at stake.

Beyond a reasonable doubt, no good can come from these monsters'

daily reign of terror; it must end.

But who will rescue the little, defenseless lambs which have not one

friend?

Fables, fairytales, pop songs, and hymns all tell of a Savior—a saving

grace.

This redeeming love is so highly praised and priceless, yet, it is

bootlegged, given as bunk and apparently can have no genuine base.

Can it really destroy internal dangers and take the most torn down of

souls to an elevated place?

Do you believe in monsters?

I do, but they don't believe in me.

If they don't believe in me, then they don't know how they are hurting

me.

I'm afraid of monsters.

Who wouldn't be if no one else believes in them either?

The entire time she performed the words to her poem, she made sure to avoid looking at the back of the auditorium. It wasn't clear to Dalesa whether the Jenkins came for the genuine support of their granddaughter or if they wanted just to keep up appearances. Dalesa performed with so much conviction and passion that she could make out the sounds of personal connection a few audience members had with her words in the form of "Ummm hmmm." For Dalesa, the emotional affirmations were a catalyst that propelled her deliverance of the piece to a riveting level. It reminded her of the church—like when some members of the congregation would talk back to the minister and say "Amen" if he said something poignant or relevant to them.

Even though the audience received the poem well and gave Dalesa a standing ovation, she was fixated on the back row—two seats from the door. The fact that the Jenkins took their time standing to their feet and looked to be on the brink of exhaustion as they clapped, it still wasn't a precise or reliable way for Dalesa to gauge their receptivity. As she bowed, she thought of some reasons why they were the last to stand on their feet. They weren't all negative ones. Osteoporosis, arthritis or plain, old age were the most optimistic excuses she could come up with as she thanked the audience and walked off the stage.

"I had written that poem specific to how the Jenkins were treating me. I tussled back and forth trying to convince myself that they were oblivious to that fact," Dalesa says to Romeo, along with a little laugh to herself.

Romeo smiles. "So, your grandparents gave you no indication that they would show up that night?" he asks.

"Nope. They weren't supposed to hear me call them monsters. Even if their aging minds couldn't decipher what I was creatively hiding within metaphors and hyperbole, they weren't meant to hear that poem."

"At some point did you get over the shock, and feel glad or have any positive feelings about them being there?"

"I tried. I really did, but that didn't last; it was fleeting."

The talent show ended three more performances after Dalesa's. The MC thanked everyone for their attendance, and the lights came up in the auditorium. Immediately, the sound level increased in the hall as little sisters ran up to their big sisters that performed, and sons ran to their mothers and fathers. Being located right by the exit allowed the Jenkins to slip out quickly and before anyone else could. Dalesa walked up to the aisle and headed to where she had seen her grandparents sitting while she was on stage, but when she got to the section, they weren't there.

Dalesa wondered to herself if she had imagined their presence. She walked into the hallway outside the school theater and saw them walking at a moderately fast pace to the nearest door out of the building. They were stopped in their tracks by Dalesa's science teacher before they could make it to the double doors.

"Mr. and Mrs. Jenkins, it's so nice to see you. I'm Mr. Reynolds, Dalesa's science teacher. We met last semester."

The Jenkins extended their arms to shake the gentleman's hand. Dalesa now had enough time to walk over to her grandparents before they vanished. As she walked towards the couple perpetrating as supportive legal guardians, Ms. Mayon spotted Dalesa amongst the scattering assembly.

"There she is," Ms. Mayon seemed so pleased to see Dalesa, as she approached her. Dalesa was equally happy to see Ms. Mayon but didn't want her grandparents to get away before she could get to them.

"Hi, Ms. Mayon," Dalesa said, with a humungous grin on her face. They embraced.

"You were amazing tonight!" Ms. Mayon said.

"Thank you," Dalesa said, as humility brushed rosily on her cheeks.

"Are your grandparents here?"

"Yes. They are over there talking to Mr. Reynolds."

"Oh, let's go rescue them. Shall we?" Ms. Mayon joked. Dalesa laughed. Ms. Mayon grabs hold of her finest student's hand. They walked over to the small gathering comprised of an enthusiastic and talkative teacher and an elderly couple who were nodding in what seemed like interest with pretentious, plastic smiles boldly displaying their dentures.

"Hi, Allen," Ms. Mayon said to Mr. Reynolds as she and Dalesa walked up on his conversation with the Jenkins.

"Oh, Hello, Patricia. I was just telling Mr. and Mrs. Jenkins just how impressed I was with Dalesa's performance," Mr. Reynolds said. "Dalesa, I'd heard about your writing, but I'm in awe. I must say you are far more gifted in your use of words and expression of emotional content than I was at your age—even now."

"Thank you," Dalesa said, as she lowered her head in modesty.

"Don't be modest. You have actual talent—a gift. I also enjoyed how you did more than just reading words on a page. You gave a performance as you recited the poem. It was very theatrical. You two must be very proud to have such a gifted daughter," Mr. Reynolds continued. "I mean granddaughter. Well, you all have a beautiful evening. I see a few more students I want to congratulate. Take care."

"See you tomorrow Mr. Reynolds," Dalesa said. She hugged him.

"Get home safe, Allen," Ms. Mayon said.

Mr. and Mrs. Jenkins gave their valediction in unison, and Mr. Reynolds quickly got lost in the sea of loitering students, staff and parents.

"Mr. and Mrs. Jenkins. So, glad you could make it. Dalesa wasn't sure your other obligations would permit you to attend our function this evening. It's nice to see you," Ms. Mayon said.

"Yes, we were late getting here because of some work we were doing for the Lord at our church. Thankfully, though, we made it in time to hear Dalesa," Mrs. Jenkins said.

"Wasn't she remarkable?" Ms. Mayon praised. "I know you two haven't made it to any competitions, but your granddaughter writes and speaks so eloquently. As I'm sure you know seeing all the medallions, trophies, and plaques she's been awarded this year."

"Yes, very impressive work she does," Mr. Jenkins said.

"We are so proud of her accomplishments," Mrs. Jenkins added.

Dalesa couldn't believe she heard compliments from the two of them. Of course, she knew they were putting on a front, but it felt good to hear anyway.

"I'm trying to work with Dalesa to expand herself as far as where she sees her writing going. At the rate her skills are developing, she could be writing novels by the time she finishes high school. She may want to consider journalism or maybe even speechwriting or public speaking as career options for her," Ms. Mayon said.

"Well, we always tell Dalesa not to limit herself. There's no telling what she can do if she just applies herself," Mrs. Jenkins.

"Yes. We expect great things from her," Mr. Jenkins co-signed.

Dalesa covered her mouth with her hand. She didn't want anyone to see her jaw drop. 'What? Have I entered another dimension? Two conversational rounds of compliments from both my grandparents in under five minutes. This is unheard of,' Dalesa said to herself.

"I'm going to miss her next year, but I hope she continues to stay active in writing, performing arts, public speaking or whatever she finds that will allow her to remain creative and put her talent to good use," Ms. Mayon said.

"We'll keep her on track," Mrs. Jenkins said. Then, if the ostentatious conversation with Ms. Mayon had not been enough, Mrs. Jenkins went in for the hard sell and laid a wet, kiss on Dalesa's forehead. Dalesa nearly fainted. She knew that that public display of affection was like the one other drink at the bar that was too much for a drinker's system to handle. There had been no physical contact between the two of them in at least seven years. Mr. Jenkins knew that Mrs. Jenkins wouldn't be able to take much more of smiling and the generosity of kindness towards Dalesa, just as much as he could no longer take the awkward twitching of his left eyelid from the phoniness.

"Well, we really must be going. It was nice talking to you. I forget your name," Mr. Jenkins said. He put his arm around his wife.

"It's Ms. Mayon. The pleasure was all mine. You all have a good night. I look forward to seeing more of you."

"Likewise. You coming with us, Dalesa? Or are you going to catch up with one of your friends?" Mrs. Jenkins asked. She and Mr. Jenkins had begun walking so quickly that they were almost out of the building as she asked this.

"I'm coming with you. I'm just going to finish saying goodbye to Ms. Mayon."

"Dalesa. Again, great job tonight!" Ms. Mayon said. "However, I'd be a horrible teacher if I didn't say that your poem left me a little concerned about you. I'm your biggest fan. I'm very familiar with your style of writing, and I know when you are eluding to something in your writing, which without literary acrobatics you would otherwise find uncomfortable to talk about." Dalesa lowered her head—feeling vulnerable and exposed but relieved that someone heard her cryptic cry for attention. "Look at me, Miss Moreno," Ms. Mayon insists. Dalesa lifted her head, partially. "If you ever need to talk, please know that I'm not a monster. I won't bite," Ms. Mayon said with a reassuring smile. "You can come to me, and I'll help you any way I can."

"Ok. Thank you. I'll remember that." There was an exchange—although, no words were spoken at that moment when Dalesa looked Ms. Mayon into her eyes. Dalesa somehow felt a support that extended past that shared between a teacher and student. Subsequently, Ms. Mayon felt a security that Dalesa was not in any imminent physical danger, and when Dalesa was ready to open about the monsters hiding in her closet, she wouldn't hesitate to come to her. "I'll see you tomorrow, Ms. Mayon. Have a good night."

When Dalesa was in the car heading back to the Jenkins residence the silence was as biting as a Nor'easter with blizzard wind gusts. Dalesa was still stunned by her grandparent's conscious choice of compliance to play the roles of caring, caregivers with no pistol held to their skull. If anything, they were led only by the quiet, social pressures that came with not indicating any non-Christian-like behavior in their ways. The Jenkins were silent because their compromised contempt for their granddaughter had sent their souls into shock. Dalesa, eventually, broke the silence. She said, "Thank you for coming tonight."

"You know, honey, that itty bitty girl that was singing that song as we were coming in tonight had such a lovely voice," Mr. Jenkins said to his wife—completely disregarding Dalesa's backseat gratitude.

"Yes, she did. That was a sweet song, too. Very uplifting," Mrs. Jenkins responded.

"She reminded me of a young, Whitney Houston," Mr. Jenkins added. "You know who else I thought was enjoyable? That little boy that read the poem he wrote about the dog at the ocean."

"Oh, yes! That was a lovely poem. He didn't write that, though," Mrs. Jenkins corrected him.

"Yes, he did. It was typed in the program that it was an original poem. Anyway, that had a nice message too."

"You're right, dear. I'm re-reading the program, now. His name was William. It says here that he's in Dalesa's class. That tiny girl's name was Tonya. She's in Dalesa's class, also," Mrs. Jenkins said.

"I know we didn't catch the whole program, but they were my two favorites of the night," Mr. Jenkins awarded.

"Mine, too. The school will be losing two of its most talented kids next year," Mrs. Jenkins said.

"I'm sure we haven't seen the last of those two. Those two young people are going places," Mr. Jenkins said.

"Most certainly, I have no doubt about it," Mrs. Jenkins said. "I like what William said in his poem. It was something about how dogs never get overwhelmed. Even in an ocean, it's still just a doggie pool for them."

Dalesa sat in the back seat of her grandparent's luxurious Lincoln Town Car and felt so insignificant and small. They spoke as if Dalesa did not get a standing ovation—that her name was not printed in the same program, only lines below Tonya and William's in the same font characters, font color, and font size. She clawed into the leather seat with her fingernails, as she refrained from yelling out of rage and crying from heartbreak.

Would Dalesa have needed to keep herself surrounded by third parties, like teachers and church dignitaries, to receive the minimal respect due to an urban, non-rebellious, young teenager who was still a virgin and a consistent honor roll student? Would the integrity of the Jenkins' personal choice to resign from advocacy in their granddaughter's life—preferring antagonism instead—have been compromised in any way if they had at least given her some credit? What did they stand to lose by giving proper merit to the budding, young woman in their care? Dalesa had managed to resist the easy accessibility of narcotics within their neighborhood, remained active in the church and if not mature beyond her years, god-like in displaying meekness and respect to the duality of their custodial authority as her foster parents and grandparents—despite their hurtful words and behavior. Then again, that may have been too much to ask of them considering they had no idea of the adverse, quite possibly irreversible damage they had inflicted on Dalesa's psyche and soul.

"Dalesa, you graduated, at the top of your class, from Columbia University, didn't you?" Romeo asks.

"Yes," Dalesa answers.

"You recently were given an editorial feature in the upcoming issue for the magazine you write for, correct?"

"Yes."

"I know that you and I haven't discussed this, yet, but according to your roommate, Coreen, you two have been friends since you were teenagers. Is that accurate?"

"Yes."

"You've been living with HIV for eight years and are currently undetectable, right?"

"Yes."

"Okay. Thank you."

"Why are you asking me those things?"

"When you were in the hospital, I wasn't able to work up a complete psychosocial profile for your chart. I just wanted to be sure of a few things. That's all."

"Okay."

Romeo knows all the answers to the questions he just asked, and they have been well documented in her profile already. He has reasons for his redundancy, but for now, it's only important that

Dalesa has a moment in history to refer back to when the time comes for his intent in asking those questions to be revealed.

"I want you to know, Dalesa, I realize that none of this is easy. There are parts of this process that will ease as we go along, but in real work, there's the greater chance that it will get increasingly more challenging first," Romeo says. "This is going to sound a bit oxymoronic, but the less comfortable you are, the more comfortable you'll become."

Dalesa repeats what Romeo's said in her head trying to make sense of it as if she sounded out an unfamiliar word before attempting to pronounce it. "You have to explain that one to me, Mr. Sylvian."

"Well, it's an observation I've made in the field. When patients are too comfortable, especially, in the beginning, that means nothing has penetrated enough in them to evoke a shift or change. A new feeling, perspective or way of thinking about familiar things must make a person feel uncomfortable, a little, at first to know something is different. That way, when a patient notices how even the slightest things don't appear the same, they will feel inclined to want to work through the awkwardness and discomfort."

"Oh, I get it! It's almost like when my editor, Mr. Glasgow, asks me to work overtime. I dread the long hours, but when I get paid, the following week, I'm all the merrier."

"Something like that. Yes."

"Weird," Dalesa says and drifts momentarily on the current of quiet thought.

"What's weird?" Romeo asks.

"Usually, I'm thinking of how I want things to get better or how I want to feel better. Now, I'm looking forward to things getting a little bit rough. It's just so overwhelming to think about some of the things I share with you."

"We're a few weeks into this. So, this is still the beginning for you."

"I wonder how much philosophical truth there was in what William said back in eighth grade."

"That's the boy who wrote about the dogs and the sea, right?"

"Yeah because this doesn't feel like a YMCA pool, I'm swimming in these days. As a matter of fact, I'd rather be on a raft with a slow leak in the East River, than on this shark-bitten surfboard in the Atlantic."

GO ON

How can I go on living like this?

I have no support for myself.

If I have not the support of myself, then I have no one.

Who is going to help push me up the last hill when I start to feel weak

and feeble from climbing the dozen before it?

The Most High Love, shower me with your aide and answers, like

rain upon the flowers and pastures on their thirsty days.

How can I go on in this handicapped condition?

I want to believe that residing within me is an indwelling good.

I want to trust that all has not been lost, but all is abiding in

storehouses, awaiting recovery and redemption.

Conspiracies of contradiction regarding love are being debated and

debunked, daily, in my head.

This stress provides the only friction which seems to ignite any fire in

me, and this flame is dim enough only for hope.

Hanging on to nothing else

Although, not defeatist, my attitude is, certainly, not progressive.

Hanging on is not the same as moving on.

I'm dangling here—tied at the wrists by my fear of falling and my fear

of flying.

Upon an organism's start of life, the instinct is survival and

sustaining that life.

I'm not going to make it this way.

How can I?

No one else seems to be convinced or can convince me that they

believe in what it is I say I stand for as a person.

Why should I?

Tell me who truly believes in the purity of my heart's substance?

The heartbreakers, liars, cheaters, and predators prevalent in society

have practically made everyone jaded victims and skeptics in the

possibility.

It appears I've been built for great things—despite the planned

debasing of my soul.

The naysayers sing the praises of celebrities and although, I may not

be ready, deny that my day of reckoning has arrived.

If all the world's a stage, how can I go on?

Throw the rotten tomatoes if you must but will I die having been

opposed to the grain all my days?

Consistency counted for something when commodity was not counted

for everything.

Now trending topics predict the whether and seasons determine the climates for cultivating compassion and charity with good will toward men exchanged through the temporal love of holidays and seasonal coffee beverages.

What I value in my life, my person and within humanity is not going viral or heavy tagged in search engine optimization.

Much of what is adored and glorified by the masses, to me, seems worthless and has no merit.

Some would say, "Be you. Embrace your truth."

Being myself is the issue I'm struggling with.

How can I go on with this burden and guilt?

It's me against the world.

In the beginning, the world was small.

Now, it's much bigger than one man can fend against.

One man cannot hold 8 billion people in his hand nor withstand the individualized blow from them.

Conformity is calling my name.

It is a temptress that is seducing me with the promise of acceptance, approval, and fraternity.

I've lost so much of myself trying to find myself.

I'm a weakling with no solidarity of self-worth.

I was given a name for the purpose of defining who I was to be called

in society.

However, I was not shown how to love in order to recognize it, given

appreciation to understand it or provided acceptance in order to

mirror it and then couple my defining name with a defining of my

heart.

I was showed how to walk, how to use the potty, how to ride a bike,

drive a car, write, cash and bounce a check but I wasn't showed how

to love myself and place no other appraisal of my worth or judgment

over that of my own.

I know that Love is the primordial stuff that the universe is made of,

but could I pick it out of a line-up?

I've been so misinformed and mislead by an illusion.

So, I see it in Nature, in the stars and the eight lunar phases—even in

materialism.

What about in people?

It's all up to me, now.

But how can I go on saying that I am Love and don't love myself?

I feel like a vestigial virgin.

I'm going into this self-discovery and self-love trek, blindly.

I have no point of reference.

I haven't seen what fulfillment looks like.

Does peace exist or is it a romanticized idea put in my head like an

unattainable piece of cheese hanging on a string above a mouse

running in a stationary wheel?

What is self-worth, anyway?

I don't want to be purchased or traded.

I want to give of myself, freely.

Are self-worth and self-esteem custom-made or customary?

I feel what little I have is based on the validation of others.

It's far more likely that people would hate other individuals as

opposed to themselves.

However, I'm the only one that seems to loathe, detest and barely

manage to keep cordiality with himself.

How can I go on?

CHAPTER 7

Six weeks later…

"Their tone always felt so cold whenever they spoke to me. A simple request to wash the dishes reverberated so much callousness that I never let them see a dirty dish in the sink or a particle of dust on the mantle. That way they couldn't ask me, and I could be spared from the coldness in their speech," Dalesa tells Romeo.

It's been several weeks since her first meeting with Romeo. Since that initial session, they have explored various components of Dalesa's past and present life. Gradually, with Dalesa's candidness and Mr. Sylvian's guidance, they are beginning to find a correlation between those chronological elements and her mental health. With each visit, she is feeling more and more comfortable exposing him to events and emotions that, up until now, she had felt to be so private and intimate, that she thought she would die with them either unclassified or unresolved.

Today, Romeo listens as intently as usual, but he has a head cold. He keeps wiping his runny nose with a tissue and sneezing occasionally. Hoping it's not a distraction, he asks, "Did the contempt they displayed towards you make it hard to stay focused when you weren't in their immediate vicinity?"

"I tried to avoid the Jenkins at all costs whenever I was home from school. Luckily, we lived in an old house. So, floorboards and door hinges would make varying noises throughout the house. I made it a point to learn what areas of the house made which sound. Just by listening, I could know where anyone was inside the house no matter where I happened to be—which was usually locked, out of sight, in my room. While kids my age were dubbing cassette tapes, I was making audio archives for the way each of their house slippers sounded gliding or flapping on the floor, the rhythmic patterns as they each walked up and down the stairs—even the loudness with which they each closed a door."

"Did you have any conversations other than clean the dishes or what not with them?" Romeo asks but then catches himself. "That's right. You made sure they didn't ask you about dishes. My apologies. Ah-choo!"

"Bless you."

"Thank you."

"There was dialogue, but their sentences were always short. They never volunteered information. The only time they ever did was when they had found—in a sick, sadistic sort of way—something to say to me that they felt would be sure to elicit a hurt feeling inside me and undoubtedly give them a surge of power by being hurtful. For example, Mr. Jenkins would say I was getting too old to be still dressing like a little girl. It wasn't my fault that I wore some of the clothes I did because they refused to take me shopping for anything new within a reasonable interval of time as I grew. If it wasn't for hand-me-downs from my older cousin, it's possible I would have still been wearing elementary school dresses my first day in high school. That's a bit of an exaggeration, but you get the point."

"Yes, I understand. Ah-choo!"

"Bless you."

"Thank you. So, I'm glad that you mentioned your cousins. What were your relationships like with the rest of your family members?" Romeo asks.

Dalesa sighs deeply. Her body language shifts slightly. Her graceful poise dissolves into a sudden slouch, and she gazes up at the ceiling. She inhales and with an elongated exhalation, says, "Oh, boy! My family." She pushes her hair from off the sides of her face to lay behind her ears. "The relationships were insidious and dysfunctional. At least with one of my cousins, anyway. My father had one brother, Nathaniel, Jr. He was divorced but had two children.

"So, it was the three of them, plus my grandparents that made up my immediate family. My distant relatives kept their distance and showed up on holidays, as most do. They didn't take an interest in building a relationship with me, but I tried to get close to a few.

"So, when it wasn't Thanksgiving or Christmas, it was just my cousins, and Uncle Nate—who I later learned was almost always near tears when he saw me because I looked so much like my father. They were always coming to the house. Many people thought we were brother and sisters. The age gap separated the three of us by only a year—one older girl, Kenya and one younger boy, Tony. Kenya didn't like me very much. Tony and I got along well.

"Kenya was always the favorite of the Jenkins—particularly my grandfather. I'm not sure why Kenya got preferential treatment, but that's how it was and remained. It could've been because she was the first grandchild. She always got to ride shotgun in the town car whenever all of us would go out. She always got new shoes and clothes before Tony and me. Tony had his share of moments in the spotlight many times too—being the only boy—but still just as a supporting role. Kenya was the star child—even though she got held back twice in school. She could do no wrong and always got her way. For her to be a tomboy, Kenya knew when to play the girlish role to be sure to get what was wanted—even if it was beating the crap out of me. No one saw how she treated me when we were away from adult supervision. She was very abusive to me for a significant period of my life, but no one believed me when I spoke of it."

"Kenya physically hurt you?" Romeo asks.

"Yes. My older, bully of a cousin went from yanking my hair in the ball pit at Showbiz Pizza Time to pulling a knife out on me my Sophomore year of high school when she accused me of flirting with her boyfriend. She was fascinated with the WWF, and as if she was Chyna or Bull Nakano or somebody, she would attack me, unprovoked, as if a demon was possessing her," Dalesa recalls. "She would push me down the stairs and kick me when I was down, in a literal sense. I couldn't talk to the Jenkins about it because Kenya was their little angel even though she was always getting into fights at school. I tried talking to my uncle, but he only saw his precious little girl and didn't believe anything I told him. Besides, he didn't make me feel comfortable being around him. Even though I didn't know then what I do now about my resemblance to his brother, I could sense that trying to love me was hard for him.

"It was remarkable to see the difference in how my grandparents treated my cousins and me. I grew to accept it as normal and expected no more than what was shown. I didn't even feel like I was part of the family. I was ostracized everywhere I went, and I did nothing to deserve it—except be born."

HEART OF A FIGHTER

The blow to my skull

The push down the stairs

This was my family, and it didn't seem fair.

To be hurt so malevolently

Without a care for my esteem or my soul

Could I erase what they did to me?

To do so, would leave the story untold.

I didn't ask for life.

Should life have been so cruel?

This was the way it was meant to be, and I was the fool.

I kept quiet when my words went ignored.

I let them do this to me.

I felt I had no choice.

Where else could I be?

There in their care

In their loving chokeholds

It came down from the top to the bottom

I had to take it.

It was only fair.

Who was I?

I was the begotten one

The mistake

The burden

The misfit

Left to the slaughter

"I'm sure you felt alone," Romeo says.

"Yes, I did. I looked forward to going to school and eventually to my part-time job," Dalesa says.

"When did you start working?" Romeo asks. "I'm sure that was a tremendous temporary relief and escape for you."

"I started working as soon as I was legally able to. So, like fourteen. My grandparents left me with no choice."

"What do you mean?"

"They said that I needed to contribute more to the household because the State wasn't giving them as much money in terms of the guardianship stipend as they were awarding them when I was younger. They forced my hand when they started buying less food and stopped giving me lunch money. There were plenty of times I had to make do with only one meal a day—and if it wasn't Sunday, then that meal wasn't always guaranteed to be adequate. Remember, Romeo. They were the Royals; I was the peasant.

"So, it got to the point where if I wanted to eat regularly, I had to feed myself by getting a job. Economically, a hug or an 'I love you,' costs nothing but it might as well had come with an exorbitant sales tax, to think I could expect that or anything else from the Jenkins."

"What kind of job did you have?" Romeo asks.

"For starters, I washed dishes for an Italian restaurant. I did that for about a year before getting a job at a bookstore," Dalesa answers. "I practically relinquished most of my adolescence to become a premature adult. My day started with school. Then, there was work, homework, and then bedtime. That was my routine for three to four days out of the week. Friends, boyfriends, TV, writing all were pushed under the rug."

"It also kept you away from the discordant relationship between you and your grandparents," Romeo says.

"That was the best part. It was a freedom that I didn't take for granted," Dalesa says and smiles.

Romeo says, "I want to go back to something we talked about a few weeks ago. If you hadn't stopped viewing your grandparents as your birth parents, do you think they would have continued the lie? Could it be that they wanted to protect you from the devastating truth? A truth which I believe would be too much for any child to handle."

Dalesa smirks and says, "The truth would have come out sooner or later."

"You said that they saw you as an opportunity to right the wrong your father did. Do you think it wrong for them to want to protect you from the truth?" Romeo asks.

"I honestly can't say. I'm not a judgmental person. It hurt all the way around," Dalesa says. "The truth, the lie, the acceptance of the truth and justification of the lie all burned in me and made every day a fight to cohabitate with the contempt that I mistook for care. They were my legal guardians, but they were also the biggest threat to my happiness."

Dalesa's grandparents hardly ever laid a hand on her. Although it didn't stop her from experiencing physical abuse from Kenya, it was one less wound that her grandparents were responsible for causing. There were only a couple of times during her childhood that she received a whipping for being disobedient but, overall, she was a good child—never doing anything worthy of an attack. However, great psychological and emotional abuse dug deep into Dalesa's soul that kept hidden the beautiful smile she had, and like a hickey made imperceptibly below the neckline, kept the secret of the misconduct from all who did not live in her home.

To be called worthless on countless occasions and insulted for just being who she was and developing to be, was unbearable for Dalesa to handle without an outlet. She found an escape in her writing and her schoolwork. The latter gave many of the underachievers in school an outlet, as well, to pick on and tease her for being nerdy, studious and the teacher's pet. However, for every two students who called Dalesa insulting names or ridiculed her, there would be two or three others asking her for help on assignments. If she got too much negativity from her other kids, she could count on at least one teacher or faculty member singing her praises before the last bell rung for the day. Even at church, Dalesa seemed to find calamity in just existing. Some of the other children would find Dalesa's enthusiasm about Sunday school and prayer to be worth a giggle, mocking behind her back and ostracism. Most of the time, if the church moms caught any of the kids picking on Dalesa, they would put a stop to it—which left one less social group in Dalesa's life for her to be up against.

Being an outcast at school, in the neighborhood, and at church damaged Dalesa's perception of self-worth but it was the persecution from the Jenkins that troubled Dalesa day and night. It was her grandparents' bullying that mattered the most to her because they were her family. Nothing she did at home ever seemed to be right—not the way she mopped the floor, not the way she dressed, not the way she addressed them as grandmother and grandfather. It was if the sight of her disgusted the Jenkins each time they passed each other in the house.

Dalesa took all the blows and held in her hurt and anger as if trying to control flatulence. The pressure seemed to have no end because there were but a few places she could go and be accepted and welcomed. She needed acceptance from somewhere.

Dalesa was always very active in school up until probably her junior and senior years. She maintained good grades for those years and never gave her teachers any disciplinary issues. She kept to herself—which wasn't hard considering it was difficult for her to make friends. Coreen was the closest friend that Dalesa had while attending school, but by the time their lives crossed paths her junior year, Dalesa had already spent most of her academic life alienated from her peers.

It wasn't as if Dalesa was mean-spirited or unlikable. She had a great sense of humor and could hold a conversation on just about any subject. It was probably her need to mature quicker than the average teen—due to her home life, and although she couldn't see it at the time, her way of coming across as needy. Other kids had no problems approaching her for help with homework, especially English papers. She was the coveted partner to pick from the pool of classmates when the teachers said to pair up for an assignment, but always the last to be picked during gym class for double-dutch or volleyball teams. She didn't wear her sexuality for the boys to go out of their way to explore. She didn't dress in the latest fashions or listen to the modern music of her age group, which would have probably given her a comfortable fit into the cliques and popular social circles but at the risk of losing her identity.

To make up for the deficit of familial attention, social acceptance, and self-appreciation, Dalesa submerged herself in academics, chorus, poetry, public speaking clubs, the school newspaper, and theater. She was on the Honor Roll and in advanced level classes all through school. Dalesa didn't realize the significance as it presented itself, but every "A" she received was a pleasant contradiction and rebellion to the psychological propaganda the Jenkins were spewing by saying she was stupid and good for nothing.

Day after day, no matter how much the yearning swelled within the valves of her heart to receive at least an "Honorable Mention" for being a satisfactory granddaughter, she maintained a desperate need to feel acceptance somewhere. After muddling through it for some time, she concluded that the best course of action was to change—since no one and nothing else was shifting.

Around the second semester of 10th grade, Dalesa decided that what she needed to do was make friends. She had seen how in the movie *Grease*, Sandy changed herself to be accepted by the Pink Ladies and ultimately, Danny Zuko. She had seen how Ariel gave up her voice for legs to get her prince in the animated classic, *The Little Mermaid*. Even Aladdin, changed his social and economic status to get the attention of his romantic interest. Steve Erkel, in the *Family Matters* sitcom, felt he had to build a transformation chamber and invent "Cool Juice" to reconstruct his DNA to gain acceptance—no longer wanting to bear the burden of loneliness and being an outcast.

Without any special serum, Dalesa attempted to make new connections and friends through imitation of her already popular peers and through the portrayal of the idolized from media. She changed her clothes, the type of music she listened to, her hair, her way of speaking—all in hopes to turn the *ridicule* into *respect*.

Dalesa did whatever she could do to fit in. She got tired of being an outsider. How could she like herself if no one else liked her? Dalesa compared her situation to something she noticed when she was working at the Italian restaurant. When the chef saw that no one was ordering the Minestrone each time he put it on the menu for a daily special, he finally stopped making it a regular soup of the day. She decided to take the old Dalesa off the menu of options for people to abuse and take advantage. She attempted to reestablish herself within her community as someone more appealing and desirable to be around. For starters, she tried to brand the moniker, 'Lesa. After a week of trying to condition everyone to her new identifier, she realized if she wanted improved self-esteem and a more valuable personality, she couldn't go around calling herself anything that insinuated "less-a" anything. So, she put an end to that.

Since she had started working at the bookstore, she was making more money and could afford to do well for herself. She stayed out late and tried to change her way of being. All her outward changes, however, did nothing for her inside. She knew that her new friends only liked her for what she could buy them and for the free food she still got from the restaurant because the manager adored her.

When Coreen transferred to her school their 11th-grade year, it was an instant connection when they met in chorus class. Dalesa's pursuit for a stamp of approval from the majority was no longer the main objective with Coreen around. Besides, it was obvious that the changes she made didn't alter perception because she was still considered the "church girl" and awkward. Now, that Coreen had arrived, she could be her quirky self. Other students took a liking to Coreen as well. So, as Dalesa and Coreen became extremely close, Dalesa was accepted into cliques—by association. Wherever Coreen got invited, automatically people knew she would make Dalesa her "plus one." The two of them were like siblings, whom unlike with Kenya, they got along with each other. Dalesa chose to confide in Coreen, who in turn chose to be an anchor and rock for her. Dalesa felt that she had found someone that loved her for who she was— flaws and all.

Dalesa's grandparents were not at all happy with Dalesa's new friend. Mr. Jenkins wouldn't even speak to Coreen when she would come by the house. After Coreen would leave, he would say things about her regarding her living in the city projects and how she was only friends with Dalesa because Dalesa was making money at the bookstore. Mr. Jenkins had it all wrong. It wasn't like that with Dalesa and Coleen's relationship. Coreen never asked Dalesa for a thing—not even a pencil in geometry class. She wasn't like the other people that had begun letting Dalesa into their inner circle—who seemed to be bartering off their companionship in exchange for outdated free copies of *Penthouse* and *Playgirl* she could get from work. Mrs. Jenkins, on the other hand, could see how close the two of them were. However, she thought their sorority was too tight to be righteous since they weren't kin. Mrs. Jenkins would make comments about them being lesbians and demanded that Dalesa's bedroom door remain open if Coreen was visiting. Mrs. Jenkins didn't want any gay sex going on in her house.

Coreen was the first and only living person—outside of the family—to see firsthand how mean-spirited her grandparents were towards Dalesa. She was a proud proponent for Dalesa's developmental rights as a teenager to stand up for herself. Coreen said that if she got treated the same way Dalesa was being treated, Coreen would have probably gotten grounded a lot or smacked around for being sassy because she would speak her mind. However, it was

Dalesa's tolerance and respect for her elders that Coreen admired about her new best friend. Coreen tried not to be a bad influence and encouraged Dalesa to stay steadfast and hang on for the little remaining time she had to be cared for by them legally. All in all, Coreen kept a smile on Dalesa's face whenever she was around. Dalesa had finally found a true friend and an unconditional acceptance that had been missing for so many years.

DON'T LIVE WITHOUT ONE

What is something easily found in the unexpected circumstances of

life but easily lost through consistent disloyalty or lies?

It can sprout like azaleas under a tree or like a lotus blossom up from

adversity's pond.

It is usually sparked by interest and like.

It can also flame into a lusty fire of desire.

No matter how it starts or as with the seasons, how it ends

Its longevity or brevity

Its romantic climax or stable fidelity

Friendship is something that many individuals cherish.

For many, it is an honored and heavily sought-after relationship as if

there is no other association or goal for one's social health on earth.

If you love him

If you trust her

Hold on tight and commit to being partners in life no matter what.

Friends, unlike family, are chosen.

Therefore, we must find value, purpose, and joy in the cosmically,

strategic placement of that someone or significant ones that enter our

lives.

Do friends indeed come a dime a dozen?

If so, how many dimes can fit in your palm?

This doesn't mean that choosing friends shouldn't be viewed as an

elitist ritual in which one judges based on credentials—worthy of

nothing but the best.

When it's all said and done, when what constitutes a friend is

perfectly placed with priority and purpose, a person's popularity,

number of tweets or friend requests and accepts won't secure just

anyone a seat at the table.

Having friendships should mean something special.

No finer building can be erected or designed when compared to what

can be built upon enduring friendship and love.

The ancient philosophers considered friends to reflect oneself.

Don't ever be lonely if it's hard to be vulnerable, trusting or have fun

with another person on your level.

It's okay.

As great as friends are, what if one day all domesticated pets become

extinct and your bloodline and family tree dry up and withers away?

Then, one must be able to find a heartfelt, encouraging and dedicated

relationship with oneself and be one's own best friend.

"I have never had a friend like Coreen," Dalesa says to Romeo.

"That's great!" Romeo says and smiles.

"You should have been there when I told her about what Kenya used to do to me. She about nearly flipped her lid. Coreen said that Kenya had better hope she never ran into her because Coreen would not hesitate to kick her behind," Dalesa says. "I made sure their paths never crossed. Coreen told me that she could understand a passive approach in dealing with the elderly, but if no one would listen to me about what Kenya was doing, then I should fight back."

"Did you ever fight your cousin?" Romeo asks.

"I would protect my body from her blows. I wrestled the knife out of her hand that one time, but I never hit her intentionally. I'm not a fighter—never have been. As soon as it was taught to me to turn the other cheek, I made it a personal commandment. Maybe, I was foolish to let someone beat on me, but I honestly felt that I deserved it in some way. When I started working at the bookstore, I wasn't around much, so Kenya's aggressiveness tapered down from physical roughness to verbal assaults whenever she saw fit.

"I dealt with it the same way I dealt with the non-physical abuse from my grandparents—I took it! Keep in mind, even though I had a blind child-like faith, I still grew up having a fervent Christian faith, nonetheless. Jesus had been crucified for his love of humanity. I remember thinking that he could have taken himself down from the cross if he wanted to, but his love asked for the forty lashes and nails. It doesn't make sense to me at this age and this place in my life, but somehow, in some convoluted way, back then I thought my family's dangerous nature was a display of love. I think back on it, now, and can rightly say it was silly of me because I loved my family and never wanted to maltreat them—no matter how much they were hurting me."

"I'm glad Coreen was there for support during that period of your life, but you must realize that no one deserves to be treated evilly… ever!" Romeo affirms.

"You know something, Romeo. At this age and based on what I've experienced, if I'm not being treated badly—in some way, shape or form—then, I would feel like something is wrong."

One day, during Dalesa's junior year, Dalesa was on the phone with Coreen after school. Mrs. Jenkins didn't know the phone was in use and picked up the receiver of the phone in her bedroom. She stayed on the phone a good seven or eight minutes listening in on Dalesa's conversation. She heard Dalesa complain to her friend about living with her grandparents and the latest misconduct in their foul custodial care. Dalesa vented about all the things she had too much respect to ever say to either one of them in their face. It enraged Mrs. Jenkins. She broke her eavesdropping silence and said, "Oh, that's how you feel?"

Dalesa panicked and hung up the phone before even saying goodbye to her friend. She thought she could just hang up and that would be the end of it. She thought she could turn on the television and pretend that nothing happened. Even knowing the attitude of her grandmother, she felt she didn't do anything wrong. She was merely expressing her personal feelings to a friend.

Dalesa heard her grandmother leaving her bedroom and walking across the hall to Dalesa's room. Dalesa could tell the exact moment that her grandmother realized she wasn't upstairs because Mrs. Jenkins bellowed Dalesa's name from upstairs so loudly that the house next door could probably hear. The sounds of the floorboards indicated immediately that Mrs. Jenkins was headed downstairs where she would find Dalesa in the living room. Dalesa didn't know what to do. She couldn't retreat to her bedroom because that would put her directly in contact with Mrs. Jenkins at the stairs. She couldn't go outside because it was too cold, but she knew she didn't want to have an altercation. So, she ran to the bathroom which was in the opposite direction of her grandmother's footsteps. Mrs. Jenkins yelled to Dalesa when she was at the foot of the stairs, "You want to talk bad about me on the phone? Who was that? Who were you talking to Dalesa? Was that your little dike girlfriend? Why don't you say something to my face, ingrate? Dalesa!"

Dalesa locked the door behind her. She sat motionless on top of the lowered lid of the toilet. She could hear her grandmother calling her name throughout the house, and it was only a matter of time before Mrs. Jenkins figured out where her granddaughter was hiding. Dalesa whispered fearfully to herself, "Please no. Please no, no, no." She didn't want confrontation, but it seemed that Mrs. Jenkins wanted to argue by the density of sound in her voice as she called Dalesa's name.

The bathroom door usually stayed open unless someone was in it. When Mrs. Jenkins got to the door, she turned the knob, but it wouldn't open. Since Mr. Jenkins was not home, the game of "Hide 'n' Seek" was over. "Open this door, young lady," she said with sharp inflection. She jerked the doorknob with such aggressive force that she rattled the door on its hinges.

Dalesa didn't say a word. Mrs. Jenkins yelled to her from the other side of the bathroom door, "You need help, little girl. I feel sorry for you. Why are you on my phone saying those things?"

"You have to know how you treat me. There's no way you can't be aware because you do it all the time. I don't know what you heard on the phone, but I don't care anymore. I'm not happy here," Dalesa answered back with a quiver in her voice.

Mrs. Jenkins laughed with cruel amusement. "Your mother was a bimbo and good for nothing. You are worthless and pathetic just like her. Look at you hiding in the bathroom like some scared puppy. Is that what you are Dalesa? A filthy mutt? A little bitch? Huh? Open this door right now!" Mrs. Jenkins hollered.

"People care about me, and they love me, regardless of what you say!"

"You don't know what love is you precious, pitiful child. If you have so-called friends…if all these nameless, invisible individuals claim to love you, as you say, then you take your burdensome hind parts to their house and stay with them. Thank the good Lord Jesus, you're graduating soon. Nathaniel and I already have somebody willing to rent your room from us. Let someone else take care of you. Let your simple-minded friends and their parents feel sorry for you. I don't.

"You strut around this house like you're entitled or something. You had no one. No one! You would have been in some God-forsaken orphanage or some terrible foster home if it weren't for us. We took you in, which is a decision we have been regretting for years. Being the Christians we are, we raised you like you were our own daughter. Now, I have to listen to you on *my* telephone, the one *I* pay the bill for each month, in *my* house talking about what horrible people we have been to you. How dare you? To hear you talking as if you don't appreciate the roof we've placed over your head is downright disrespectful. Your father—God, rest his coward soul—sure did dodge a bullet not having to care for you. He's the one that should be putting up with you—not me and not Nathaniel, at our age." Mrs. Jenkins bangs on the door hard with her fists.

Dalesa screamed out, "Stop it! Stop it!" She started to cry.

Mrs. Jenkins yelled back, "You stop it! You stop! Stop being you. How about that? Be somebody else for crying out loud because nobody cares about who you are. You'll see. As God as my witness, you'll see someday. Hey, you know what? While you're in there, do yourself a favor and flush yourself down the toilet. That's where waste goes. You ungrateful little brat." Mrs. Jenkins opened her eyes widely, and her arms gesticulated with exasperation in the air. "You are lucky to have us. Open this door, now!" she said, as she yanked on the doorknob again. She paused and heard Dalesa sobbing. "Don't you get it? Nobody wants you. Nobody wanted you when you were born, and nobody wants you, now."

Dalesa dug her knuckles into the temples of her head and continued to cry profusely. Then, she began hitting herself in the back of the head with her hands—alternating between swift hard punches from her left and right fists. Mrs. Jenkins stood on the other side of the door laughing as she listened to the weeping. Dalesa had to get out of the bathroom. She stopped beating herself up and went to open the door. Mrs. Jenkins was a blurry figure in front of her, as the tears were impairing her vision. However, with determination in her voice and shallow breath, Dalesa said, "I may not know what love is, but I know that this isn't it." Mrs. Jenkins slapped Dalesa's face so hard she hurt herself also, but that didn't stop Mrs. Jenkins from preparing to smack Dalesa again. The dilapidated teen didn't give her a chance to strike a second time and rushed past her. Dalesa went upstairs and barricaded herself in her room until the tempest quieted.

Imagine there is only one mirror in your home. This mirror is the sole means with which you have to view yourself. Now, imagine that same mirror covered with smudges or water stains that no one can clear away with a strong cleaner. You could still see your likeness but not as clear as you did before with all the filth now obstructing your view of the reflection. In your imagination, replace the dirty mirror with one of those trick mirrors like the ones found in a fun house at a carnival or county fair. The image of yourself in the mirror would have a contorted likeness, and you'll not have an accurate view of yourself. For years, you have only this one mirror to see yourself. Afterwhile, you grow accustomed to the view and believe you look as you appear in the deceptive mirror. You become so convinced you look as you seem in the reflection, when the mirror is replaced with a regular, clean mirror, you don't believe the undistorted likeness.

No matter what stage a child has reached in his or her development, to say to that child he or she is pitiful, worthless or any other devaluing insults is cruelty which the laws of any land should find felonious. To treat a child as if he or she is nothing is detrimental and as lethal as poison to the child's self-esteem and psyche. Is there any disparity between that and brutally whipping a child? There is no real difference except for maybe the recovery time of the inflicted wounds from each assault. Bruises and broken bones are unfortunate injuries that can heal with time, but the psychological and emotional scarring that accompanies those contusions do not mend with a bandage. Whether there is a corresponding physical component to emotional abuse does not diminish the reality that internal damage from psychological assault and verbal torrents of abuse lingers—handicapping victims, in some cases, for a lifetime.

Dalesa didn't want to believe the harmful words that scorched from her grandmother's lips were true. She couldn't validate them because her teachers didn't say those things. Coreen didn't say those things. Why was it her loved ones did? Dalesa heard silence outside her door and was relieved with the thought that the enraged woman she left downstairs had tired herself out. Dalesa began to pray with an earnest plea for salvation.

Romeo jots down a few notes in Dalesa's file. Dalesa looks at him with expecting eyes. She wants him to say something that will take the pain she is feeling away as she recalls such dark times of her life. She wants him to tell her that what she feels is temporary. She wants him to assure her that when those feelings leave, they will never return.

Romeo asks, "Do you believe the things your grandparents said to you throughout your youth, right now? You don't think you're worthless, do you?"

"Why shouldn't I believe them?"

"Because it was nothing but unsubstantiated bull, Dalesa," Romeo says with an emphatic accentuation. "Excuse me." He catches himself and continues, "I don't' know your grandparents, but I know this. You are the only person who can determine your worth."

"But if they were my teachers and the ones responsible for showing me the path I should go in life, shouldn't I trust their judgement?"

"Do you hear yourself? I could tell you every day that your hair is blue but what do you see when you look in the mirror to comb it?

Somebody else can tell you that your hair is red. The reality is that your hair is neither of those colors. Belief in the truth is a choice, just like, belief in a lie is a choice. You don't have to accept the lies your grandparents tried to brainwash you with, but you can't believe the lies you tell yourself either. No matter how people perceive it, no one has the power to alter the truth because it is what it is."

"I can't trust what I see. I know what I feel, and I feel like sometimes my grandparents were right. My mother is dead because of being pregnant and giving birth to me," Dalesa says.

"No. The complications your mom had was because of your half-brother's birth. Not yours."

"Yeah, well I didn't help any. I made it worse," Dalesa argues.

Romeo crosses his arms and goes to speak but sneezes. Then, he says, "You can't continue to…"

"My father loved my mother in his twisted way enough to kill himself because of how my birth caused her to die," Dalesa interrupts.

Romeo says, "Dalesa, listen to me…"

"No, you listen to me, Mr. Sylvian. Up until I was 18 years old, I had spent my life in the care of two people who hated me because an entire portion of my genealogy disowned me. That's the truth," Dalesa says, as she begins repetitiously tapping her foot out of anxious impulse. She looks up at the ceiling and closes her eyes. Romeo waits before saying anything, since she's cut him off twice already. Dalesa continues, "Why shouldn't I believe them? Especially, if they were right. Look at me." She lowers her head to look at Romeo, teary eyed. "I'm a mess. I'd rather be sitting in sorrow accepting reality than be at peace in denial."

Romeo rolls his chair closer to her, and in a soft voice, says, "Listen to me. That is not reality you are accepting. It is a phantom truth that is haunting your self-image and infiltrating your ecosystem of belief. The fact is you are a talented, intelligent, amiable and resiliant woman who is a valuable asset to her community."

"You forgot to add, post-suicidal, severely depressed, HIV-positive, unattractive, lamentable and hopeless," Dalesa says, as her gaze drifts off.

"Stop it! Stop talking about yourself in such a negative way. Look at me. Please?" Romeo says with excitable compassion. He wants to grab her hand but tries to get eye contact with his client instead.

Dalesa averts her eyes and looks down. Then, she says, "My grandfather said that no one will ever love me. He told me that people would be kind to me only because they want something from me. He said once they got it, they will leave me alone because I don't deserve anything else. And wouldn't you know it. That's all everyone has ever done. Who knows?" Dalesa looks up at her therapist. "Maybe my grandparents were prophets because you can't sit there and tell me despite the corroboration from my historical life experiences that their 'unsubstantiated bull,' as you put it, doesn't reek of truth."

"Yes I can. It is absolutely not true. Their words were 100 percent fallacious rhetoric," Romeo says.

"Then explain why no man wants me. Explain why out of 8 million people in this city, I only have five numbers stored in my phone, which are mostly coworkers. Explain why Carson raped me. Explain my life! Who has ever been there for me, Romeo? Tell me that. Coreen. That's the only one who would miss me if I died tomorrow. She's the only one who has stuck around and some days I wonder if that has been out of convenience."

"I would miss you. I'm here for you. Are you there for yourself?" Romeo replies. "Yes, you are HIV-positive but healthy. You are taking your meds and taking good care of yourself. Yes, you are depressed, but you are here seeking help. Yes, you are single. And yes, maybe you have only a few friends, but Dalesa, you are not alone. You know what else you are?"

"What?" Dalesa asks, as she wipes the wetness from her tears off her face.

"You are here. Notwithstanding everything that has happened, you are still here. You are alive. You were strong enough, brave enough, beautiful enough, worthy enough and powerful enough to make it this far. Only you can stop yourself from doing more."

"I want to do more," Dalesa says. "I've tried to do more. I've tried many times, but I always end in the same place. There's always something getting in my way—making it impossible to go any further."

"Then you keep trying. Try again and again if you have to," Romeo says.

"Don't you think a person will get tired of doing that? If you go down a road that always leads to a dead end, then you stop going down that same road. Wouldn't you? It would be stupid to continue down that path."

"Right! You go down another road, Dalesa. There's more than one way you can travel to reach your goals but there is only one path to recovery. Let's stop using the word *trying*, and from now on start *doing*."

"You think it's that easy?"

"Of course, I don't. I know it's not easy. Psychologically you have many barriers, but that's why you are in treatment. Getting treated is the only road that leads to recovery."

"So, I'm supposed to believe that after all these years of heartache, abandonment, lonliness, and persecution, I can someday expect to have peace of mind?"

"If you keep working toward it, you can have anything you want," Romeo says.

"I want to believe you," Dalesa says. She has calmed down quite a bit.

"Then, believe," Romeo says. He quickly snatches up a tissue from the box on his desk to put over his nose, as he sneezes loudly. "Excuse me."

Doubt can be born from several different conceptions. There is fear, previously failed attempts at something or external stimuli, to name a few. Doubt's range of impact is broad. A person can question him or herself or be doubtful of a plan, a mindset, the future or the intentions and benefits of offered help from another person. Love, however, always hopes. To hope, one must cling to possibilities and eject doubt from active feelings. A person walking abundantly in love brightens the darkness of doubt with the light of expectation shining brightly at the end of the tunnel.

Romeo and Dalesa talk for several minutes more before their session ends.

Later in the evening, Dalesa stands center stage at the Ether Lounge. She smiles at the audience, with her fans eager to hear what she will convey with her spoken words tonight.

BE GONE

I could have easily died with her at birth.

I survived.

While she passed on

I could have had a father.

He couldn't "Man up."

Let the chance pass on

Their responsibility was to take care of me.

Their neglect was like a meal to me.

While they fed like gluttons on foster care charity

This is what's left of me.

I fight each day, hoping to fulfill some part of my destiny.

Look at me and how I've done so much but gained so little.

I feel so lost, but I find myself in the middle

Sandwiched between bitter and sweet

Chaotic and neat

Glorified and meek

They said I wouldn't make it.

You were all I had.

You wouldn't hold me.

Your emotional torment has driven me mad.

You let me dangle.

My pride and self-assurance were strangled.

There is no other angle.

Perception is clear.

The web of confusion is untangled.

You didn't love me.

I'm at the edge.

Go ahead!

Shove me!

I'm holding on by a thread.

Even though, I think I'm strong enough to hold on.

I feel the need to let go.

Something's got to give.

Time to be gone.

CHAPTER 8

Romeo looks at the clock. It's 5:45 pm and Dalesa is 15 minutes late for their session. He rings the front desk to see if he might have missed her call. The receptionist says he has no new messages. At 6 pm, the front desk transfers a call to Romeo. It's Dalesa.

"Romeo, I'm sorry I'm just now calling you, but it took every bit of strength I had even to dial your number," Dalesa says.

"Are you okay?" Romeo asks.

"I'm just not feeling well. It's one of those days when the fatigue is just unbearable," Dalesa replies.

"Is it purely physical or emotional as well?" Romeo probes.

"Both. I feel weak and don't feel like moving. My body aches, and I feel down."

"Well, I hope you feel better. Thanks for calling. Do you want to reschedule for maybe tomorrow or Friday? I can make time for you."

Dalesa hesitates and says, "I don't know, Romeo. I could use a break this week."

"That's okay. It's been an intense few months. I get it, but I want us to stay consistent. Don't lose stamina, now. You are making swell progress."

"Don't worry. I'm not losing stamina. I'm still committed," Dalesa assures.

"Good to hear. Well, if anything, call me if you need to talk or utilize your support system and talk to Coreen."

"I will. Have a good evening."

"Take care, Dalesa."

The two of them hang up their respective ends of the call. Romeo is remiss in his miscellaneous typing on his computer's keyboard. He is disappointed that he will not be meeting with Ms. Moreno today. She is his last client of the day each Wednesday, and he's grown quite fond of her, her story, her temperament, her beauty and, although— she doesn't do it often—her smile. Perhaps, it's the scarcity of its display that makes it even more beautiful when she does eventually show it.

Romeo knows there's nothing wrong with caring for patients, but he feels he is standing at a caveat where his ethical integrity could collide with his heart and professionalism. There is something about Dalesa that oddly attracts him to her. From their first meeting, with her in merely a hospital gown, Romeo has taken an interest in Dalesa. He doesn't lust for her, and he doesn't have romantic motives but counsels himself—trying to make some sense of feelings. 'Is it sympathy?' he questions, but he knows that is not what Dalesa needs right now.

If he could remove himself from his body or at least be a double for himself right now, he would shake himself by the shoulders and tell himself to pull it together. What Dalesa needs is a strong support system. Without operative familial connections and only her co-workers and Coreen by her side, Romeo needs to be the catalyst that helps her establish a firm footing in society and reconstruct her tampered psyche.

SMILING

The smile that you wear with such grace

How the warmth there in your smile brings peace.

I meet you in the circumference of your security.

It is held in my memory of you abandoning that dreadful place.

Chosen by fate to put you in my care and so I had to let your gloom

settle.

The treason of your heart was to that truth that kept you running

away from yourself.

Growing weary, I provided a canister to quarantine and capture your

fears.

The hydration of your saline tears was short-lived before becoming

the vapors from the kettle.

It's not about yesterday but rather "yes" today

The Fools play.

The Wise meditate.

The Learned study.

The Hopeful pray.

No matter what you may be going through—even if the waters protest

being still

Smile, if you can with only sparing use of the upper muscles of your

mouth—sit down, stand up, walk about, run or lay still.

Just smile.

It's a guarantee that you are still trying.

What can be more beautiful to see?

Like a rainbow appearing after a Category 3

I'm sure you miss the smile when it's gone.

The days can't all be seized each moment to their capacity.

However, it shouldn't be a hindrance to keep from smiling and

always vigilant for more.

Dalesa is alone in her apartment feeling exhausted from that brief conversation with Romeo. The fatigue and lack of motivation from her depression are intense. She doesn't want to eat, but she forces herself to fix a bite for dinner. She drags herself from the bedroom to the kitchen where she slowly and reluctantly prepares a sloppy peanut butter and jelly sandwich. Eating seems like bench presses to her as she lifts the sandwich to her mouth. Chewing is draining, and her favorite comfort food tastes like cement. Pretending that she was emotionally better off than she let on to Romeo was an Olympian feat that has left her wanting nothing more than to fall asleep. This week has been one of those weeks reminding her she's sick.

Earlier that day, Mr. Glasgow sent Dalesa home the minute he laid eyes on her at the office. She felt close and comfortable enough with their relationship to explain absences and frequent needs to leave early because of inability to manage her emotions and not jeopardize her job performance. Mr. Glasgow has been understanding and makes reasonable accommodations for her depression. He knows that when he asks, "How's it going, Dalesa?" and she would say, "It's not a good day, Mr. Glasgow," that he will either keep her workload light or let her have a personal day off. Today, Dalesa must have seemed in need of some R & R. She wasn't pleased to have her condition today be so transparent, but she was elated that she didn't have to ask him for the day off.

When she came home, she got undressed and went to bed. She attempted to catch up on some daytime television, but to keep her attention on anything for too long was draining. Iris leaped onto Dalesa's bed. The cat got comfortable on top of the bed's comforter and pretty much stayed put as Dalesa rested. Dalesa wasn't going to call Romeo at all to cancel therapy, but she knew that would do more harm than good. She may have called thirty minutes late for their scheduled appointment time, but for Dalesa it was the best she could do. She too has gotten used to the weekly meetings.

When she is at work, Dalesa is a talented journalist, who is a delight to her co-workers. At home, she is a caretaker to a pet, a best friend and a tenant responsible for fifty percent of the rent. When she is at the Ether Lounge, she is a talented poet and performer. When Dalesa is alone, she is the vestige of heartache and heartbreak.

However, when she sits in Mr. Sylvian's office, she can be without form. There are no expectations, but it is a protected place that her insurance co-pay secures to be available to her for an hour, weekly. She feels it is the safest place in the city and she's grateful to Romeo for making it so.

Although she knows him to be understanding, she can't help but feel guilty for not mustering up what strength and energy she could, to make it to the appointment today. To not feel that guilt or feel anything for that matter—especially the creeping thought that she would also be disappointing those who were probably looking forward to her poetry tonight—Dalesa lets her eyelids drop shut as she drifts off to sleep.

CHAPTER 9

The following Wednesday, Dalesa arrives right on time for her appointment with Mr. Sylvian. "I'm surprised I made it here on time. You know how the trains can be," Dalesa says. She's breathing a little heavy—as if she's been running. "I practically flew from the train station.

"I didn't come last week and didn't even call to cancel right away. So, I didn't want to show up here late and have you thinking that I'm not taking this seriously," Dalesa explains. "I'm committed to this work. I didn't want to leave any room for doubt if there were any in your mind."

Romeo is pleased to see her enthusiasm but wants her to catch her breath. "First things first. Breathe, Dalesa," he says.

Dalesa sits and pays attention to her breathing with Romeo's coaching—as if it were a Lamaze class. Relieved to see Dalesa calming down, he places the "In Session" sign on the outside of his door and closes it shut.

He says, "I'm glad you made it. I don't doubt that you are committed to therapy, but I was concerned that it got a little too intense for you the last time we met. I apologize if I added to any intense emotions you may have felt."

"I can't lie and say that it didn't feel a little overwhelming the last time I was here. It startled me a little. The truth isn't glamorous—liberating maybe—but it isn't always pretty to see. You didn't do anything that you should feel the need to give an apology. If I recall, I was the one that got upset."

"Truth is, Dalesa, although it may not have seemed that way, I was a little unprofessional in the way I was speaking with you," Romeo says. "I allowed my concern for you to overtake my professional obligation to you to remain compassionate but somewhat emotionally at a distance."

"So, how can you show compassion without showing emotion? It's been a couple of months since a man has shown half the warmth and concern you showed."

"I do care. I have a problem when lovely people do not recognize their beauty. They live lowly lives instead of superior ones."

"Thank you, Romeo. You know what they say. Beauty is in the eye of the beholder. Maybe one day I'll see myself the way you do," Dalesa says. She smiles, modestly.

If it weren't for the professional distance keeping them apart during their sessions, Romeo would hold Dalesa's hand during every appointment if he could. He would even hug her if he felt compelled to do so. He is intrigued with who he's come to know in Dalesa, and he's rooting for her to heal and get out of her mental suffering victoriously.

Romeo asks, "Have you had any suicidal thoughts as of late?"

"No," Dalesa replies.

"That's good. What about depression? I know last week you mentioned that you were feeling down."

"Yes, but that's nothing new. I'm used to depression. It's been a part of who I am for so long; I can't imagine a time when I wasn't depressed. If I wasn't depressed about my grandparents, I was depressed about not having any close family ties or living parents. I was depressed about my inadequate social life as a teenager. If not that, then it was just general melancholia about being Dalesa Moreno."

In high school, Dalesa's writing skills advanced tremendously. She knew if Ms. Mayon had any idea how much Dalesa's ability to effectively communicate with written words had developed as if her writing virtuosity went through a pubescent growth spurt, Ms. Mayon would've been quite proud of Dalesa's progression. Ms. Mayon would have also been happy to know that Dalesa had expanded her writing repertoire beyond poetry to include journalism and creative non-fiction.

In addition to writing, Dalesa enjoyed participating in the drama club. Becoming part of a performing arts group was a great outlet for her. Reciting poetry in the way that evoked standing ovations and awards in middle school was not too far from delivering impressive dramatic performances in a stage play. So, Dalesa fit right in. She enjoyed having scripted lines to say and being cast as characters to portray that was unlike herself. That is until the day when the drama club was rehearsing a one-act play that was an adaptation of Langston Hughes' *Soul Gone Home*. In the one act, originally a story of a mother and her son, Dalesa played the son's character as the woman's daughter. Out of all the performing arts students in the school, the drama coach thought of Dalesa as one of the star performers, which is why artistic liberty justified in changing the character's gender to showcase Dalesa. In the play, the mother mourned and grieved over her deceased child. Dalesa's character came back to life, in a haunting spirit, that berated the poor heartbroken woman for the all the years her child helplessly degenerated the mother's ill-fated and inauspicious child-rearing. The resurrected daughter later irremissibly revealed that it was the main cause of her demise.

The coach called for a ten-minute break, and as the girl playing Dalesa's mother extended her arm to help Dalesa get up from off the floor, Dalesa said, "I wish I were dead." The dialogue in the play was hitting too close to home. While the personal experience was helping Dalesa in the role, it triggered emotions she couldn't quickly shut off just because the director ended the scene.

The girl playing the mother didn't know how to respond to Dalesa's comment, and Dalesa didn't think it needed a response. The girl, however, told the drama teacher what Dalesa muttered. The solicitous instructor didn't want to say anything while the students were still around. With a hidden concern, the coach proceeded to direct the remaining portion of the scene when the break ended. Once they were finished, and as the club members dismissed themselves, the drama instructor asked Dalesa to stay back for a brief chat.

Dalesa was expecting performance notes, but instead, the teacher cast aspersions on Dalesa's emotional stability by immediately interrogating her about her morbid red flagging comment earlier. Dalesa had never felt so betrayed and anxiously wondered who else the girl might have told.

The drama coach asked if Dalesa needed to talk to anyone—if everything at home was okay. The teacher mentioned talking to her grandparents and setting up something with them and the school counselor. Dalesa knew anything involving her feelings and the Jenkins would not be comforting or reap any positive results. She panicked and then ran from the activity room—no words, no valediction, just an abrupt exit.

Dalesa left the school and wandered the streets to avoid going home for as long as she possibly could. She had managed to bottle up all her emotions about living life the way she had for so long. Up until then, she had the remarkable stealthiness to keep everyone at school and church from noticing any red flags that could be indicative of something awry in her weary life. Anxiety swelled within her as she violently worried over all her sorrow and troubles that had finally lured from out of the shadows.

She had nothing stopping her. It was her chance to run away but where would she have gone? She didn't want to live on the street. What family did she have? Even if her uncle were to let her stay at his place, Kenya would make it a hell just as painstaking as it was living with her grandparents. What friends did she have? No one. Dalesa couldn't even go to Tiffany's house; they weren't speaking those days. Coreen wasn't an option because she was still a school term away from entering Dalesa's life. It was heartbreaking to realize she had nowhere to turn. So, all those smiles to other classmates in passing in the hallway, all those essays she ghostwrote for them, they had not led to any friendships or bonds that could help her with an emergency sleepover or bus ticket on the Greyhound. Dalesa had to go home. She began to feel her grandparents were right about no one wanting her. She didn't want herself that night.

The next day at school, the school's counselor called Dalesa into her office. The Drama coach had already informed Ms. Stephans, the school counselor, of the previous night. Ms. Stephans was a soft-spoken woman whom Dalesa had never met for a one-on-one. Dalesa knew her to be sweet from her talks in assemblies and when she came to visit the classroom. In the counselor's office, that day, was also an on-call, crisis psychiatrist who wanted to ask Dalesa some questions about how she was feeling and her overall mood from day to day.

Dalesa was hesitant at first, but eventually, she opened to the idea of speaking with someone, finally, about the emptiness she'd been feeling inside. The doctor seemed to be non-threatening. The more questions the tall stranger asked, the more convinced she became that he could help with the disassociated and unsettling emotions she struggled had been struggling with for so long. He wanted a few sessions with Dalesa before giving a final diagnosis that Dalesa had Major Depressive Disorder.

In conjunction with regular sit-downs with the school counselor, Dalesa was finally starting to address some issues, and it was apparent the problem was not the teenage blues. It was darker and deeper than a hormonal shift. Dalesa's condition, if it weren't treated would become disabling. All aspects of her life were at risk, but the psychiatrist couldn't prescribe a minor with medication and not consent from her legal guardians.

Dalesa had not told her grandparents she had weekly visits with the counselor or sessions with a doctor that came to the school. So, when she invited the Jenkins to come to a conference and learn about treatment options for her condition, they laughed. They teased her about having emotional problems and took no ownership of their culpability to her unstable situation. Ms. Stephans sent an official letter to the house and made it mandatory that the Jenkins attend Dalesa's upcoming appointment.

They were compliant and met with the counselor and doctor. The doctor explained what clinical depression was and provided them standard information about his pharmaceutical recommendations for Ativan and Paxil. Quietly and amused in their opposition, the Jenkins listened as both the counselor and psychiatrist talked about the child in their care that was in serious need of support emotionally and psychologically. The Jenkins were not interested in what either of them had to say. At the end of their informal orientation of mood disorder and psych medication, Mrs. Jenkins only responded that Dalesa was okay, seeking attention and all she needed was to go to church and pray.

They would not sign any release paper and refused to allow Dalesa any more sessions. The doctor stated how he understood the cultural stigma on psychiatric treatment, but then he probably provided the right selling point but to the wrong people when he said, "It's not healthy or typical for a person, let alone a child to wish they were dead, Mr. and Mrs. Jenkins. I'm a spiritual man, and I've seen how sometimes medication and therapy can work alongside prayers."

Mr. Jenkins asked, "She wishes she were dead?" Shocked, he put on his fedora and tapped Mrs. Jenkins on the arm. "We're done here. We'll talk with Dalesa and have her sit with the pastor of our church. Good day."

Mr. and Mrs. Jenkins left the counselor's office, and Dalesa sat numbed by the entire encounter. She was curious about the medication but not too disappointed that she wouldn't be able to try the pills. Dalesa had enjoyed talking to someone about her feelings. So, she hoped that her grandparents' guardianship couldn't truly prevent her from talking to her school counselor whenever she wanted. Ms. Stephans assured Dalesa that as her counselor, her role in her academic life was just as fixed and substantial as the principal and school nurse; she would be an anchor.

Dalesa couldn't help but feel that her grandparents' performance in the counselor's office was proof that they didn't want her to have peace; even though, she made no strides in disrupting their lives.

"So, you wish you were dead, huh?" Mr. Jenkins asked Dalesa when she arrived home from school later that day.

Dalesa didn't respond.

"Do you want to hang yourself as your father did? In a couple of years, you will be 18 and can do with your life as you want. For now, you belong to your grandmother and me, and we will not have you embarrass us like you did at your school today," Mr. Jenkins said.

Dalesa for the first time sensed an elusive concern from her grandfather about her life in his reprimand. Although, she couldn't help but wonder what it would be like for him if she were dead. Would it be his granddaughter he would miss or the foster care subsidy? She wondered if she would have successfully run away and not come home last night if her grandparents would have taken the town car out looking for her.

COME FIND ME

I never knew the road to love would be this lonely.

I feel betrayed by those who should be the closest to me.

I have no one.

Many days I fantasized about what real love felt like.

I dreamt of what it would mean to have it in my life.

In that world of make-believe, love is in everything I touch and see.

The colors of love look vibrant and gay.

Disenchanted reminders of life without love entirely dissipates in my

fantasy.

However, within the disillusioned reality that coexists alongside my

body, all around me is melancholy and disarray.

I accept that perhaps contentment is only something to be yearned for

but nothing that I'll experience.

Tell me, please.

Why has love forsaken me?

It is the only thing that can rescue me from my sadness.

Imitations of love—selfishness marked with a forged signature of real

love—have left me to drown in the waters of depression.

The same song plays over and over in my ear.

It is a battle song – an anthem for liberty and revolution.

The war for peace of mind was waged many years ago.

Love can end it all and bring salvation to my soul.

The enmity I feel towards myself can be lifted with love.

It seems though that love doesn't love me.

Love doesn't want me.

Love doesn't know me.

If only those around me could become possessed and drunk with love.

The humanitarian in me would be met by the humanitarian in them.

I would be able to give love liberally and receive love lavishly.

I wish dreams actualized.

I could then live in a world where love rules, royally, and not fear,

tyrannously.

Love does not live here where I am.

It has abandoned me and left me in a cold, dismal place.

I'm on some unmarked, desolate road searching for it—using

anything I can to find it.

I must keep looking because if I stop searching, it means I have

accepted it's nowhere to be found.

I'm a miner cutting and blasting to extract emotional and spiritual

ore looking for cosmic currency.

I view my life as a commodity.

I'll barter for just a touch of love.

There must be a bit of love for me, and one day I'll find it.

I don't want to give up hope like the ones I love who tend to do so.

I hope one day love comes and finds me.

"Jesus is the answer. Prayer can heal anything," Dalesa says. She begins laughing lightly. "That was their answer to everything. Lose a pen? Pray about it. Got a hole in your sock? Pray about it."

"Why does that make you laugh?" Romeo asks. It is the first time in all their sessions that she seemed extremely amused.

"It's funny that they claimed to be Christians—devout soldiers of God. Get them away from other people, and the love and charity that Jesus preached about didn't guide or order their steps. They were hypocrites – decrepit, unvenerable hippos," Dalesa says. "I did it their way. I let the minister at church pray for me. I let him rub holy oil and holy water on my forehead to exercise the demon of depression from my body.

"It changed nothing in me. I felt no closer to God or happiness after the Holy Ghost visited me than before. What I was experiencing was more than my spirit could bear." Dalesa was no longer laughing. "I wanted to believe that I could sing a spiritual song, chant a prayer, partake in communion and find joy waiting for me once the communion wafer was digested in my stomach.

"I've had what seems like fleeting moments of happiness. If I can call them that but what I tend to feel regularly has been such a constant in my life that I've taken wretchedness to be my natural disposition. That's why I never actually sought professional help. I've learned to mask it from coworkers and seldom allow Coreen to glimpse it. Would things have been different if I had gotten treatment earlier? I don't know.

"What I do know is that I have a problem. Is it a disease? I know it is a disorder and something that I detest. Whatever deficiency of neurotransmitters, serotonin or what have you, it's not just chemical imbalance; I feel it in my body – in my bones, my hair follicles, my teeth, my muscles, my appetite. It affects a part of my spirit that I thought only the Most High could touch. I call Major Depressive Disorder the mental version of AIDS. Self-esteem, motivation, the libido, interpersonal relationships are all affected. You saw what happened to me just only a few months ago. A man broke my heart, and it drove me to become suicidal. Just the other day, I got overcharged a dollar at a department store, and you would have thought the world was coming to an end. I couldn't handle my failure to pay attention or the event of losing any amount of money. As small an incident as that was, it was as if it were an opportunistic infection. It was something that a person with good mental health could have easily gotten over, but someone like me gets broken down by it. I feel so inferior and worthless sometimes that just the thought of my cat having to rely on me for food each day can have me in tears or have me banging my head against the wall like a lunatic."

"Mental AIDS?" Romeo asks.

"Yeah."

"I've never heard anyone call clinical depression that before. So, with you having put that out there, how does it make you feel to have both HIV and psychological AIDS?" Romeo asks.

"Helpless," Dalesa says. "Hopeless." Her left wrist begins to itch. She starts scratching it.

"Are you okay?"

"Yeah. I think it's psychosomatic, but when I have depressing thoughts sometimes, the marks I have on my wrist starts to itch. It's got to be a mental thing, right?"

"Marks? Marks from what?" Romeo asks.

"I don't do it now, but from time to time I would cut myself with a knife or shaving blade. The scars are my reminders of how dark it can sometimes get for me," Dalesa confesses.

"You said that you haven't tried to kill yourself before a few months ago," Romeo clarifies.

"That's true. I wouldn't cut for fatality. Even though I've thought about it and contemplated ways of doing it over the years, up until last month, I've always been scared to attempt committing suicide," Dalesa explains.

"People cut for different reasons. You said you didn't do it to end your life. Why hurt yourself? Why mutilate your body?"

"Control. Romeo, all the pain, and suffering in my life came to me. It found me. I didn't ask for it. No matter how bad it would hurt, and no matter how the sight of my blood made me almost faint, it was a pain I inflicted with my own hands. As I would put the blade against my skin, I would be in complete control at that moment. I have never had a feeling of power like that. I have never been able to command myself to be happy. It seemed like pain and suffering were all I was ever going to know. Why not inflict it on my terms?" Dalesa says.

"Can you show or tell me where you would cut?" Romeo asks.

Dalesa rolls up the sleeves of her blouse. With her palms facing upward, she extends both arms toward Romeo. So, he can examine. Romeo notices horizontal and diagonal marks on both her wrists and forearms.

Romeo thanks her for showing him her scars, and she pulls back down her sleeves. "It's been almost a year since I last cut myself," Dalesa says. "When I was younger and for some time in my adult years – around the time I found out I was positive and maybe once or twice since then – instead of cutting, I would find myself banging my head against the wall. Sometimes I would do it repeatedly with my forehead and other times with the back of my head. I would hit my head so hard that it would leave bruises and lumps. Only once did I cause an abrasion that let out blood."

"This control you had by doing this, did it make you feel better in some way?"

"It seemed to intensify the pain I was feeling in my heart. It made whatever I was suffering through more complete. There would be the internal agony, depression, and despondency—all uninvited feelings—at the table for supper with my soul and then the corresponding physical twinge and torment that I welcomed to dine as misery's company."

"Thinking back on past feelings and moments when you were down, do you feel that same need for control is present now?" Romeo asks.

"Anytime I feel defeated or overwhelmed; I usually get an urge to cut or want to hit my head against the wall. This past year I attempted to try something a little less painful when those ideations come. It's disgusting, but it gives me the same sense of control as before. Remember how I told you I have an adverse reaction to shellfish? Well, what I have done only a couple of times, is order a pint of shrimp fried rice and let myself vomit for an hour. That's freaking demented, right?"

"You know I don't judge. The question is why do you feel that you have to harm yourself to have a sense of control?"

"I don't quite understand my logic behind it all, but in some strange way I feel safer if I'm the one causing the pain."

"Have you ever taken notice to how you are repeating patterns of the same baneful behavior received in your past? That's what appears to be happening. Sure. The pain may be from your hands but are you genuinely in control?"

"What do you mean?"

"The other day you were saying how you have no one and are worthless. That's what your grandparents used to try and make you believe. You even force feed yourself food to induce vomiting as your grandmother did to you on at least one occasion you've shared with me. You have made self-inflicted lacerations on your arms and banged your head against the wall. It's hard not to believe what you're describing is reverberant of how your cousin Kenya used to abuse you and once threatened you with a knife."

"Wow! I never really looked at it that way before."

"So, looking at it this way, do you still feel that your injurious behavior is still being in control or can you possibly see how you are merely following a program?" Romeo can tell that Dalesa is considering what he just proposed. "I have an alternative for you." He opens one of his desk drawers and takes out a rubber band ball. The ball is about the size of a baseball.

"I've never seen one of those that big before," Dalesa says.

"Yeah. Collecting rubber bands is a little hobby of mine." Romeo removes several bands trying to get to the perfect one to remove. He must take off seven or eight rubber bands before getting to one with the right breadth he wants. Once he takes it from the ball, he hands the rubber band to Dalesa. "Put it around your wrist. Are you left or right-handed?"

"Right."

"So, put it on your left wrist."

Dalesa follows his instructions and puts the circular band on her wrist.

"Whenever you feel the need to be in control or that you want to harm yourself, pull back on the rubber band and pluck yourself. It won't break the skin or cause you to bleed, but the slap on your wrist should sting a little. Compared to gastrointestinal pains you may experience as you vomit or pain from a laceration, the harm from a rubber band pluck is a one on the pain-o-meter but…"

"Will this work?" Dalesa asks skeptically.

"It depends on you. If you want the pluck of a rubber band to stop your feelings of loneliness or make you see rainbows and butterflies in the middle of a hurricane, then no. If, however, you want to have always accessible, a sense of control over pain when other harmful things are overwhelming, it's a start in a more positive direction."

"Thank you. I'll give it a try."

Dalesa and Romeo say their goodbyes, as this week's session comes to an end. Dalesa makes her way to the Ether Lounge afterward. When she enters, many of her fans told her how much they missed hearing their words last week. She told them, she missed being here but glad to be feeling better.

As Dalesa enjoys the performances of the entertainers ahead of her on the artist list, she browses through the pages of her notebook trying to find something to read tonight. Instead of some of the topics discussed in her session with Romeo this evening, she rediscovers a piece that she wrote a few years ago that seems most appropriate to her headspace.

ANATOMY OF SADNESS

Feet of gloom

Heart of contempt

Stomach ailing

Consuming

Intestines disposing

Ears curved but not bent

Hearing words of one sent

Chest broad with pain

You can call me built because my tears fall like rain.

Teeth yellow with fear

Grinding joy

Genitalia of a hermaphrodite

Warm, moist womb of misery

Penis a knife

Soul torn to shreds like that of a goat's bite.

Nose aware of the stench of foulness filling the air.

Arms and legs long

No power

No strength

Keeps me weak unable to carry on.

My hair's not nappy but wooly like Jesus' who just like me was at

times unhappy.

Waited for a resurrection three days too long but my angels sing a

melancholy song.

My mind full of thoughts

Getting heavier

My eyes change color like the leaves in fall and glow like a cat's

when night falls.

CHAPTER 10

"Can I ask you a personal question?" Dalesa asks. She settles herself in Romeo's client chair after entering the office and exchanging regular pleasantries to ease into today's session—of which she has decided needs to begin with an ice breaker.

Romeo clears his throat and says, "Under normal circumstances, Dalesa, you could ask me anything. However, this time every Wednesday I want you to use the opportunity to talk about you but... Sure. What do you want to know?"

"Do you believe in God?"

"I do."

"I don't."

"So, you're an atheist?"

"No. I wouldn't say that. I don't believe in the anthropomorphic God I was taught about in church growing up or the one under which this one nation stands indivisible," Dalesa explains. "I believe in an omnipresent, omnipotent, omniscient power that is the source of all things material and spiritual in the universe but not a man that holds the world in his hands or says that vengeance is his. The Most High as I like to call the All, doesn't have a gender and isn't made in man's imagination. I believe the Most is the perfect embodiment of love. I believe love to be the building blocks of the entire universe."

"Interesting. Okay. So, what role does this All have in your life? Well before you answer that. Tell me why you have chosen to bring your spiritual beliefs into therapy, now?"

"I was thinking back to our session last week," Dalesa says. "I realized that I was losing hold of my belief system. There's a reason I never tried to kill myself, despite all the anguish I've experienced. There's a reason I was able to suffer silently for all those years. It was my faith in the purposefulness of life."

"You said last week that prayer did not alleviate the gloom and sorrow you felt," Romeo says.

"No. It didn't seem to as a child, and for the most part, I don't think I've seen the benefits of prayer manifesting any miracles in my life currently," Dalesa replies.

"So, what keeps you hanging on if not prayer? Is it hope or faith?"

"It's a little of both. It's because of my faith that everything that occurs in my life has a significance and that keeps me hoping against hope that things will get better for me," Dalesa says. "I didn't always feel this particular way. Growing up in the church caused me to have expectations of what having a life in the arms of God was supposed to feel like. When I was younger, I believed in God and that the supposedly most powerful being had arms like a man." Dalesa chuckles. "Anyway, I couldn't understand why I was experiencing sensations and compulsions so dark and oppositional to the peace and love that the evangelists and ministers promised.

"When my grandparents flat out called me a heathen and said my soul was damned for wanting to be dead, I relied heavily on salvation from the church and the all-powerful God who always seemed diminished by his attributed human characteristics. I was praying daily and going to church weekly. I did these ritualistic things in adoration for this man-like God, and I was still unhappy. I cried constantly and often for no apparent reason. I had a fear of people and life.

"I honestly felt abandoned and forsaken by this highly recommended and overly promoted God that seemed to have had acquired all the inhumane characteristics of a God made in man's image. What was I doing wrong? I asked myself. I got so angry with the God of the Jenkins. People advertised him as the perfect embodiment of love, but somebody sold me a lemon. It didn't seem fair."

Romeo probes, "So, you lost your faith at that point?"

"I did, and up until a few months ago, it was still a bit disoriented. I, a few years ago, had to start reprograming myself from the extremely religious faith that I was forced into believing as a child," Dalesa says. "As I got older, things become clearer, and I could understand them better. It was more than just a mood disorder that kept me depressed. I came to see that I was the way I was due to the factors in my life – like in math how a plus b equals c. It's taken me up until recently to see that I wasn't being punished. I had toggled back and forth the concept for years, but in talking with you, it makes, even more, sense. If you mix yellow with blue, you get green. I was green because of things that happened to me, because of circumstances, because of yellow and blue – a and b. It's the law of existence—cause and effect.

"In my soul searching and my plain search for understanding the enigma that is life, I saw that some old guy with gray hair on a throne was a fanciful idea. The Most High lived inside me and in everything," Dalesa explains.

Romeo is intrigued by her philosophy, and comments, "That is so profound. You have stopped blaming the 'Most High' as you say, for your clinical depression and troubling life?"

"I had to. If I didn't, then I could never see the things I had no control over and accept the ones that were placed in my hands like a ball of clay, to shape and sculpt to my liking."

"I still believe in the Most High, but I have a new relationship with my faith. Love is all there is, and I know that there is divine love and I'm a part of that whole. Faith is trust in something or a person, right? Well, I want to stop looking for the Most High to rescue me from myself. I want to save myself," Dalesa shares.

"When it comes to physical and mental health, do you believe you can save yourself?"

"I believe anything is possible, but realistically, I know I need medication to treat my HIV. Therapy to do what prayers cannot alone, and Chardonnay for everything else." She chuckles.

"Oh, Cool. I still have a job as your therapist. You seem to be so enlightened today. I was worried you didn't need me anymore," Romeo says, and they both laugh.

"As long as I need you to be, is what you told me."

"That's what I said, and I meant it."

"I think everything works together for the greater good and there's nothing but the Most High – the All Good – everything in one."

"Would you consider starting a regimen of psych meds?"

"I would."

"Why now after all of these years? I know you may not have been able to when you were younger because of your grandparents, but since then, there's been college and a career. You've had plenty of time to have sought treatment."

"I thought I could make it without them. I'm only considering it now because the suicidal ideations I have had over the years, escalated from thought to action. That frightens me," Dalesa says, beginning to feel her wrist itch, slightly. She plucks the rubber band.

"I think I've only been coasting along all this time. I don't think I've been managing the depression well. Not to be grotesque, but it's been like feces that floats instead of sinks in the toilet bowl."

"Well, I don't prescribe medication, but I can have you talk to a doctor, who works out of this office. I will coordinate with you both and see if I can get you in to see him ASAP."

Dalesa smiles and says, "I think I'd like that."

"I used the word enlightened a moment ago, but optimistic is another word I would use to describe the Dalesa Moreno you've presented today."

"It may be a short phase I'm going through. We'll see how long it lasts, but I'm trying to find strength in my faith. I'm scared to the bone that I'm only fooling myself to believe that things can get better."

"Things are getting better. They have been for some time, now," Romeo says. "What did I tell you? You are in the restoration period of your life. Changes in how you feel begin with changes in how you think, and already your thinking is different than when we first started."

"You're right. What do I have to lose by hoping for the best? If I'm disappointed by love, it will leave me no worse off than where I started."

Romeo and Dalesa talk a little more in their session about Dalesa's philosophy on Divine Love and her struggles with faith and hope. Romeo initially wasn't sure where Dalesa was headed interrogatively with her question to him earlier about his belief in God. The truth of the matter is if the setting was informal and they were just friends talking to each other on the street, he would have told her that he believes firmly in God. So much so, that Romeo sees God in her—when she speaks and when their eyes meet. Romeo would tell her that he prays for her spiritual healing, regularly.

It isn't to say that Dalesa receives any preferential treatment from Romeo. There is no sliding scale for her insurance. Her sessions are the same length as his other patients. He is just as invested in the well-being of Dalesa as he is for all his clients. He secretly prays for each one of his patients before their session – hoping that they each reach a higher level of awareness.

However, whenever Dalesa enters his office, Romeo is overcome with a feeling of awe that is inexpressible – almost transcendental in its crux. He can't understand it and doesn't know what it is. Her story is lamentable, and each week he prays she comes to realize her resilience, as she sits on the cusp of a more triumphant life—filled with all the love she's been longing to own for so long. Perhaps, that's what it is. It's her innocence and insufficient experience with real love—an ailing heart void of healthy self-love, self-esteem, and self-worth. She claims not to know love, but something is unbeknownst to her; she has vicariously loved herself through her teachers, co-workers, and anyone who has enjoyed her writing and performances and sweet personality.

He sees what she can't see. Others see it, too, Romeo believes—everyone must. How can they not? Romeo agrees with Dalesa's trust in the purposefulness of life. He sees that Dalesa has a loving essence so pure that it radiates off her skin and is incandesced through her irises so brilliantly, that her dark-spirited parts of her genealogy chose to disown and discredit because they couldn't deal with the beauty.

How can a person tell someone that's been abused like Dalesa that they are destined for greatness without them thinking the messenger is delusional or trying to play on their vulnerabilities? It's a delicate territory to tread. So, Romeo continues to pray, privately—waiting for her to come to the discovery on her own.

Imagine love as pure energy. Then, it wouldn't be hard to justify the claim that love is in everything because as physics confirms, everything is energy, and everything vibrates at various velocities. Even though she suffers, Dalesa believes that love never fails. It is a constant; it endures and can conquer all things. The statutes of love are never changing. To this regard, there should be admission into belief, as this is the truth and not an opinion. "To be or not to be" is not the question. It does not apply here. People change and conviction waivers but rest assured that when it comes to the laws of love and the Universe, what "is" will always "be."

Dalesa is trying to connect herself to a greater love than she has known. If God is love, then like the Most High, love is inside of everyone. It is true that many people act contrary to the mandates of love. They move under the influence of a perverted, deviant version of the same authoritative force. This vibrating energy can positively change and uplift lives if allowed to do so and if it is used constructively – just as quickly as it can disintegrate and tear down if used to destroy. To know true love is to know divinity – even if you don't believe in God.

People are so eager to charge the Most High Love with the transgressions and felonies of life committed against their economic status, mental and physical health, ego and being – or whatever else.

They cry out, "Oh, Lord, why me? How could you let this happen?" Dalesa has been no exception. The thing that many people forget is that the Universe is made up of systems and a matrix of laws.

The systems that regulate the revolving of planets, the change in seasons, the formation of clouds, digestive and respiratory systems and the vast number of other structures – from the molecular to the astrological – are all manifestations of creation and evolution. They follow natural laws within their idiosyncratic design. There is not a great "man upstairs" that sits in his celestial veranda disrupting or manipulating laws of nature to bring misfortune to randomly picked individuals. Things happen, and the outcome is merely a result of varying factors—cause and effect.

Dalesa doesn't see The Most High as some passive-aggressive deity that she had been taught God was, in her youth, who would decide, perhaps, out of boredom to drown cities with hurricanes or tsunamis. In cases such as these, the devastating events are the result of impersonal laws of condensation or displacement of water. Even on the biological level, congenital disabilities are not from an insensitive creator experimenting with an embryo trying to architect a deformed child. Such a phenomenon occurs by a perversion of fetal development in the womb. If anything can happen, for anything to be possible and the scope of the unknown inclusive of an infinite number of reasons, why is it that people judge the circumstances and events of their life purely by what they see or can cognitively fathom? If the flap of a butterfly's wings can affect somewhere on the opposite part of the world, why couldn't the thoughts, words, and actions of a person set into motion the blessings and curses that may fall upon that or another person's life?

Dalesa and Romeo end their session for the day. Romeo tells her he will contact her by tomorrow afternoon with an appointment time to meet with Dr. DeShazor, the psychiatrist. Dalesa leaves the office and makes her way to the Ether Lounge. She wrote something last night that she was eager to share with the crowd.

She arrives and takes her seat at the bar. Her name is called, and the audience welcomes her with warm applause.

THE MOST IN MY LIFE

Who are you?

Who am I when I contemplate myself in you?

I know I am made of you.

I'm made in your mind—an image you've created as if a thought.

At times I feel so disconnected from you – like a faded memory.

I live and breathe because you have blown the breath of life in me.

I exist because of you, but still, I don't know you.

You are an enigma – a complex power in which I try to place all my

faith and trust.

I feel like I don't know what you are.

So many countries want to know you too, and many lands have fought

over you in brutal wars over the years.

Nowadays, the battlefield requires less bloodshed, but people are

murdered and martyred all the same.

The soldiers are in combat with propaganda, music, politics and

spoken words.

One group calls you one name and another something else.

Over the seas and beyond the valleys, a group calls you this and

somewhere else over the hills they call you that.

It's evident they speak of the same greatness.

Their culture, superstitions and vernacular will only allow them to

perceive you in their own way.

I have dedicated so much of my life to you.

Your celestial pull at my heart began many years ago.

Even though I have strayed many times from the Divine path, I still

hear your voice calling for me to come back.

I still feel the tug at my spirit to return to your grace.

How many years have gone by that I haven't acknowledged your

touch in my life?

I should have been dead, yet the mercy of karma has kept me stuck in

the web of circumstance created by my biology, genealogy, and

planetary influence.

Some situations seem so splendid while others appear to be a cruel

practical joke.

"All things work together for good."

"Everything happens for a reason."

"Patience is a virtue."

"I won't be given more than I can bear."

All these axioms are on repeat in my head.

Sometimes I fall short in my faith because I feel so far away from you.

Your greatness can be intimidating at times.

I know that you are the Most High and you are not like a man.

We, the earthly gods draped in the flesh, act unfairly, irrationally or

under the influence of dark and unpredictable emotions.

You don't gender or sexual orientation, so you don't make decisions

based on libidinous impulses.

You are love.

Everything that exists is because of you, Love.

You live inside me, and I'm a part of you, Love.

I don't know you, Love.

I long to become intimate and be consumed by you.

Ultimately, I just want to know you.

You are love.

You are the Most High, the Most Love, and I want to know how to

love the way you do because you are the Most in my life.

CHAPTER 11

Three months later…

"This is a question I already know the answer to but your friendship with Coreen…is that the most meaningful relationship you've had with anyone either at school, church, work, etcetera?" Romeo asks.

"By far, yes. I still find it hard to believe we are still friends – especially, after the senior year separation," Dalesa answers.

"What was the senior year separation?" Romeo asks.

"Well, after 11th grade, there was a school re-zoning, and Coreen had to transfer to another school. I felt so lost without her. Coreen was my rock. No one understood me the way she did. No one hardly spoke to me unless we happened to be together.

"Once we got separated, I had a void that needed filling with some companionship. I used sex as a means of getting the attention that I was now craving having spent the prior school year with someone always by my side."

"If the basis of your relationships with boys was purely sexual, didn't you still feel something missing?"

"My teenage lifestyle had me so enthralled into promiscuity that I didn't allow myself an opportunity to feel the lack of substance in all my temporal relationships," Dalesa says.

"So, you found a way to receive acceptance and be desired?"

"Outside of Coreen, acceptance was like a merit badge of social evolution for me. Coreen wanted to be around me and my quietness and quirky demeanor. These boys, however, showed me that I had desirability worth fighting over. There wasn't a strict dress code at my school. So, I was able to alter my appearance with more revealing and provocative, which really got the boys to talk.

"I was already dependent on praise and encouragement from teachers and members from the church like an infant needing a bottle of milk. Now, with my lasciviousness as a cover for my insecurity, I found multiple sex partners to dilute my neediness. In lowering the torch, the sentiment and love I longed to have got replaced with passion and licentious conduct. I had spent so many years wanting something that seemed reluctant to come. It was pleasurable and placid for me to accept my sexuality and eradicate sentiment, " Dalesa says.

"Do you understand the difference in being accepted for who you are versus being desired?" Romeo asks.

"I guess you're asking if I felt used. Yes, I know what those guys wanted, but it made me feel good that they chose me. I had something that someone wanted – a nice behind, bouncy breasts, soft lips, a sweet smell, an enticing walk – even if it was for just a few minutes of fornication and lust."

"I remember you said you had a boyfriend leaving high school going into college," Romeo says.

"It was a summer fling. When I got to college, I wanted to calm things down a bit not to be as loose. The goal was to focus on my studies and not a party for four years and disappoint the teachers and mentors that had helped me make it to that point."

"Then you got infected."

"Right and my whole outlook on sex shifted from being something I would carelessly engage in, to something that I considered somewhat sacred."

"I know you were violated in a reproachful way, but do you think that you will ever be able to love with your heart or your body in a way that is harmonious with your mind and emotions?" Romeo asks.

"That's a loaded question, Romeo. Richard showed me a life with the love that I had never known before. So, I thought. Then, to have it leave quicker than it came leaves me scared and very reluctant to try again," Dalesa says. "I'm damaged goods. Who's going to want me anyway? It's not cool or sexy to just say on the first day, 'Hi, I'm HIV-positive.' The guy probably won't even want to talk to me anymore.

"It's been 30 some years since AIDS was first discovered and people still don't know how to deal with this disease. Then, if you don't say anything right away, get close and get to know a person, hearts get involved. So, I haven't had any luck with this. When you disclose your status, it isn't pretty. You can't win either way.

"I don't want to deal with it anymore. This is my punishment. I understand that, now. My hell happens on earth. Who knows? Maybe I will be forgiven when my soul no longer has this body. I still believe this body caused my mother's death. This body was fondled and penetrated by lots of men. This body was infected with HIV. This body has been mutilated and poisoned by its owner. This body might be keeping my soul from touching the divine. Maybe heaven waits for me after death or maybe not. I don't know. If love is out there for me, I hope it happens before it's too late for me to enjoy it." Dalesa takes her hand and wipes a tear from the corner of her eye.

Dalesa knows all too well, that if a person wrongs another person, in any degree, the effects on the victimized can take a length of time to cease being disadvantageous. The saying goes, "Forgive and forget." However, any person that has been on the receiving end of any misconduct knows that turning the other cheek is a feat best accomplished by apostles and saints. It's hard to forgive and even harder to forget.

No doubt, it's difficult for Dalesa to refrain from feeling the puncture and pain from the hollow tips of heartbreak, darts of disappointment, and chafing of calamity. There are long-term effects from the hangover of betrayal, and another's wrongdoing. However, love keeps no record of wrongs.

Love is kind and merciful. To love effectively and powerfully, one must take on the arduous task of learning how to accept the bad and be grateful for it. Perhaps even more formidable is holding no animosity or blame. In Dalesa's case, this would include not directing resent towards herself. To do that is to realize that everything in life has purpose and necessity. Every adversity, if properly assessed and integrated into the psyche, can help build a stronger individual—a person that is shielded from detriment with the safeguard of love.

"You speak about acceptance and being wanted by others. Do you accept yourself?" Romeo asks.

"If nobody else wants me, why should I?" Dalesa replies.

"A few months ago, we spoke in depth about the purposefulness of each person's life. Doesn't that purpose practically warrant self-acceptance?" Romeo challenges.

"I have only the value others give me. I'm kind because others say that my actions and words are helpful. I'm generous when others are grateful for what I give them. I can go on and on but without validation, what good am I to myself if not anyone else?"

Her Senior year before going to college and being subjected to a new group of people whom she felt would more than likely reject her, Dalesa changed her personality, again. She returned to her woes about wanting to feel part of the majority.

With Coreen gone, so too was Dalesa's easy pass into the same social circles as the year before. Dalesa kept experimenting with versions of herself. She had already started with her sexuality. So, she began smoking cigarettes and weed to gain some "cool" points. Dalesa played the role, and like the phenomenal actress she was known to be, she was finally accepted by the "cool" kids – at least so she thought.

She altered her tastes in life, her likes and dislikes, and some of her passions. She dropped out of Chorus class and didn't go out for the Forensics or Drama club. She even shoplifted. She did whatever she could that regardless of ethical compromises would allow her to fit in.

Dalesa saw Ms. Mayon one Saturday afternoon in the bookstore. She didn't have the heart and was too embarrassed to let her former teacher know, she wasn't writing or performing much anymore. It would have broken Ms. Mayon's heart to know that Dalesa had dropped out of extracurricular activities – not to mention a couple of Honors and college prep courses. So, she hid behind bookshelves and kept her head down so Ms. Mayon wouldn't see her and ask, "Why?"

What would Dalesa have told her? Would she proudly say how she was a little floozy with a third of the Senior class boys and even some college kids she'd met, getting high in dark and vacant parking lots, stealing even though she made money? Dalesa wanted to ask if that middle school invitation to talk to her was still valid after almost four years. If so, she would tell Ms. Mayon how she felt she was about to be swallowed up in a new, reckless identity that didn't belong to her. Dalesa couldn't look into the same eyes that once looked back into hers when at a time all she was seeing was a promising future. This present identification was the was one that she sacrificed, researched, studied and even paid, in ways, to take on – just so she could obtain "cool" points, instead of college credits.

One night during Spring break, Dalesa was hanging out with a few girls and boys in her neighborhood. They were passing around a couple of cheap bottles of malt liquor that one of the boys' older brother had purchased for the group. They were enjoying the music playing from Dalesa's radio and just enjoying Spring break. After a while, a few more kids from the neighborhood came around to hang out, too. One guy was flirting with Dalesa. She tried to act like she wasn't enjoying the attention, but her reputation preceded her act at coyness. So, knowing she was into the sweet talk was turning him on.

One of the girls asked Dalesa if she wanted to hit the bottle and Dalesa said, "Sure. It's about time." Dalesa was enjoying the gathering – she felt as elated as she did when she finally made it to a chair at the big kid's table at Thanksgiving. She was bobbing her head to the hardcore music pumping from the stereo she bought with her last two checks from the bookstore.

Had Dalesa not already been drunk with the bliss of social acceptance, Dalesa would have noticed the sly grin on the girl's face as she was handing her the bottle and most of everybody else staring at her as she grabbed the bottle. She put the opening of the bottleneck to her lips. Dalesa took a big gulp, and if the snickering wasn't indicative of something mischievous, the bitter, warm fluid that was cascading down her throat sure did. She had swallowed urine.

While the guy was flirting with Dalesa, one of his buddies was refilling the bottle with his piss. Everyone in on the prank broke out into laughter. Dalesa was disgusted and embarrassed. She thought these were her friends. What friends would make their friend sharing her music device to deejay an underage, mini-block party drink human waste?

"That day, I remember thinking that maybe my grandparents weren't being mean at all. Maybe they were right the whole time. Maybe they were just telling me the truth about myself and other people," Dalesa says.

"What truth was that?" Romeo asks.

"That I was a nobody and people didn't care about me," Dalesa says.

Romeo says, "You can't say that those kids didn't care about you."

"They ridiculed me."

"No. Those people ridiculed a personality you created and presented to them. Those kids weren't befriending or bullying the real you."

"The really messed up thing is that the very next day, the caricature of a cool person that I was, tried to hang out with those girls again—as nothing had even happened. Isn't that pathetic?

"I didn't want them to think I was mad at them. I still wanted to be their friend. I didn't have the self-respect just to leave them alone. They had no respect for me, but I just wanted to belong – even if it was to be a source of entertainment for a while."

"What about in college? That was an entirely new environment—away from the Jenkins, away from Kenya, away from high school immaturity. Did you make any friends at Columbia?" Romeo asks.

"I did. I lost touch with most of my friends after graduation, but the social experience was much different."

"Better?"

"It was no different than the work relationships I have now. We connected as friends as it related to a common goal—in college, it was to graduate, and at work, it's to meet deadlines."

"Try not to downplay those relationships. Did you hang out with college friends after a lecture or do you hang out with your co-workers after work?" Romeo asks.

"Yes, to both," Dalesa replies. "I went to a few parties in school and my co-workers, and I go out for drinks from time to time – especially after the latest issue of the magazine is published."

"How did it feel or how does it feel to hang out with people who have similar goals and interests as you? Each of those people you attend parties with or have cocktails with could just as easily keep their engagement with you within the classroom or office, but instead, they invite you to hang out."

"That's true, but the relationships I have with them are depthless—genuine but superficial. I don't have any close relationships with any of them."

"Well, isn't that Coreen's responsibility—to provide sentiment and be a deeply invested part of your life? Do you want your co-workers asking if you took your HIV or psych meds today or if therapy is going well? That's your best friend's job."

"That makes sense. Seems fair to let the person I'm closest to maintain exclusive rights to my insides and behind-the-scenes," Dalesa says with a smile.

"You look like a weight has just been lifted off your shoulders. Or am I reading too much into that lovely smile of yours?"

Dalesa blushes at Romeo's compliment and observation. "Truth of the matter. College was a tailgate to high school in which I struggled with relationships. So, I wanted my college friends to be interested in me on a deeper level. I put so much pressure on myself for feeling like no one cared about how I was doing as opposed to the redundant query into what I was doing on any given day."

"Do you care about how you do each day?" Romeo asks.

"Is that a trick question? Of course, I care about how I'm doing. I'm usually doing badly."

"If Coreen was having a bad day, would you try to do anything to make her feel better?"

"Surely, I would."

"Like what? Can you give me an example?"

"I may ask her what's wrong," Dalesa begins to illustrate. "See if there was anything I could do to help. Then I'd be a friend and support her in any way I could. If it's guy trouble, then I sit and man-bash with her or take her shopping. It would depend on the situation and if she felt like talking about it."

"So, you take the time to analyze, with her permission, what the problem is, and then you try to help her sort through her emotions. You see what can or cannot be done, and then you work with your troubled friend so that she takes action to cope and move on?"

"I never broke it down so methodically but yeah. That's basically how it goes. She'd do the same for me."

"Is the reason that neither one of you wants the other to suffer is that you care enough for each other to not want unpleasant feelings to saturate not to want to allow the other to be saturated with unpleasant feelings?" Romeo asks.

"Absolutely!" Dalesa exclaims.

"Well, Dalesa, why is it that you aren't a friend like that to yourself?"

She is caught off guard by the question. "What do you mean?" she asks.

"I mean, you don't handle your bad days the way you help your friend with theirs."

"Maybe I don't consider myself a friend to myself—obligatory maintenance and responsibility are more like it."

"Then, how could you expect your college friends and co-workers to give you the kind of relationships you wanted from them? I'm sure your colleagues have days or nights at the bar when they are stressed over their kids or spouses or a Con Edison electricity bill."

"Yes."

"They probably open up to you, and with that endearing compassion of yours, you listen and try to help in any way you can. However, seeing yourself as a burden means not allowing others to get to that innermost part of you because it's possible, you're afraid that the deep-seated feelings you have regarding yourself will be reciprocated."

"So, what you're saying is that I have been the reason I haven't had many intimate relationships?"

"Look at it this way—a couple of *ways* actually. If an artist is saying over and over to themselves that something, they've just created is horrible, they aren't going to be receptive to people who in their encounter with the work find it beautiful. He or she will continuously be discrediting their opinion or finding more and more reasons to dislike an undeniable masterpiece. Pretty soon others will be convinced to share the same feelings."

"That makes perfect sense," Dalesa is amazed at the discovery.

"Also, keep in mind. We've already seen how you mimic the poor examples of conduct, neglect, and abuse inwardly that your family presented to you growing up."

"So, that's where that saying comes from about only being able to love others once you love yourself."

"Loving yourself means being the same kind of person to yourself as you are with others. Allow yourself to work through emotions instead of accepting that it is just the way you are feeling. For many instances, emotions and moods are chemical reactions in your body and brain. How you process circumstances, and those feelings are controlled by thought and your perception."

"I feel like you are handing me over diamonds and pearls right now—jewels of wisdom I wish I could have been meditating on and growing from all these years instead of my soul feeling like it has been deteriorating."

"I'm glad you said meditate because this work we are doing is completely reprogramming what was programmed in you and rebuilding your foundation on essence and light—not darkness."

"So, it's not wrong that I want to be accepted and to have people that love me in my life, but I also have to mirror those desires internally?"

"Yes. Why, Dalesa Moreno, I think you just had a breakthrough," Romeo says.

Dalesa doesn't know how to respond. She smiles. She agrees with him that she has seen something that she hasn't seen before. Dalesa has been searching for love, but love isn't placement beneath someone. Love isn't showering others and neglecting yourself. Love is generous and far from vain. Love is being able to receive love and be filled so that it can be given back to others.

If Dalesa has voids—cavities or craters where self-love and self-admiration are lacking—then the love that her friends give her would have to be enough to fill the holes to get Dalesa to normal capacity. This can't work long-term because her friends are doing what she should be doing for herself. Dalesa misses out because all that love she could be relishing in and giving back to her friends is used up on giving her self-worth and a reason for living.

Unless she should happen to receive an abundance and outpouring of high magnitude to not only compensate for the love lacking and see a carryover and reap a profit, Dalesa cannot survive off her friends' love. Her friends need love too, and until she loves herself, the love she gives them will only be the love they give her, regurgitated.

If love was a car and everyone had one, how would they care for their automobile? Would they use it for carpools, road trips or keep it in the garage? Would they keep up with oil changes and rotate tires? Would they pay their insurance for full coverage or liability? Would they go for luxury, speed or practicality? Would they follow the rules of the road with their vehicle, be defensive drivers or be reckless? Would they wash it regularly, get chrome rims, equip it with a state-of-the-art sound system or tint the windows? Will they take care of it themselves or make their personal property the responsibility for someone else? Will they pick up hitchhikers? Will they make out in the back seat? Will they fasten their seatbelts with every drive? Will they fill up the tank with regular gasoline or premium? Will they let their friends drive if they are too intoxicated?

This metaphorical love-mobile is registered in each person's name. Each driver has insurance. Each person can decide which passengers to let ride and who to let wait for the bus. This love-mobile is a birthright—assembled exclusively at an assembly facility upon conception. It's then sent to a lot to be parked until the owner is born. The parents or guardians hold on to the keys until the owner is licensed but every day teach the new owner about maintenance and eventually how to drive.

When the owner is of age, they are taken on test drives in parking lots and graduate to the road when the caregivers feel they are ready. Until they can drive on their own, the guardians teach by example—theoretical and practical methods. Some get their license earlier than others because they have great teachers, but others still need practice. Poor teachers produce poor drivers. People can't grow and evolve if they don't know how to drive and take care of their love-mobile. Other people have their own to tend to from day to day.

Unprepared drivers and owners of love have accidents because they aren't paying attention – wear their heart on their sleeve with no shock absorbers, bumpers or emergency breaks. Careless and reckless drivers drive under the influence and potentially hurt their love-mobile and those of others. A person can never lose their license to love, but it can become restricted if the laws of nature and the universe find them guilty of inverting love to destroy instead of build—this destruction would apply to victims as well as to the driver. When a person doesn't love themselves, they can't love others without co-dependency. The obvious problem with that is that there is only one gas pedal, brake pedal, steering wheel, ignition, and driver's seat. There can only be one navigator in love, and it starts with independent drivers sharing, not hogging, the road.

Dalesa was given her love-mobile, the keys and left to transport herself through the highways and byways of life and this world has received a poor lesson in Lover's ED. If she continues to let others take the wheel or backseat drive, she will always get lost. Those enabling her self-deprecation and lack of self-love, by siphoning from their love-mobile to hers, may one day grow tired and drive home. Thankfully, as Dalesa is beginning to see, she has friends that are excellent drivers and don't mind giving her a few lessons. Practically nine months have gone by, and the two of them can see progress. She's still swerving a bit, but she is getting more comfortable being behind the wheel. This is her journey, and her love will get her to her destination safely in time—with rest stops every seven days on Wednesdays at 5:30 pm.

Romeo and Dalesa continue to talk until it is time for their session to end. Dalesa leaves his office with a smile. She discovered something today. Realizes how special friends are. Hers have been hand-picked to share her life. She is grateful for that, and she will work on being an example of the love she wishes to receive towards herself—the "concrete" rule.

The golden rule states to treat others as one wants to be treated by others. The platinum rule maintains that one treat others as those individuals would like to be treated. With the understanding that all buildings have foundations and footings, of which concrete cylinders are typically used for deep foundations, the "concrete" rule would be as follows: "Do first for yourself what you would do for others." Friends reflect oneself. Dalesa's friends have already shown her love—the love that Dalesa owns; only now she must discover it for herself.

It's about a quarter past eight. The second performer for the night sings an upbeat love song on the Ether Lounge stage. Dalesa isn't sitting on her unofficial reserved stool at the bar. Tonight, she has invited Coreen and a couple of co-workers to experience the creative underground at the Ether Lounge. As has always been, her poetry is something she regards as a sacred expression of her raw emotions and private thoughts. Rarely, did she share them with anyone outside of the Ether Lounge—a place where she'd found comfort and safety to be her authentic self? However, she now wants her friends to hear her perform. They are all in good spirits, and after her enlightening session with Romeo, their presence there with her has a deep overcast of sentiment and is met with sincere appreciation, as they enjoy their beverages and listen to the vocal belts coming from the baritone singing on stage. Dalesa doesn't even have to sign the performer's list anymore. Once the hostess spots her—which is ordinarily at the bar— she just waits for a discretionary moment in the night to call Dalesa to the microphone.

Dalesa's co-workers, Yusef and Lucy, vibe well with Coreen. It's as if Coreen had known them before meeting them for the first time tonight. They are on their second round of drinks by the time Dalesa gets called to the stage. Dalesa already has her fan base that catcalls when she is about to perform, but tonight, she had her cheerleaders whistling as she walked from the table; the admiration made her blush.

She usually likes the band to feel the piece she performs and play something complimentary, but for what Dalesa has chosen to recite tonight, she's requested a cappella. Coreen shouts out, "We love you Dalesa!"

Dalesa's cheeks had just returned to their normal color, but the outburst made her blush all over again. "That's my best friend ladies and gentlemen. She just ordered her second Cosmopolitan, so please excuse her," Dalesa says playfully. She laughs with the amused crowd. "I also have some co-workers here tonight as well. I want to dedicate this to the three of them and to anyone else that can relate. Thank you." Dalesa begins reciting her spoken word poetry.

MORE THAN JUST A FRIEND

You don't know the depths of my feelings for you.

If it takes the rest of my life, I'll see it through.

Showing you in every possible way.

I smiled when you said to someone that you were mine.

If I could catch a melody from the air, I'd hand it to you.

With love and faithfulness, I'll always deliver to you.

There is no limit.

There is no end.

There is nothing I wouldn't do.

If only you believe

Believe in this fellowship.

Believe in my lifetime assurance policy of camaraderie and fidelity.

I look forward to our regular conversations.

I can't wait to tell you what's happening in my world.

I can't wait to hear what's going on in yours.

I trust you with my secrets.

You get me when no one else seems to understand.

You don't judge me.

You forgive me when I utter the wrong thing and catch me when I can't stand.

So many days go by, and I'm grateful for each day I have you by my side.

The bond we have is unbreakable.

I could ask for no better friend.

Time forces us to change.

I've seen how you've grown.

One thing remains the same.

It's my love for you.

It's deeper than you'll ever know.

Always on my mind

Always in my heart

Time can never weaken my respect and adoration.

This right here

What we have.

It is strong enough to hold me in my time of need.

More tenacious to reciprocate that same support in yours

Brave enough to go against the odds

Reliable enough to always be on-call

Secure enough to stand beside me

Support me

Laugh with me

Cry with me

Succeed with me

Yusef and Lucy raise their cocktail glasses in the air in saluting regards to her endearing words when Dalesa finishes. Coreen stands from her chair, joining in the audience's applause. Dalesa comes to the table and walks right into Coreen's outstretched arms. She gives Dalesa a tight, bosom-to-bosom bear hug and kisses her on the cheek. As Coreen sways Dalesa from side to side in their hug, Dalesa smiles and closes her eyes—imagining that it is herself giving herself the robust and loving embrace. Then just as that image imprints in Dalesa's mind, Coreen says, "I love you."

Dalesa responds, "I love you, too."

CHAPTER 12

One month later…

"I'm gonna die," Dalesa says after an invitation from Romeo to start their session with whatever was on her mind.

"I don't know any human who doesn't die at some point," Romeo replies with light-hearted sarcasm and chuckles.

Dalesa doesn't share in the laughter. Romeo straightens his smile and clears his throat. "Sorry," he says.

"Awe, C'mon, Romeo. You don't have to get all rigid, Mr. Psychotherapist," Dalesa says. She tries to give at least half a smile. "I know you were kidding. It's just that I haven't had much of a sense of humor these last several days."

"What's been going on? Are you still taking your meds?" Romeo asks—adjusting his position in his chair.

"Yes. Well, let me clarify. Are you referring to my HIV medication or the meds that Dr. DeShazor prescribes me?"

"I was thinking your psych meds, but you can answer for both."

"Yes. I'm taking them all. That's part of the problem I'm having. Dr. DeShazor keeps changing the pills and the dosage. I feel like a lab mouse he's testing drugs on."

"I'm sure he has explained to you that when it comes to medicating psychological issues, it can take some time to find the right medication that will work for you. How has your mood been since the last change?"

"About the same. Okay. No. I can't say that. At first, when I was on Paxil, there wasn't any noticeable difference for a few months. Some days, I seemed to be doing worse. So, he just recently started me on Effexor, and I have noticed a few more moments of sunshine in my week but not enough moments to be able to say it's because of the medication, though."

"Well, it could be a matter of time before you see the effects, or with your honest feedback to Dr. DeShazor, maybe you'll find the efficacy is not there at all, and the dose may change, or maybe another pill will be prescribed all together," Romeo says. "I had one patient, whom it took about a year working with another doctor to find the combination of medication that did what he and the doctor wanted the medicine to do."

"That is so frustrating to hear. I'm tired of taking medication," Dalesa says.

"You can tell the doctor you want to stop the medication at any time. Don't feel that you have to include medicine in your treatment."

"I know, but I want to use therapy and medication to deal with my condition. I've lived so much of my life without help; I don't want to shut myself off to any avenue at this point. I'm trying to be positive that we'll find the right medication that works," Dalesa says. "It's just that it seems like my life, or rather my survival is being managed by reliance on my HAART cocktail for my HIV and the antidepressants for my mental AIDS. My liver and kidneys must be working overtime.

"Then there are the side effects. The HIV meds have gotten me to an undetectable status, as you know, according to my lab results but the toil these potent drugs are taking on my body will only get worse with time.

"I take back what I said before about the latest medication from Dr. DeShazor. He and I both agree that I've gone from severe to moderate. I'd say at the higher end of the scale when it comes to being moderate, though. It's definitely closer to being severe than it would to be mild, in my opinion."

"It sounds like you are disgusted with having a dependence on the pills, but you see a benefit from taking them," Romeo summarizes.

"Yes, I do, and you said it right when you said I'm disgusted. I don't know about the antidepressants but my other meds I must take for the rest of my life. It's been eight years, and I'm still in denial about that sometimes," Dalesa says. "It's not an option. I must drink those pills every day, or I could risk developing a resistance to the treatment. That scares me because I haven't been consistently taking them.

"It's not something I've been doing intentionally. I know the risks. That's why I think I'm gonna die sooner than if I had remained consistent with my meds starting about six weeks ago."

"You know the risks and have managed to comply with the regimen for years. Why suddenly this inconsistency?"

"I don't know really. It started so subtly. One day I forgot to take them, and the same thing happened on the next day. This day was better because at least I remembered by the time I was getting ready for bed. I ate a quick snack and took them right away.

"I don't know how it slipped my mind. I guess I was preoccupied with a new story for the magazine or something. Anyway, as the weeks went by, I noticed that a day or two would go by every week where it was like I had a mental block wedging out the medicinal habits of almost a decade and its importance. I just had some lab work done and thankfully, despite my sloppiness, and because of my retroactive prayers, once I realized my sloppiness, my viral load is still undetectable. The only thing that the doctor did mention was a slight decrease in T cells, but he said not to worry; it's still in a good range.

"It just scares me that I became so reckless, but to be honest, the thought of having to take pills for the rest of my life is devastating. It's sad to know that my life support is drinking these chemicals every day. I didn't ask for this disease."

SWALLOW

Press down

Twist

Top off

Dump out

Pop in

Sip

Swallow

Body aches gone

Headache relieved

Fever lowered

Press down

Twist

Top off

Risk took for heart attack

Stroke

Heartburn

Rash

Press down

Twist

Top off

Dump out

Pop in

Sip

Swallow

Clear nasal passages

No itchy, stuffy nose

Press down

Twist

Top off

Risk took for spiked blood pressure

Irregular heartbeat

Unusual nervousness

Press down

Twist

Top off

Dump out

Pop in

Sip

Swallow

Higher CD4 counts

Lower viral load

Less likelihood of virus-related illnesses

Press down

Twist

Top off

Risk took for diarrhea

Appetite loss

Fatigue

High cholesterol

Mood changes

Sleeping problems

Press down

Twist

Top off

Dump out

Pop in

Sip

Swallow

Stabilized mood

Decreased psychosis

Lowered anxiety

Press down

Twist

Top off

Risk took for joint pain

Muscle aches

Nausea

Migraine headaches

Daytime sleepiness

Weight gain

Suicidal ideations

Decreased sex drive

Press down

Twist

Top off

Dump out

Pop in

Sip

Swallow

Pain alleviated

Press down

Twist

Top off

Liver damage

Constipation

Osteoporosis

Dizziness

Swelling

Weight loss

Blurred vision

Press down

Twist

Top off

Dump out

Pop in

Sip

Swallow

Wait four hours

Press down

Twist

Top off

Dump out

Pop in

Sip

Swallow.

"I may have been sexually uninhibited as a teenager, but I was always safe. I always made sure my partners wore a condom. This jackass, Carson, takes what I didn't want to give to him and doesn't use any protection. If he didn't know he had the virus, Carson was stupid to screw me and not strap up because he had no idea of knowing if I had any STD's or whatever. He seemed to have planned everything so meticulously. Carson should have picked up a Trojan, Magnum or whatever condom when he got the ruffie. He invaded my body and poisoned my blood," Dalesa says, angrily.

"So, it sounds like you still have animosity towards Carson for infecting you," Romeo says.

"After all this time, I have a quiet rage but not towards him. I'm angry with myself for allowing myself to be put in that situation. I should have known something was not right when he wanted to make sure his roommate and I didn't cross paths. He flirted with me all the time. I should've been smart enough to know he would want more than to watch a 60-year-old movie with me. If only I had not procrastinated and gotten the movies on my own sooner. I wouldn't have needed to watch his copies."

"I'm sure you have replayed the events of that night a million different ways in all these years. One thing you have to remember, no matter what could have, should have or would have, means it was your fault," Romeo says. He knows this is a difficult subject for her, but, every time she feels the need to talk about the incident, he reminds her that, "He had no dispensation. If anyone had entitlement, it was you, and he took your right to give consent away. That's not your fault. Even without a toxicology report, there is beyond a reasonable doubt that he took away your sound, and conscious mind by drugging you. Carson is to blame. If you don't want to or if you do want to forgive him, so be it, but do not place any blame on yourself for any of it."

"I understand my mother. Had she lived, she may not have wanted to abort me, but she didn't want to be bound to me for the rest of her life from my cradle to her retirement home. She didn't want me sucking on her chest for milk, swaddling me and trying to get me to sleep. She didn't want me growing up and looking more and more like Stanley. She didn't want to pay for school uniforms, daycare, clothes, and shoes, for an illegitimate child that would be a physical reminder to compliment the traumatizing memory of the man who assaulted her—in his twisted act of love.

"Why did this happen, Romeo? Why did Carson do this to me? Why do I have to live off meds? Why are men scared to touch me? Why do I always have to suffer? Why? Why? Carson left me with the Mark of the Beast!" Dalesa begins to pound her fist on her thighs several times and lets out a frustrated grunt. She hits herself harder and shakes her head, roughly, from side to side – as if someone had asked her a question to which she was responding "No." She starts to cry profusely.

Romeo intervenes. He gets up from his chair and holds her by her wrists, but Dalesa is resistant. He holds her until she stops fighting against him.

After a minute or so, she stops jerking her head and relaxes her hands. When Romeo is confident, she is calm, he releases his grip and returns to his seat. Dalesa's crying subsides, and she sits still and silently. Romeo places the box of facial tissues he has on his desk closer to her. She pulls out a few sheets and dries her face. After she balls the tissues up and tosses them in the wastebasket, she pulls up her left sleeve a little—revealing the rubber band Romeo had given her.

He is glad to see Dalesa putting the therapy to work. He allows for there to be a few minutes of silence—a quietness of speech that is—because there is a sound resonating with a dry reverb in the office, which is the smack and slap of the rubber band hitting against Dalesa's wrist.

"You started our session by saying you were going to die. My delayed response to what you said is do you want to die?" Romeo asks.

"I don't want to be sick anymore," Dalesa answers.

"I understand that. Not to put my personal beliefs into the mix or not to sound like a conspiracy theorist, but between you and me, I know there must be a classified cure for HIV and AIDS. I just pray that the day comes sooner than later when the powers that be make the remedy available to the general population – instead of forcing lovely people, such as yourself, to indefinitely be subjected to quarterly blood tests and toxic, highly active and effective combination antiretroviral cocktails.

"I wish you didn't have to depend on medication to survive with this virus. I would like it if you didn't have it all. I realize you go through your periods of denial, but the reality is that you are HIV positive. Currently, you must manage the disease daily. You were lucky with your most recent lab work. I'm glad, but if you fall off again, it could be a different story for you next time. I'm sure your doctor had some choice words for you already. So, I've said my piece," Romeo says. He feels a little emotional but doesn't let it show outwardly. "Suffice it to say, not taking your meds can be harmful and dangerous." He clears his throat and takes a sip of water from a water bottle beside his computer monitor.

Romeo has allowed his compassion to lead him and not his profession. It is not the first time when his heart speaks and not his degree. He can see that Dalesa is near tears again. He takes a couple of tissues from out of the dispenser and hands one to her. He rolls his chair towards her, leans in close and with the other, takes it and wipes a tear from off her cheek. "I can sit here as a cultivated and educated man and tell you that everything will be just fine. I can say for you to not worry about a thing," Romeo says. "However, at this very moment, being a man that has grown immensely fond of you, with humanity in his heart, I can say that I'm not the least bit concerned with the generalized everything." He makes quotation marks with his fingers on the word "everything." "I'm concerned about you. So, as a person that cares about you, I will tell you that you will be just fine."

"Will I, Romeo? I seem to be retrograding every other week," Dalesa says. She wipes a tiny, drip of mucus from her nostrils.

Romeo takes her hand and holds it with such genuine care and warmth that a shiver rushes up Dalesa's arm. "All that you are going through and have been through has been one ultimate test—a crucible. Just like the crucible used for melting gold, you are reaching the liquefying point," Romeo says with a comforting smile. "By any chance, do you know how much heat it takes to melt gold?" Dalesa shrugs her shoulders – not knowing the answer. "Let's just say the heat would need to be over half as much as molten lava. To put it into even more perspective, I know you're familiar with the Bible. Well, to melt gold, it would take the heat more than twice as hot as the lakes of sulfur in Hell. I'm not sure if you've ever felt now or in your past like you were in Hell but…"

"Plenty of times," Dalesa interjects.

"Well, listen here Ms. Moreno. That gold nugget heart of yours is in that crucible being melted down to the undefined state which will later be molded into a beautiful crown to adorn your head like you are the queen of your destiny," Romeo releases her hand and rolls his chair back closer to his desk.

Dalesa is no longer in tears inflamed by feelings of hopelessness but is overwhelmed and trying to process all what Romeo has said to her. "I don't know what to say to that, and I'm seldom at a loss for words," Dalesa says.

"I probably said too much, but it was from the heart. I've been trying to get you to open up your heart and emotions in each of our sessions, while mine has remained hermetically sealed," Romeo says. "I couldn't sit across from you another evening and not speak to you as a man that has a heart that hurts for you with each new story you tell or tear you shed. I hope you took nothing out of context. I hope something I said resonates well within you."

"You definitely gave me some concepts to think about and process for a while. I thank you," Dalesa says. "Honestly, I'm not entirely convinced of the validity of some of your comments, but I'm not dismissing anything without some contemplation."

Dalesa can still feel the warmness of Romeo's clasp of her hand on her skin. It felt so soothing, and Dalesa felt that Romeo was not just a therapist doing a job but someone who sincerely cared about her. She doesn't want to think of it beyond a professional predilection, but she dares to think in her mind that he was speaking as a friend.

"How do I adjust to everything that's happened to me and continues to happen to me? You saw what just happened to me a few minutes ago. I feel like I'm losing my mind," Dalesa responds.

"Have you ever heard of counting your blessings?"

"Yeah. I've heard that a lot."

"Start doing that. Take it seriously. Write the things you are grateful down if you must and keep it with you. Refer to it whenever you doubt that life can get better."

"That doesn't work. The bad outweighs the good all the time."

"It doesn't have to be that way. Good and bad are relative concepts—purely subjective and are in cahoots together—they work for one another," Romeo says. Dalesa has a smug look on her face but still curious to see where he is going with his philosophy. "What I'm about to tell you is way easier said than done but if you change how you view life, how you live, and experience life will also change. How you, or any person, look at situations—their perception – has a lot to do with what they go through. You're staring at me like I'm a lunatic."

"I'm listening. It is interesting to hear, but so far I definitely agree that it sounds simpler said than actually executing it," Dalesa says. She straightens her face and takes in what Romeo is sharing with her.

"Take a fox preying on a rabbit. Then, see the fox successfully killing that rabbit and having it for dinner. Reality says the death of the rabbit is merely the passing of a rabbit. A person's perception determines if the fact is good or bad. Considering the rabbit's life, the rabbit's mate or maybe some, now, orphan bunnies, a person may see it as probably a bad thing that the rabbit died. However, the fox has a tasty meal and doesn't go hungry for the night— which a reasonable person can consider being something right to come from the rabbit's death; it's the circle of life.

"As you said in one session, you don't take your corporal self with you when you die. Love resides in your essence; it lives in your soul. Focus on connecting with that, Dalesa. Stop looking to other people, other projects, other circumstances, other false perceptions, for what's waiting to be discovered within you," Romeo says with all his heart.

"And you're saying that this starts with how I see myself and the world and things in the world around me, right?" Dalesa reiterates.

"That's right!" Romeo exclaims.

"It seems to all come back to me and something I must do. I'm starting to wonder if I've truly been a victim. You and Dr. DeShazor seem to give me a lot of credit and authority." Dalesa starts to play in Romeo's Zen garden.

There is silence. Romeo watches her rake the sand with her diverted attention from his eyes. He says finally, "You have been victimized, and I'm sure you've been made to feel the victim. As you sit in my office today—as you have for a few months short of a year—you are no longer the victim. You are the progenitor of a new life for yourself."

"You see good, but all I see is bad," Dalesa says. She looks up from the sandbox. I try to be an optimistic person around my friends, but when it comes to myself, I'm such a pessimist. It's like your positive affirmations and little fox and rabbit ideologies and the wrist whippings with rubber bands and the blessing counting and the melting in the crucible and all of this…all this that we do here each week seems right. You know what, though, it feels like malware or some virus is corrupting my mental hard drive. You even described what we're doing as reprogramming. I'm not built for this. Life has not been good to me. I can't believe that life can be better, now. It just doesn't seem fathomable." Dalesa crosses her arms and looks Romeo dead in the eyes.

"None of this process is easy. If you recall, I mentioned to you early on in our sessions that this will be difficult. I can see in your eyes that you want what I'm saying as being possible for you, to be real. It may be out of your mental capacity to conceive of the possibilities right now but hold on to that hope. If nothing else for now, just hold on to that, please." Romeo petitions.

Dalesa sits with her head down but mutters "Okay." She is taking in all of what he's said today. She wonders if her life can indeed be changed with perception. She admires the patterns on Romeo's Persian rug. Romeo writes something in her file.

How can a person that's infected with an incurable disease be optimistic about his or her future? Can a person have peace of mind, knowing each day the risk of living while a destructive virus is continuously replicating itself in his or her blood?

It seems impossible that such a person can have joy or know serenity with so much against them and everything looks bleak. However, love always perseveres. This is not a hope, wish or fantasy. It is a fact. It's a Universal law that says if a person holds on to love and clings to the god or goddess within, he or she can weather any storm.

Romeo looks at the time. It's time for their session to end. They say their goodbyes and Dalesa leaves the office more pensive than she's ever been. Has she been looking at things all wrong? Could there have been peace during all those years of turbulence and misery? She leaves – contemplating life, death, and the in between.

The evening has slipped into the night. The streets lamps glow along the streets of Spanish Harlem in the city with insomnia. Inside the best-kept secret of New York, with her notebook in hand, Dalesa walks onto the Ether Lounge stage. She greets those in attendance. She tells the band to play something solemn but smooth. She steps up to the microphone stand and speaks with conviction and intensity.

TOO DEEP

I gaze into the mirror.

The reflection I see is supposed to be me.

Is it really me that I see?

Can this piece of glass with its reflective, silvery backing honestly

show me?

I'm looking at the image, and this can't be me

Is that my hair looking like that?

Are those my lips I'm licking?

Have my ears always been that size?

I hear this voice in my head.

It's not a thought.

It doesn't sound like me.

It says, "Look deeper."

"Beauty is only skin deep."

Oh, how I wish to be beautiful.

I hear people in their casual dialogue.

They ogle and obsess over models on TV and those in magazines with

idolizing fascinations and scrutiny.

The perfect body, with a perfect face, wearing the perfect clothes

Always in style

Always with good taste

I look into the mirror.

What a disgusting piece of skin and bone I am

How I would love to be the sexiest person in the room now and then.

It would be nice to have a few admiring stares when I walk on the

train.

Yet, this voice keeps speaking to me.

It interrupts my thoughts.

Invades my mind

It insists I look deeper

I don't understand how.

The mirror isn't an x-ray machine.

If it showed anymore, you'd see my kidneys and spleen.

Skin deep; that's as deep as it goes.

The mirror shows no more than what I see.

"A deeper love is inside," the voice says.

My mirror must be rigged 'cause things look bleak.

I thought I knew love.

I've been searching and have found nothing remotely close.

Just ask my family, they know.

They treat me like an outcast.

They judge with no rational logic.

They give but only with conditions.

They don't deal with an issue.

They dodge it.

They stand nearby to watch me suffer.

So, at the end of it all, they can say at least I was there.

They don't care.

They think the molecular bond of DNA is all they need to claim me.

Blood may be thicker than water, but at least water is pure and transparent.

My family holds on to lies and harbors resentment.

They coerce me into believing in their home is loyalty and refuge.

Only to betray me and leave me with nowhere to turn.

That's not love.

The belief that genetics is enough to secure family ties is a stupid

philosophy.

Love is not based on surnames or twigs from the family tree.

So, if I can't get love from my family, how can I expect it from

anywhere else?

The voice is still here.

It continues to push me, "Look deeper."

I sought love in romantic relationships.

I thought that just maybe I'd find it.

I learned the hard way that romantic love has its expectations and

prerequisites.

There tends to be an imbalance.

I give 100 percent and get in return only a portion of it.

I sacrifice and do my best to make my partner happy and only get

complaints and requests for more.

I offer a non-judgmental ear to my lover's worries and woes.

Yet, in my time of need, I have no shoulder to cry on.

No one's there to comfort me.

Selfishness shows.

I give of myself and my income, but it is as if I'm paying to be loved.

The love between two people should not be a commercial transaction.

It should be organic and everlasting.

"Deeper! Deeper!" the voice commands.

I don't want to look deeper!

What does it matter anyway?

No one loves me.

Look deeper?

I won't dare!

Why, should I care?

If we learn by imitation, then my teachers were inadequate.

I have no idea how to love myself.

I'm mentally sick.

Spiritually and emotionally impaired

Delusively snared

Caught in the matrix of self-doubt and fear

There!

Voice, are you satisfied?

I've looked deep.

In the mirror, I see someone needing love, and I'm praying love finds

me.

After the showcase ends, Dalesa decides to hang around a little longer than usual to have another glass of wine. She sits at her usual spot at the bar. She tries to reflect on her session with Romeo earlier, but she gets a little distracted by patrons coming up to her praising her work and her performance. The showcase crowd eventually dies out, and she can be alone with her thoughts and her glass of top-shelf, Merlot. Everything he said seemed too good to be plausible. Pondering the analysis and philosophy he presented has put her in a strange place mentally and emotionally. Could she be on the cusp of finding the cure to mental AIDS? Is there something to the perception concept that Romeo spoke about? Has love been standing at her door knocking, ringing the bell, and sending registered mail for all these painstaking years while she's been trying to maintain? Mentally, going around in circles, she almost doesn't notice that she has finished her wine.

As she waits for the bartender to finish with a customer, she feels a tap on her shoulder.

"Does Dr. DeShazor know you are consuming alcohol?" Dalesa turns around and is surprised to see, Romeo.

"Busted! I don't believe you're here. Why? I mean, how did you know I would be here? Or did you even know I would be here?" Dalesa has a little buzz but is so happy to see Romeo. "Bartender! Can I get another glass of wine? Thank you."

"Well, I called your apartment, but Coreen said you were here. I was a little concerned about you after our session and wanted to check in," Romeo says. He sits on a stool next to her and orders a rum and Coke.

"That's sweet of you. You know, right? If you had gotten here a little earlier for the showcase, you could have heard me perform," Dalesa says. She can't stop smiling.

"Who says I didn't? I like when you said that blood might be thicker than water, but at least the water is transparent. The whole piece was fantastic. You have a way with words, and the way you perform when you speak is mesmerizing," Romeo compliments. The barkeeper has returned with their drinks. They toast. "To going deep."

"To going deep. ¡Salud!" Dalesa echoes.

"I must say you managed to curate much of what you and I have discussed over months into several minutes of orchestrated, spoken word. Amazing!" Romeo takes another sip of his drink.

Dalesa is so glad that Romeo admires her work. "So, is it safe to say that I've just earned a new fan?" She nudges him on the arm and bats her eyes.

"I've been a fan since Montefiore Hospital when you told me that you could die another day." He winks at her.

"Oh really? So, my hair hadn't been combed, no make-up. I was fresh out of a coma, on suicide watch. Gave you a little bit of resistance at first if I recall correctly and you mean to tell me that you considered yourself a fan with all the mess that was Dalesa Moreno back then?"

"Yup. I sure did."

"Whatever you say, Mr. Sylvian. Even though I think you are full of bologna." Dalesa laughs playfully.

"Had I known you came here every week—at least that is what Coreen told me—I would've been here supporting you."

Dalesa blushes and pretends to play naïve to his covert flirtation. "You would do that? Come see me speak here? Even though not long before I walk on that stage, you would have just listened to me probably crying, or throwing a fit or telling some intimate detail about my sorted past?"

"I love supporting a good artist—especially ones with whom I have a close and personal connection. I bet no one here that cheers for you each week can say that." He winks at her.

"Romeo, you are too much. What am I going to do with you?" When Romeo first came up to her, she was shocked. She hopes he didn't sense the weirdness she was feeling when they were first talking and ordered drinks. 'Who has drinks with their therapist?' Dalesa had thought to herself. Now, however, with her refreshed goblet of libation and seeing for the first time more of personality than professional from Romeo, Dalesa is allowing herself to enjoy herself. "So, what will the office say if word got around that you are out fraternizing with clients?"

"Who me? Fraternizing? Oh, no. No. No. Not me." Romeo smiles. "This is a professional courtesy to ensure you are okay. It would've been a phone call, but you weren't home." He leans in about an inch of her.

"Well, how come you didn't just call my cell phone?" She smiles. Feeling he has no way around that, she too leans in about an inch.

"After talking to Coreen, I looked at the time and figured if I called you right then, you may have been performing and couldn't answer. Then I thought you could have been listening to other performers and still couldn't talk. So, I figured I'd show up in person. That way there would be no game of phone tag and no intrusiveness. Then, I could go to sleep tonight knowing that you were okay." Romeo moves in another inch closer. This time he takes a swallow from his beverage feeling sure his explanation was iron-clad and free of any motives that could be construed.

"So, at what point did you have that assurance you needed that I was okay?" Dalesa leans in. "Was it when you sat down beside me or after you ordered your first drink?" She stands up and waves for the barkeep.

"Correction. First and only drink." He sits back straight up on his seat and waves a napkin as if surrendering with a white flag. "You win. You win," Romeo chuckles. Dalesa snatches the paper handkerchief from out of his hand and giggles.

"I know I win." She orders her and Romeo another round.

"A phone call would have been sufficient to pass as an appropriate gesture of professional courtesy and concern. However, the way you were talking earlier I was almost sure that after 6:31 pm when you left my office, I wouldn't see you again—at least not for a while."

"Awe, Romeo."

The bartender brings their drinks. "Since you ordered us more drinks; I guess I'll hang out for a little while longer. All I ask is that you don't think of me as your therapist tonight. Think of me as your friend."

"Friend?"

"Yeah. You can even call me Romie like my buddies do. Just remember that what happens in the Ether Lounge stays in the Ether Lounge. ¡Salud!" They clink their glasses and move their bar stools in closer to one another.

"Just for the record," Dalesa says. "You ceased being my therapist tonight the minute you winked at me and shamelessly started flirting with me. Ha ha."

Romeo smiles. That comment makes him second guess his decision to pop up in an unofficial capacity. "Please know I was only playing. You did know that, right?"

"Sure," she says. Dalesa doesn't believe him, that he was kidding around, but she will flow along with his redirection of intent.

"While we won't have titles, we will still have boundaries. Cool?"

"I understand. No problem."

The two of them drink in merriment, enjoy the music and talk for at least another 90 minutes. During which time, Romeo opens about his family and his hobbies. Dalesa listens intriguingly and laughs at his jokes—even the corny ones because that's what good dates do. A date is what this night has been for her. Even Romeo's had a few moments tonight when he was turned on by the conversation, Dalesa's attractiveness, and her reassuring display of enjoyment.

Dalesa does not go out anymore, socially, since the breakup with Richard. Except coming to the Ether Lounge every week, she hasn't been out in a while. She doesn't typically stay past the showcase hours at the lounge. She recites a poem or two and heads home shortly afterward.

As she sits with Romeo tonight, she feels safe and relaxed. Dalesa stands to her feet and feels woozy. She realizes that she may have had one glass of wine too many.

"Are you okay?" Romeo asks. He stands up to offer her assistance as she wobbles.

Dalesa insists that she is fine. "I'm going to the ladies' room. Will you be here when I get back?"

Romeo says, "Yes but I have to be heading home soon. It's almost 11:30."

"Yes. Me too."

Dalesa goes to the restroom and returns a few minutes later. When she returns, she seems a bit more contained than before stepping away from the bar, but she is done consuming alcohol for the night.

"Let me take you home, Dalesa," Romeo says. He waves for the bartender to settle the tab. He walks Dalesa out of the building. The air feels good in her lungs and on her skin. As she inhales and exhales, Romeo raises his arm and tries to hail them a cab. One pulls over within a few minutes. Romeo opens the back door, and Dalesa gets in. She scoots down to the other end, and he follows. They arrive at Dalesa's apartment building rather quickly.

"You don't have to see me up. I can manage from here," Dalesa says, as she exits the taxi.

"I'll feel much better if I came up and saw you to the door." Romeo pays the fare and follows Dalesa into her building and takes the elevator to the 11th floor. Once inside her apartment, Dalesa turns on a few lights, and her Iris immediately makes an entrance – welcoming her back home. She takes off her jacket and doesn't bother to hang it up; she tosses it on the couch. Romeo looks around the front room and comments, "You have a quaint home. It's very modest and warm. You and Coreen have the whole Feng Shui thing down."

"Thank you." Dalesa exits to the kitchen. Romeo walks down a moderately, long hallway. On one of the walls are hung a couple of framed articles Dalesa has written for American Memoirs that have won awards.

"Is the bathroom down this hall?" Romeo asks.

"Yes. On your right. Can I get you some coffee?"

"Sure."

Dalesa puts on a pot while Romeo uses the bathroom. When he comes out, he can smell the coffee brewing, but Dalesa is no longer in the kitchen and not in the living room. He sits on the sofa and patiently waits for his hostess to return.

Romeo thinks back on the night he just had with Dalesa. He thinks of how he wanted another rum and Coke but had to set that limitation for himself to respect the boundaries. With alcohol, it took more self-control to deny himself any chances of feeling that it wasn't just about her but about him, too. He dreams about Dalesa in his waking hours. He thought he almost lost her today all because he loosened the reigns on his tender feelings for her.

He has never been inside a client's home before tonight, and of course, he's never had drinks with one either. It was an intense session for both, and Romeo had to go the extra mile to ensure she would continue treatment and take in what was discussed like she'd promised and not dismiss anything prematurely.

Sitting on the sofa, Romeo keeps looking over his shoulder for Dalesa to come into the room any second. After several minutes of sitting in the living room alone, Romeo begins to wonder what is taking her so long to return with the coffee. "Dalesa, is everything ok?"

"Yes, everything is just fine."

Romeo hears her voice coming down the hallway. He turns to face the corridor and his jaw drops. Dalesa has disrobed and wears nothing but a lace bra and panties – holding a cup of coffee and creamer in her hands. Romeo turns his eyes away quickly.

"Are you sure you are feeling okay? Where are your clothes? I don't need coffee. I think I should leave."

"Don't leave, Romeo, isn't this what you want?" Dalesa places the coffee and creamer on the glass table in the room and walks towards him.

Romeo is already to his feet and lowers his head, as he walks towards the door. He keeps his field of view directed downward to the hardwood floors. "Dalesa, let's get something clear. I am your therapist. I'm not a boyfriend or one-night stand." Romeo feels extremely nervous and uncomfortable. 'What have I done?' he thinks to himself. "My compassion and admiration for you are sincere, but perhaps I led you on and did not realize that I had compromised the integrity of what we were building as counselor and client."

Dalesa's bottom lip is quivering as her eyes begin to water. "You held my hand today in your office. That was the first time a man has touched me in nine months. I felt something between us in your office—something that you can't deny has been there since the beginning. Per your own admission, you've been a fan ever since."

Romeo walks back to the sofa and grabs the coat Dalesa had tossed down. He hands it to her. "Can you put this on, please?" She puts on the jacket. Romeo finally can look at her. "Dalesa, perhaps there is a bit of transference occurring here on your part. It's not uncommon in therapeutic relationships such as ours."

"Really, Romeo? Transference? From what? From whom?"

"From the boys in high school. Richard. Carson. From any guy that has seduced you with compliments, praise, acceptance, and attention just to have sex with you."

"We're not talking about my past. This is about you and me right now and these past several months."

"I'm not trying to hurt you, Dalesa. Maybe the attention I give you may make you think there are romantic interests here, but as your therapist, I want only what's best for you. I apologize for any displaced feelings I may have caused you. Perhaps, by clasping your hand during our session and winking to you at a cocktail lounge sent the wrong message. Dalesa, there is something I feel when I get lost in your stories or your eyes. Something has broken through the invisible divide that should separate us—especially myself from becoming attached emotionally to what has always been and needs to remain a top priority – your mental health. My care for you comes from my humanity. You don't owe me your body for that."

"Once a slut, always a slut I guess," Dalesa says. She laughs at herself out of shame and wallops her forehead with the palm of her hand. She lets out a frustrated grunt. "I'm so embarrassed. You're right. I'm so humiliated. Just like you tell me all the time, I repeat negative patterns of behavior. Tonight, being the most humiliating as I throw my tits inside some Victoria Secret and throw myself at my therapist."

"I should have been more mindful of my interactions with you knowing what your issues and struggles are. I'm embarrassed as your therapist for my behavior. Please forgive me. I'm sorry. I'm going to go now." Romeo lets himself out.

"Dalesa follows behind him and stands at the door. As he walks toward the elevators, she says, "I'm pathetic, Romeo. You know that, right?" Romeo doesn't respond. He presses the down button. "I always have been. My legal guardians were freakin' prophets. They told me." The elevator doors open and Romeo walks inside the car. Dalesa goes back inside and sits on the couch. She wants to cry, but she's all cried out over herself. She tries to have a dialogue in her mind about how devastatingly climatic the last six hours have been. It all started the early part of the evening with Dalesa telling Romeo in therapy that she was going to die. She finds it ironic that during his cameo appearance at the lounge, she learned that Romeo officially became her supporter when Dalesa told him in the hospital that she wanted to live. She can no longer stand the strain of thinking and the ache of feeling and decides to take herself to bed. She will have the next seven days to process and evolve from this night. There's so much to assimilate emotionally. Between the impassioned words exchanged and the undignified things that were done, she hopes that a week spent repenting and reflecting will help her with her "Walk of Shame" into Romeo's office next week. She will need to have gained something of merit to replace the dignity lost tonight.

Romeo, on the other hand, sits in a cab heading home. He can't believe he let things get this far. Dalesa was right. He had truly formed a connection early on. Up until today, Romeo justified all his interests in Dalesa and constantly did a spot check with his quality of care towards, her compared to his other patients. Romeo should have made some considerations months ago when he realized the vehement intensity of his fondness for her. The day he wanted to hug her and rock her sorrow away, he should have known that if he didn't do something, his ability to keep his feelings concealed would be met with greater challenges—especially when he became more attracted to her essence with each hour-long session. "Dang it!" Romeo blurts out in the backseat. The cab driver glanced behind him using the rearview mirror. Embarrassed by his random outburst, Romeo apologizes and asks to be let out at the next block. He's going to walk the rest of the way. It is only a few more blocks to his apartment, and besides, it is the warmest December night the city has seen in years.

He didn't ask to have this compassion for Dalesa, but it's not her fault either. Her mental health matters more than Romeo's attraction to her. What he wants Dalesa to understand is that it's not nor ever has been about lust. However, he has never been so enthralled by a woman who is unable to see—near or far—even with a set of gorgeous eyes, how the quintessence of love that dwells inside her, transcends all worldly, superficial beauty and circumstance.

NO VACANCY

Heard you have company.

I already know who it is.

You don't have to tell me.

She came to me once before, asking to stay a night.

I don't remember inviting her in, but I must have.

It wasn't long before she had squatter's rights.

I know you may feel all alone right now.

It may feel like what you are going through is a solitary fight.

Sunrises may even seem less regular than sundowns.

Does it seem like days didn't use to linger and drag as they do of

late?

Is there a prevailing pressure to persevere intense in you like a boiler

soon to burst?

She won't let you succeed from your current state if that's the case.

She will make you feel like all you've accumulated and accomplished

is coming to a premature end.

This dame is very cunning, and she'll make excuses for everything.

I can help you get her out of your space but don't let her back in

again.

She re-arranged all my structures and forcibly threw my hope out the

window.

She volunteered to water and fertilize seeds that were going to reap

beautiful fruits.

When my harvest didn't come, I knew she had to go.

Like a ring slipping off a swollen finger that's lubricated with butter,

better days seemed to slide off the future of chances from a sad past

when you're with her.

I know you're feeling the pain, but it's good that all things must come

to an end—just do what I say, and it won't happen again.

Tell her you saw me today, and she'll probably start packing

immediately.

Who knows?

I know I'm still in litigation trying to restore my life and regain

everything that was kept from me.

Just remember she is manipulative, and she embellishes the reality of

things.

She never calls with good news and thrives off affliction, so let the

phone ring.

She is a predator and saw your situation and that you were down.

Ms. Misery offers nothing but depreciates everything to the ground.

Two is company.

I had no one to help me when she came knocking, but you have me

now.

She prefers engaging in wretchedness and distress, one-on-one.

So, keep me around because three's a crowd.

You don't have to vacate her alone.

Just come and find me.

Misery only loves company.

CHAPTER 13

"Hi," Dalesa softly says to Romeo as she enters his office the following week. All she has thought about for the last seven days is having to come through his office doors, today. She wasn't sure what to expect or what he expected. She takes her usual seat at his desk and looks for a new pattern to trace with her eyes on his Persian rug. Romeo places the "In Session" sign on the front of the door. He sits down in his chair and puts his hands in his lap. Dalesa refuses to look up at him.

"It is good to see you, Dalesa. Happy Hump Day! I hope this week has been going great for you so far," Romeo says. Romeo is impressed with himself for not sounding as uneasy as he feels – especially, considering he can still picture his adored client in her brasserie. Today is the first Wednesday he has not looked forward to 5:30 pm since Spring. He's been dreading this day since about midnight on last Thursday morning when he stepped into the elevator leaving the eleventh floor of Dalesa's apartment building.

Dalesa feels that her salutation is as generous as she is ready to be with words for the time being and doesn't respond. Still afraid to make eye contact, she does manage to lift her gaze above her ankles and to her hands on her lap. She admires her freshly manicured and French-tipped fingernails and makes a mental note to increase her technician's gratuity on her next visit.

It is apparent; neither party wants to address the elephant in the room, but it's a purple one, with yellow polka dots. It cannot be ignored for too long. Romeo knows that he should take the professional initiative and sensitively bring up at least one of the concurrent issues, but he is embarrassed for her also—as if he too were seen in his underwear that night.

He's had to undoubtedly approach what is a precarious situation and shift in the dynamic between them both personally and professionally. He sighs silently and picks up a business card from off his desk. He knows what he must do. Although it will be in the best interest of his patient, it was not his first consideration – nor one he finds favorable.

"Dalesa," Romeo says to get her attention. She looks up—eyes still falling short of direct contact with his. Even with a lowered brow, Romeo sees that the usual gleam in her eyes is dim. His heart is breaking. He hands her the card. Dalesa takes the card and silently reads the name on it. It's a card for Wayne Duvall.

"Who is Wayne Duvall?" Dalesa asks.

"He's your new therapist. That is, he will be if you agree to my referral. I've spoken to him, and he's decided to take you on as a new patient."

"New therapist? So, you are dumping me?" Dalesa places the card on his desk and crosses her arms. Now, she assuredly wants to make sure her eye contact is direct with Romeo.

"I wish you wouldn't put it that way. This is not an easy thing for me to do. Choosing to let a client go is probably the most difficult decision I've had to make in my career within at least the last two years. Dalesa, I should not have been in your apartment last week. That was a bad judgment call on my part. I take full responsibility for what happened there. I should've just stayed in the taxi and went home, but I wasn't thinking. Then again, when it comes to you, I don't think. I mean, I don't use my brain really. That doesn't sound right either." Romeo is flustered. "When we are together, I react with my heart. You compel me to think with my heart. I don't know why it's so easy to turn off Romeo Sylvian when I'm listening to you and be Romie.

"There's something so very special about you Dalesa. There is also something so fragile and bruised. As a mental health professional, I took on as my responsibility to offer help, tools, and counseling for you to heal from severe emotional and psychological trauma. I don't get to play with your vulnerabilities the way I did, unintentionally. I was careless with my own emotions to have not been more careful watching out for and handling yours. For that, I'm truly sorry."

"If half the guys that said they didn't want to see me anymore had broken up with me like that, maybe I wouldn't need therapy now." Dalesa laughs to herself. Romeo smiles. "I'm the one that should be apologizing. It sounds like you've made up your mind about this. So, there is not too much more I can say but thank you. Thank you for being an excellent therapist and a great guy.

"I wish there were more guys like you. Preferably, ones who won't be compromising their professional integrity by holding my hand while I tell them about my psychological, emotional, sexual and physical abuse. I wish there were more guys, who when I tell them I'm infected, still, wink their eye at me, give a swagger smile and openly flirt with me in a public place. I want to meet a guy who would look as cute as you did even in shock, seeing me serve him coffee half near naked and still respect me enough to say that ensuring my wellbeing and mental stability meant more to him than having an unbridled, one-night stand. What would be the likelihood of me finding someone like you on the streets? Next to impossible. Now, you say that I can't have you in a therapeutic capacity either. I'm willing to forget last week."

"That's the problem, Dalesa. I can't forget. I have a job to do. My commitment to the field and my obligation to you cannot be put in jeopardy. You deserve to be treated with the highest quality of care. I honestly can't risk even the slightest indiscretion in how I may speak to you, which could have a direct impact on your recovery. That's why I've set you up with one of the best therapists in this office. I'll be checking up on you from time to time."

"We can make this work, somehow. I'm sure," Dalesa pleads.

"No, I think it's best we end things before they escalate. Don't worry, Duvall is a very dear friend of mine. I'll give him all my notes. You'll be just fine. Then, too, you'll still be seeing Dr. DeShazor every month. Remember, therapy wasn't about me and won't be about Duvall. It's about you."

Dalesa can't believe it's over. She is heart-broken. She looks at Romeo sitting across from her, but Romeo seems so emotionally removed, they might as well be in two different rooms. "This professional relationship although clinical was more intimate than any relationship I've had with anyone in my family and boyfriends—making this the longest, close relationship I've had with a man. You can't just pass me on to another therapist and expect me just to open up about my darkest feelings and experiences. I messed up last week. I get that. I'm sorry but don't leave me, Romeo." Dalesa is crying because she is sad, but also in her tears are molecules of madness.

Romeo passes her the tissues. "Dalesa, don't cry. It's going to be okay," Romeo says.

"How can you say that? You're acting like you don't care."

"Of course, I care. I don't think you understand how this is not your fault. None of this is. Do you remember what we talked about in our session last week? Anything?"

"Not off hand," Dalesa wipes under both her eyes with the tissue.

"You see? That's a problem. What happened after the session replaced what happened in the session. You only reacted to what I put out there, and my behavior created something it shouldn't have. What was important from the events of last week should have been the things you discovered and discussed in therapy—not the act of me winking at you or holding your hand.

"I hope you can one day come to understand this for what it is. If you aren't benefiting from therapy, then there's no need for it. When I see you crying like this, I want to do this to you." Romeo rolls his chair close to her and begins stroking her hair softly. "Then, I may want to say in a gentle voice how it will be okay, and I pull my chair closer. I may then want to do this because you are still crying." Romeo wraps his arms around her shoulder. He is close enough for her to lay her head on his shoulder. "Shhhhh…It's going to be okay." He pulls back. "How did that feel, Dalesa?"

"It felt good. Your touch was tender."

"Did it feel like your therapist was stroking your hair?"

"No but…"

"Exactly. What I just did was inappropriate for a therapist to do to a patient. Small circular rubbing on the back or shoulder is okay, but in some practices, even those actions are prohibited. Today, not unlike other times, I felt you needed more attention from me than me handing you a few facial tissues. Whenever I have seen you hurting as you speak your truth, I quietly pray that your non-anthropomorphic God comforts you and I want to make you feel better in my distinct way. That's why I speak so passionately to you from time to time because I love you.

"As your therapist, I cannot trust myself to remain objective, detach myself emotionally while remaining appropriately empathetic or refrain from showing affection with feelings that are so deep for you. As your therapist, I can't have drinks with you or invite you to my apartment to watch sports with my friends, just to get you out of the house because I know you've been nowhere but to home and the office all week. As your therapist, I cannot do this either."

Romeo leans in towards Dalesa. Carefully placing one hand, longways, on the lower part of her head and nape of her neck, he pushes her head forward and kisses her on the lips. Dalesa rolls her eyes back as her eyelids close. They kiss for about five seconds before Romeo sits back in his chair and pushes away from her. He can't believe he just did that, but Dalesa isn't complaining.

Romeo says, "This is why I can no longer be your therapist, Dalesa. Today, I was just supposed to speak to you about Duvall, apologize and give you my best regards. However, the more I tried not to react and speak what my heart was telling me to say, the harder I found it to think of myself walking out of your life. I would miss knowing how successful you were in starting to love yourself.

Romeo's lips no longer press against hers, but she can still feel his soft flesh on her mouth folds. She heard Romeo speaking but time is standing still for now and nothing in the room—in the world—matters except his confession of love and his challenge for her to do the same—to love herself.

Dalesa feels like damaged goods. Her life has been nothing but heartache and heartbreak. Romeo loves her despite this. He knows things about her that no one else knows—things that she would never tell another living soul. She has poured out her innermost feelings, shared dark experiences, immoral behaviors and deplorable attacks to herself to him for months, now. He knows her better than even her closest friend. It's an incredible wonder that he can say he loves her knowing all that he knows.

Dalesa looks at Romeo. He is smiling, but there is a look of expectancy in his eyes. She knows she should say something—but what? She expected to receive counseling, not fall in love. She is trying to process this as quickly as possible, but she knows the next words to come from her mouth are crucial.

"Romeo," Dalesa finally says.

"Yes?" Romeo responds.

"You just told me you love me."

"I do immensely, Ms. Moreno. I didn't stutter."

"I don't understand how."

"The reason you don't understand is that you don't love yourself."

"Then, you kissed me." Dalesa can't help but smile, coyly, as she says that.

"Yes. I did. It felt appropriate. I'm sorry if I was out of line," Romeo says, apologetically.

"I didn't stop you, did I? It was nice. You have soft lips."

"So, do you. Thank you for not slapping me." They both laugh. "So, we're good?"

"I'll call to set up an appointment with your friend."

"Don't worry about that. I already have. It will be the same as ours used to be. Changing therapists is already a significant shift. We didn't want to add another one by changing your schedule."

"Thank you. I'm going to miss you." Dalesa stands.

"Stay in touch, please. My cell number is on the back of the card." Romeo gets up from his chair, and she stands, also. He hugs Dalesa. Dalesa practically melts like butter on a freshly toasted slice of bread in his arm. She inhales his scent that smells as soothing as scented oil burning. "Take care of yourself," he says.

Dalesa leaves his office, and Romeo hopes she is not leaving his life and their acquaintance. As she walks to the train station, her heart swells within a kaleidoscope of emotions. Various, patterned thoughts rotate about in her mind, and her soul swims in a pool of sensibility. Ambivalence is like a crown of thorns pressing around her head. 'Love. What is it?' she thinks to herself.

A person that trusts in something has that something to hold on to when there is uncertainty. A person that believes in nothing has nothing and is left searching for something but unsure of what. When apprehension and fear come to the surface in this person's life, he or she, without a doubt, will fall into a dark abyss of insecurity and instability because there is nothing to hold – nothing that can help lift him or her up and be stable. Despite the dismal, frightening threats of gloom and the spontaneity of hardship, confidence in the promises of an almighty love is what keeps Dalesa's hope alive. She may feel she doesn't know what love is, but it is her trust in the power of love that above all else keeps her afloat as she drifts along life's oceanic currents of the unknown. When the earth is quaking beneath a person's feet, the waves crashing against the boat, or a breeze becoming a gusty tempest, a person that trusts in love can use it as ballast and defense.

THIS IS...

This is how I am.

I wish I could say I'll be okay.

This is who I am.

I wish I could fly away.

This is what I do.

I pray for a change to come.

This is what I get.

The same situation

The same circumstance

The same source of sadness that leaves me in regret

This is why I say.

There is no hope for me.

This is why I cry.

I have a tendency.

An uncontrollable urge to seek refuge from life's storm

In my fear and inertia

I can't seem to break free from the norm.

A commonplace of complacency, discontent, and gloom

I don't want to be here anymore but where else can I go?

I'm doomed.

This is why my faith sways.

I've given up.

This is why I pray.

I see no other way.

I need some assistance.

I won't be resistant.

I throw up both my hands.

Anxiety erupts in worry, and my feet fall in sinking sand.

This is it.

The final hour

Tell me, can I take any more?

This is how it is.

I grovel on bended knee.

Banging on Mercy's door

This is too much.

I think I've had enough.

It's been rough.

But I've been tough.

There's no denying.

I'm through with it all.

You can call my bluff.

There's too much violence.

Me, fighting against the world

Against the odds

Against what isn't

Now, I know exactly what this is.

This is life.

CHAPTER 14

Dalesa sits on the floor in her bedroom with her back leaning against the side of the bed, and the lights turned off. The evening twilight is fading into the dusk, and the darkness of her room offers a gracious invitation to her circumventive thoughts. She has an article that needs to be completed and submitted shortly. She doesn't have much of it left to type, but she is in no way motivated to send the email. She can't stop thinking about Romeo, their farewell kiss, and his confession of love to her in his office.

It's been almost twenty-four hours since Dalesa said goodbye to Romeo, possibly, for the last time. She is still processing the whole thing. She loved her sessions with him. She loved kissing him. She realizes that she loves him, also. The invocation she sends up to the heavens on proverbial bended knee asks the universe how she can, and if she can love herself. She had hoped that Romeo would show her the way in their sessions. They were making progress in the treatment, but now she feels she is back to the beginning. 'Will I have a good relationship with Duvall?' Dalesa asks herself. She misses Romeo already. Romeo made it clear that it wasn't enough that he loves her but that she loves herself, too. She doesn't know how she can do that.

Dalesa fears that she will never be able to love herself the way Romeo petitions. She recalls Romeo saying to her in one of their sessions that if she doesn't love herself, then she will never know real love. He suggested that she try loving herself vicariously through her friends and then it may become easier for her to appreciate herself as a thing of itself independently.

Dalesa never actually tried the exercise. She had the utmost respect for Romeo's guidance but didn't think this suggestion would work. She always felt that when it came to love herself, it was hopeless. She begins smacking her wrist with Romeo's rubber band, over and over. She is frustrated and attempts to think of how to start the experiment. Now, it is better than never. What does she have to lose, except Romeo, if she isn't able to make baby steps to loving herself?

She decides to start with her fans at the Ether Lounge. She thinks of how they love her spoken word poetry. They adore her for being the one who writes it, and they love the emotions she shares. 'I love that I write beautiful poetry. I love that I can incite emotions in people with my words.' Dalesa thinks about what she's just done. It was simple—took all of three minutes in thoughts and a few seconds to speak to herself. She felt nothing out of the ordinary but does notice she now has a smile on her face, as she thinks of patrons and staff she's grown to adore at the lounge. Baby steps.

Next, Dalesa thinks about the people she's helped in her volunteer work. She thinks about how she does service for the Girl Scouts and how the girls look up to her. She thinks about her time helping at the food pantry and a nearby homeless shelter. Dalesa donates clothes and offers to tutor people trying to get their GED. 'I love that I am someone that people can be helped by in their times of need. I love that I take the time to give back to the community and that I'm someone that inspires the next generation.' Knowing that she doesn't have much, she has a sense of pride as she thinks to herself that not many people can say they give without expectations to receive. The smile is still there.

She continues by thinking of how Mr. Glasgow considers her to be a remarkable journalist and an asset to the American Memoirs team. She thinks about how he shows her that he cares about her as a person—not just as a professional. 'I love that I'm a hard worker. I love that I've had a positive impact on the magazine. I love that I'm a person worth my boss actually caring about when I have to take a sick day.'

Dalesa is starting to feel something inside that she can't explain. It's a feeling that isn't foreign but so infrequent that it feels odd. She has stopped plucking the rubber band. She proceeds with the exercise, next with thoughts about Coreen and how Coreen has been the most constant figure in her life. Dalesa thinks about the encouragement Coreen gave to her at a pivotal point in their adolescence and how she was there when Dalesa got sick with HIV. She thinks about how Coreen never judges her and is always there to support her. 'I love that I am someone who has made a friend that although not related to me has treated me like a sister for decades. I love that I am someone worthy of someone else's time and energy when they have their own life to live that requires the same.'

She continues to smile as images of her and Coreen flash through her mind. She is enjoying this exercise. That indefinable feeling is still there and increasing in intensity. There's a warmth in the sensation, like what she felt when Romeo first touched her a couple of weeks ago. 'Is this love that I'm feeling? Is this what love feels like?'

Now, she thinks this exercise would be done a disservice if she doesn't address the ghosts of her past—continuing in the nature that she had been doing with Romeo in therapy. She thinks of the Jenkins and everything they put her through growing up. She thinks of how they said she wouldn't make it in life, and she looks at where she is now. She's not that same little, friendless girl who hid in her room listening for creaks in the floorboards to know when it was safe to come out. She is no longer afraid of monsters, and she has been working hard for some time to slay the beasts roaring in the wilderness of her soul.

When they died in the car accident thirty days before her thirtieth birthday, Dalesa did not shed one single tear. The loss of life is mournful no matter who the person is, but she did not want her foster parents to evoke not one more iota of sadness from her heart—especially, in their death. She thinks of how she has had a successful career, maintained healthy relationships in her life and found her way to the light despite the years of darkness they contributed to in her development. 'I love that for each day I live, and with each volume of air I breathe, I'm vilifying the ministry of negativity and cold-heartedness the Jenkins preached.' Dales takes in a deep breath. That was a huge baby step, but she is still smiling.

Now, Dalesa thinks about Romeo. 'I love that he can look beyond the tons of baggage that I carry and all that follows me as if being blown like debris in the wind. I love that he loves me for who I am.' Romeo has seen Dalesa stripped down raw—both in the flesh and emotionally. 'I love that I can be myself and talk to him about anything, even share thoughts and feelings that no one living knows. I love that he doesn't see a broken spirit but sees a blossoming lotus coming up from the murky darkness of my past and current struggles. I love that I am me because that is who he loves. Me.'

Dalesa feels amazing right now. She can't believe that she just said those words to herself. She stands to her feet and shouts, "I love me!" She turns on the room light and goes to her dresser. She looks at her reflection in the mirror. She stares at herself straight in the eyes. For some reason, they look bright and lighter to her than they've ever.

She is feeling so warm inside that she can't help but shout, "I love you! I love you! I love you, Dalesa Moreno!"

Dalesa looks at the time displayed on her alarm clock on the nightstand reflecting in the mirror. She needs to finish the article. She immediately gets to work.

It's taken thirty years for Dalesa to be able to say those three words to herself. Being ostracized from her family and not having too many close friends, she hasn't been told for years that she's loved by anyone except Coreen, Richard several months ago and most recently Romeo. It was amazing to hear those words come out of her very own mouth. These were not mere syllables but a pronouncement—a declaration of independence from the enslavement of her damning thoughts that devalue her and her belief that her life was without purpose.

As she multitasks in her mind—writing and proofreading her article but thinking about love—she realizes that she can, now, live the rest of her life not ever having to hear another person say, "I love you" to feel loved. She has found real love, at last. She recognizes love within herself. Seeing for the first time how she had hunted her entire life for love to come from without, when all the while, as she will day by day grow to understand more, the greatest love is within. From here on out, she can truly give and receive love.

Dalesa finishes her article and emails it right away. She feels that a miracle has happened. She has connected finally to love – the same love force that created the Universe. 'How is this possible?' Dalesa asks herself. It was such a simple therapy exercise, but it has managed to purge her soul. She must call Romeo.

Dalesa looks in her purse for the card Romeo gave her yesterday. The longer it takes for her to locate the card in her congested pocketbook, the more eager she becomes to want to hear his voice. He of all people would grasp what a marvelous thing has happened inside her. She finds the card.

IT BELONGS TO ME

I found it!

It belongs to me.

It's been here all along.

In my weakest hour

It came thru and proved to be strong.

I found it!

It belongs to me.

It is never boastful or loud.

It is meek and gentle like an innocent child.

I found it!

It belongs to me.

It is not envious, proud or rude.

I ignored its bellow for many years.

I'm done being the fool.

I found it!

It belongs to me.

It is not self-indulgent.

It is altruistic.

If I'm selfish and vain, I may lose it.

I found it!

It belongs to me.

It is slow to anger, patient and kind.

I'm devoted to it.

Give me the papers and I'll sign.

I found it!

It belongs to me.

It is merciful and loyal to actuality.

In the battle for sanity and mental sovereignty

Fear and doubt are the main casualties.

I found it!

It belongs to me.

It always protects, trusts, hopes and perseveres.

With it, the storm soon passes.

The coast is clear.

I found it!

It belongs to me.

It never fails.

It will never let me down.

I can rest assure it won't bail.

I found it!

It belongs to me.

When my spirit feels poor

Heaven is in my grasp.

It blesses me to the core.

I found it!

It belongs to me.

With it, I can forgive.

Thus, I can receive forgiveness.

Life has more promise, and I choose to live

I know it will take time.

Our relationship has been shaky for a while.

I realize now the potential and want my light to shine.

It won't happen overnight.

I've been beaten badly by difficulty.

With time helping to heal, victory will remain in sight.

I know if I were to have it all

Then, one day lose it

Without love, I would have nothing to catch my fall.

I found it!

It belongs to me.

My life was void of meaning.

The truth in love has set me free.

This is a new beginning.

Dalesa dials Romeo's number. As her call is connecting, her apartment intercom buzzes. She wasn't expecting anyone. She hangs up the phone and goes to the intercom box. She presses the "Talk" button. "Who is it?" she asks. She presses the button to listen.

"It's Romeo," the voice replies.

Dalesa presses the unlock button to release the door downstairs. Dalesa wasn't expecting to see him so soon after their farewell yesterday, but she's glad he's here. She opens the door and stands at the entrance to see when he gets off the elevator.

He gets off the elevator and walks towards her apartment. "I was just now calling you. What a coincidence," Dalesa says.

"Coincidence? No. There's no such thing," Romeo says. He is smiling brilliantly.

"Come in," Dalesa invites.

Romeo enters. As soon as she closes the door, he pulls her in and hugs her. "It's so good to see you."

"Likewise. Come into the living room and have a seat." They each take a seat on the couch. "Can I get you anything?"

"No, thank you. I wasn't sure if you were going to call me. So, I hope you don't mind me popping up at your residence like this."

"No, not at all."

"Why were you calling?"

"I wanted to tell you that someone I've known my entire life confessed their love to me today," Dalesa says

"Oh, wow! Really? Who and should I be jealous?" He chuckles.

"Me, silly. It was me!" Dalesa gushes with joy to be able to tell him that – to be able to tell somebody.

"That's remarkable, Dalesa! What happened? I know you've been struggling with that."

"Well, I did an exercise you suggested some time ago, and it worked. I feel fantastic."

"That's great!" Romeo steps closer to her and gives her the warmest hug she's ever received. He is so happy for Dalesa. "I'm really proud of you," he says. "You can build on that, now. You have taken the relationship you have with yourself to a new level. Maintain it."

"I will. I will. Thanks to you. I wouldn't have been able to make it this far without you. I didn't say this yesterday, but I love you, too."

"If you had said that to me yesterday, I probably wouldn't have believed you but knowing what milestone you've accomplished today, I can welcome your love with open arms." They kiss, and so it begins. A new version of life emerges from then on for both.

Dalesa continues to build on her relationship with herself, and she and Romeo take their relationship to a more romantic level – spending more time together and becoming closer with each passing day. Romeo continues to be a support for Dalesa as she still works through bouts of depression. He is committed to her, and she is committed to loving herself—rebuilding her foundation on the essence of love that dwells in her.

Without a doubt, their relationship can last, as its basis is from something real and not hidden behind masks or riddled with tawdry games. They both believe in love, and it is that yoked conviction that will carry them through years of friendship and fidelity.

Everything a person does has a connection to love – from the way he or she takes care of material things, to the way he or she respects his or herself, and to how he or she honors his or her friends and family. Many people forget that love is a powerful force that can be transferred by touch, words, emotions, thoughts, and intentions. For every person that loves, love does not return to unto them void.

People must stop viewing love as something merely sentimental. Love is energy. It is vibratory. Love *is* everything and *in* everything. You can love folding your clothes as they come out of the dryer or you can love having a good conversation. Even to like something is to love it in some capacity. Although described differently, they are the same thing. There is only variance in degrees—hate, dislike, like love, and everything in between. All relationships are affected in this way, whether it be a connection with a person, circumstance, feeling, thought or an object. As Dalesa has learned, the most significant relationship, however, is the association a person has with him or herself—all others are relative.

Loving one's self can be physical, in the way one cares for their body with medical attention, hygienic maintenance, or clothing. It can also be mental, in the way one facilitates positive or negative thoughts, or it can be spiritual, in the way one tries to obtain equilibrium and peace.

To make love the driving force in one's life means to create an alliance with it—have a personal relationship. Once an intimate life with love has begun, a person can share the love and be a personified example that out of faith, hope, and love, "the greatest of these is love."

For more content by R. Antonio Matta, visit:
https://www.rantoniomatta.com

Other titles include:
- *Destiny's Stereo*
- *Your Genesis*